CAMPUS BONES

CAMPUS BONES

VIVIAN BARZ

Text copyright © 2021 by Vivian Barz
All rights reserved.

Published by Thomas & Mercer, Seattle

www.apub.com

Amazon, the Amazon logo, and Thomas & Mercer are trademarks of Amazon.com, Inc., or its affiliates.

ISBN-13: 9781542027939
ISBN-10: 1542027934

Cover design by Shasti O'Leary Soudant

Printed in the United States of America

For Kevin, King Toad of Lily Pad Kingdom

Prologue

Goody Two-shoes.

That's what friends at Lamount University called her, and not only because she was always first in class to raise her hand, even when the questions were meant to be rhetorical, or because she didn't curse and said things like *gosh darn it* and *oh fudge* on the occasions she was exasperated, or because she rarely put out—she'd slept with only one boy in her entire twenty-one years of living, and that had been after spending three and a half years as high school sweethearts. No, it was mostly because Samantha was a lightweight; she couldn't hold her alcohol if her liver had a set of handles, they teased her at parties she rarely attended, as if being a drunk was a status to strive for.

Samantha was on her second house margarita, which was more sugar and artificial lime flavoring than anything else. Despite its wateriness, she'd worked up a decent buzz (or what was decent for a lightweight) and the nerve to do what she'd been putting off for weeks. One more round should just about remind her of the backbone she'd once had. No need to be dramatic about it. Just a few simple words, and she'd be free.

Her gaze drifted to her blustering companions, Kimmy, Miguel, and Marty, whose cheeks were aflame with outrage over the latest exploitation of Earth. Forests had been slashed, fires ignited, animals slaughtered . . . and capitalism was at the root of the evil. That's what she envisioned, anyway. She'd learned to tune them out over time, just as she was tuning them out now.

Good evening, friends—what shall we be outraged about tonight? she mused silently and then immediately felt a pang of remorse over being so dismissive. It wasn't like she didn't care about these issues—it was a great priority of hers to make the world a cleaner, better place for herself and future generations—but irate conversations such as these always marked her with depression that lingered for days, even weeks. She was having trouble sleeping because of it. It would be nice if, only just *once*, they could discuss topics that weren't so doom and gloom, even if it was something as vapid as their favorite films.

There was that, plus Rodent and his devoted band of cronies' insistence that the times of armchair activism were over, that TALK WAS CHEAP—that any poseur could post memes and political rants on social media, but true warriors didn't hide behind computers. They put their money where their mouth was—the key being *their* money and never *his*—used connections, and never backed down from a fight. They created narratives that fit the cause, stretched and bent the truth so frequently that the lies came out as easily as saying one's own name. Samantha, who avoided face-to-face confrontation as much as she avoided making enemies, had been wanting to distance herself from the group for weeks because of it. While she suspected they'd begun to sense her growing anxiety and displeasure for some time now, she'd been struggling to find the nerve to start an actual conversation with them about it.

Good thing that she had those watery margaritas to fall back on.

Her vision went blurry around the edges as she screeched her chair away from the small splintery oak table they sat crammed around. The bar stank of pre-exam stress, ancient beer spills, and bigheaded sweat (the lacrosse team, sporting their soiled game-day jerseys, was celebrating a 0–15 win against Fresno). It was an unpleasant, but not unusual, collegiate potpourri that never failed to make her nostrils flare in distaste, though tonight it was making her downright nauseous. Samantha halfheartedly asked her crew if they needed another round and then sauntered off before anyone had a chance to reply. As a broke college student—well, as someone who *played* at being a broke college student—she'd wisely ascertained that requests for alcohol tended to take on an extravagant note when it was somebody else doing the buying.

Bryan was giving her his full frowning attention from behind the bar, hawk eyeing her as if she were a frail old woman in grave danger of falling down on a patch of ice. She focused hard to keep her gait from straying sideways, smiling at him as if she didn't have a care in the world. He pursed his lips in disapproval, clearly not buying it.

With a long sigh, Samantha aimed her eyes at the ceiling. That *he* should be the one casting dirty looks *her* way was ridiculous—it had been Bryan, after all, who'd ended their relationship two weeks into junior year. Yet, in the time since, he'd behaved as if they were still together, quizzing her jealously about the males he'd seen her walking with around campus.

His frustrating behavior only validated her parents' disapproval of their daughter attending the same university as the boy who'd been her high school sweetheart. Explore your options, they'd hounded her relentlessly; get out and meet new people. Which, of course, was their way of saying that they didn't think Bryan—who was more blue collar than blue blood—was good enough for their sweet baby girl, who deserved nothing short of a prince. How ironic it was, then, that it was ultimately he who'd thought that she was not good enough for *him*. To save face with her parents and friends, she'd implied that she'd done the dumping.

She would have avoided speaking to Bryan altogether now, but he was the only one available to furnish her a drink. Keira, the other bartender on duty, was busy breaking up a blossoming fight between a territorial frat boy and a lecherous middle-aged sleazebag who was far too long in the tooth to be trolling for a romantic hookup at a college bar, which was exactly what Samantha had insinuated to him earlier when he'd tested his luck hitting on her. She'd heard that you can't blame a guy for trying, but she certainly did.

Despite her petite stature, Keira was fierce, and anyone with half a brain cell knew better than to mess with her. Samantha watched the drama with woozy interest as the two drunk buffoons, chests puffed like gorillas, swore that, no, they were absolutely *not* going to have a problem. To ensure this, the bartender lingered nearby.

"Don't you think you've had enough?" Bryan cut into her thoughts.

She nearly quipped, *Who are you, my father?* But it seemed like too much effort in her buzzed state and would undoubtedly instigate a debate. She settled on "Okay, Dad," though, in truth, she was wondering if maybe those margaritas weren't as watery as she'd thought. She was feeling rather . . .

Funky, she decided.

Bryan grunted. "If I were your father, you wouldn't be allowed to slum it in this rathole."

"Because it's so *uncivilized* in here," Samantha said with a snort, ignoring the irrelevant dig at her family's wealth, which had been an exasperating bone of contention during their relationship. As if she could change the family she'd been born into. She plopped her empty glass down on the bar. "And I've only had two drinks—"

"Or hang out with *those* maniacs," Bryan continued right over the top of her, hurling a dark look at her friends. "What could you possibly get out of spending your time with them? You're going to land yourself in jail, if you're not careful. Or worse."

Samantha raised an eyebrow at her ex, who was looking irritatingly handsome in a tousled, informal sort of way; it would have been far easier to extract him from her life had he not always looked as if he'd just returned from a photo shoot at the beach. Despite their split, he did still care about her. This was something he'd told her on multiple occasions, though Samantha would have known it without the reassurances—Bryan had always been decent like that. She reminded herself not to read too much into it now. Just because he felt love for her on some level, it did not mean that he was *in love* with her.

Had they still been together, she might have felt obliged to reveal that she shared his unflattering opinion about the individuals he believed were her friends and that she was planning on cutting ties with them tonight. But, he'd broken up with her and had therefore lost the right to question her personal relationships. Who she kept company with was none of his business.

He removed her empty glass from the bar. "You want the same?"

She nodded. He turned his back on her so that she couldn't see how he was making her margarita. Adding as little alcohol as taste buds would allow, no doubt, or maybe none at all. He twisted around and set the glass down on the bar. She picked up the drink, sniffed it suspiciously, and took a long swig.

"Good?" he asked, watching her closely as if offended.

"Good enough," she answered vaguely and shrugged. Both she and Bryan were aware that she was not an experienced enough drinker to confidently argue that she'd been hoodwinked with a virgin drink without sounding paranoid.

Samantha cast a glance back at her table, where it took only one look at her companions' flushed faces to know that the angry tirades had not ceased. She weighed her options—a stilted conversation with her ex or the indignation she'd face at the table—and decided to remain standing at the bar. Of the two devils, it was the one she knew best. She was aware that she was stalling the inevitable, but what did a few extra minutes matter as long as she cut ties with the group before going home?

She made a move to set her drink down on the bar, but it was her butt that she parked on the closest barstool instead. The fact was she'd had enough. The sweetness of the drink, initially as tasty as candy, had become cloying, and she chastised herself for being excessive, for not stopping at two. When she finally did rest the glass on the bar, Bryan was there to take it away in the blink of an eye.

"I wasn't done," she said, more out of irritation than anything else.

"Yah," he said, placing a glass of cold water down in front of her, "you are. Drink this. You'll feel better."

Had she mentioned that she was feeling off—hot, sticky, confused? She couldn't remember. She rubbed her temples, swallowing down the bile that was beginning to burn up her throat, a reminder of why she never drank.

Bryan appeared at her side suddenly. "Come on—I'll take you home."

"But . . . my stuff." She peered at her table, not really caring if she left her things behind. Not when she was in imminent danger of throwing up in front of everyone inside the bar.

Bryan lifted an arm, showing her the jacket and purse he was holding. "I got everything."

"My friends—"

"I told them I was taking you home."

Without further debate, they left the bar, and not a moment too soon. A few yards from the entrance outside, she bent at the waist and retched into a row of bushes. The invigorating San Francisco air was cold and dewy against her skin, yet that didn't stop her from throwing up again as they reached Bryan's car on the street. Samantha no longer cared that her ex was judging her as he made a move to hold back her hair, or that she'd failed to tell her so-called friends that she wouldn't be seeking out their company anytime in the near future (nor after that). As the world around her dimmed, she could think only of home, her bed, and the bliss of permitting her eyes to slide closed—forever, for all that she cared.

She couldn't recall the drive to her condo, yet here they were pulling up in front of it. And now here was Bryan at the curb outside, laboring to extract her from the passenger seat. Her limbs, warm and oozy as melted caramel, slackened against his struggle. "Christ, help me out a little, would you?" he growled, but to her ears, it sounded like something else. Something sweeter.

I love you.

"*Iloveyoutoo,*" she slurred in an exhalation of breath, a sentiment that garnered her one of Bryan's notorious fed-up frowns. It was a look she'd grown accustomed to near the end of their breakup, though back then it would have gotten a rise out of her. She blinked at him slowly.

They were at her front door lickety-split—or what seemed fast to her, though Bryan might have argued about the time and effort it had truly taken to get her up the flight of stairs—and she searched in her handbag for her keys, dropping her hairbrush, wallet, and cell phone onto the ground as she rooted. She didn't bother to pick anything up, either not noticing or not caring.

Bryan fished Samantha's keys out of her handbag and picked her items up in what seemed like one fell swoop. She stumbled over her own feet as they crossed into the entryway, where Bryan didn't bother turning on the lights. He knew her place so well that he could locate her bedroom within darkness. Limp as a rag doll, she let him drag her down the long hallway toward it, her eyes dropping closed as soon as he laid her down on the bed.

CHAPTER 1

Had it not been for the mysterious and, more crucially, wealthy bene-factor who'd swayed the dean of students at Lamount University to take on a new professor, Eric Evans never would have landed his prestigious teaching gig. While the benefactor in question had insisted on remain-ing anonymous, identifying themselves as simply J. Doe, the reason behind the donation had been made perfectly clear: the philanthropist had a keen interest in the paranormal, and they felt that LU students could use some long-overdue clarification on the topic.

Also made clear was the sole condition that had accompanied the endowment, which was to be utilized for campus improvements at the school board's discretion: Eric, a small-town college professor who'd used his otherworldly intuition to assist authorities in capturing perpe-trators in two high-profile West Coast cases, must be granted a full-time teaching position . . . *however.* He was not to act as an expert in geology, a subject he'd spent over a third of his thirty-seven years either studying or teaching. He must, J. Doe had insisted, focus his lectures solely on solving crimes through supernatural means.

Eric, who was absolutely flabbergasted that a complete stranger would drop seven figures just to see him standing at the front of a class-room in San Francisco, had initially balked at the idea. He wasn't some performing monkey, eagerly waiting to shock and amaze the crowd with his curious talents at the snap of some stranger's fingers. (Yet, he realized with some chagrin, he also wasn't employed.) That he would be throwing away years of training—never mind the small fortune he'd dropped on tuition—was the least of his concerns. What vexed him most was that accepting the teaching position on the new terms would only validate the ludicrous speculations the media had and continued to spout about his purported supernatural gifts.

He'd been fighting an uphill battle with the press for more than a year. It started around the time he'd become embroiled in the Death Farm case, which had received international infamy after twenty-three murder victims were unearthed on a private residence in Perrick, a bucolic town just off the Northern California coastline. Later offering his expertise to the FBI to expose why so many locals in Clancy, Washington, were disappearing without a trace had only added fuel to the fire. Reporters who'd elevated his status to that of a quasi celebrity, albeit one known most in amateur sleuth circles, had called him an assortment of names in the time that had passed: psychic, hack, or just plain crazy. While some reported that he talked to ghosts, others insinuated that he might have even committed a few of the grisly crimes himself, for no other reason than to seek attention.

It was partly because of these vulturelike journalists that he was obliged to take the offer at LU once it arrived seemingly out of nowhere, despite his initial displeasure with the topic he was being sought to teach. Eric couldn't have remained at Perrick Community College, the small campus he'd been employed at after his relocation to California from Pennsylvania, even if he'd wanted to; the media's relentless obsession with uncovering a truth that could never justly be explained—that he used cryptic messages from the dead to help solve murders—saw to that. He hadn't been at the institution long enough to develop friendships, let alone garner allies, and his welcome had worn out swiftly once the press had started stalking him on campus. Students and professors alike were cornered with questions, classes were interrupted in the middle of lectures. Then came the lookie-loos who'd begun registering for his course in droves, their interest in geology nil but their desire to catch a glimpse of a real live psychic immense.

Eventually, the media circus died down, but the resentment the faculty held for Eric remained. Students on campus who believed they were being sneaky when they snapped unsolicited photos of him were equally insufferable. While the college never officially terminated Eric's position, the powers that be had dropped more than a few glaring hints that his talents might be better utilized elsewhere. He'd been questioning what he was going to do for money when along came Lamount University with their offer. Although he'd mildly fussed over the changing of his curriculum, he was hardly in a position to tell them no, which he suspected they might have known.

Still, he had his pride, and he managed to make a couple demands after a board member let it slip that the disbursal of the benefactor's funds was contingent upon him accepting their offer. There was that, plus the revelation that more than a few board members were happy—thrilled, even—to have him join them at the university. The first demand was that he be allowed to dictate his lesson plans without any university interference. He'd made the request for the simple reason that he loathed bureaucracy and being micromanaged to any degree. Dean of Students Alan Williams, who hardly went out of his way to disguise his mortification over having to bring a "fortune-teller" (actual term used in an email chain Eric had mistakenly been copied on) into an institution as respected as Lamount University–San Francisco, was willing to accommodate the request. The further he distanced himself from the professor and all his "mythical woo-woo" (again, actual term), the better.

The second request took a little more finagling. Jake Bergman, Eric's friend and former star pupil—a "mature" student at age thirty— would need to be allowed to enroll at the university without having to go through the lengthy application process. He would also need to be permitted to serve as Eric's teacher's assistant, a position usually reserved

for grad students. This Eric did not view as nepotism, as Jake was qualified for the transfer, having fulfilled the lower-level class requirements
with near perfect scores at Perrick Community College; it was also
something Jake had been planning to do before the deaths of his two
close friends derailed him. Eric was hoping that making the transition
easier would get his friend back on track and help ease the depression
he'd been trying so hard to mask. Naturally, Alan Williams had taken
umbrage at the stipulations. However, LU higher-ups ultimately yielded
to what they considered audacious demands for a nontenured professor.
Tolerating a little bit of insolence was worth the hefty payout, it seemed.

Eric and Jake sat in his office now, reviewing the essays some of
the students had opted to submit in lieu of an exam. (They'd been
given the option of one or the other.) Eric had elected to name his class
Nontraditional Crimes and Investigative Procedures in the hope of giving it more academic legitimacy than Jake's proposed title: Psychics Are
as Real as the Crimes They Solve. Not that the professor would ever
label himself a psychic, although he supposed by definition he might
be just that, despite having fought against the notion tooth and nail
when his visions first began to manifest. Resist as he'd tried, over time
he'd realized that, whatever problem it was that he had—and having
individuals who'd been dead for weeks or even decades reach out to him
from beyond the grave was certainly a problem—it wasn't one that he
could ignore in the hopes that it would go away.

Eric had eventually come to grips with reality: he saw and sensed
things "regular" individuals didn't, which occasionally helped him solve
crimes. While he had no true explanation for it, he figured the ability
(or disability, depending on how you looked at it) was a by-product
of the schizophrenia he'd been living with since the age of nineteen.
With medication, he had the disease under control, though the rare
episode occasionally plagued him. Still, because his brain was wired
differently from the standard model, he could access information the

average person couldn't—while he had no way to prove this theory, it was the best explanation he could come up with.

"They've got imagination; I'll give them that," Jake said, sorting through the heavy stack of papers they had spread out before them on Eric's gargantuan metal tanker desk, which had to be at least fifty years old. An enterprising soul might tout the furniture as "vintage," but Eric recognized it for the paradox it was: a silent yet screaming loud statement on how the university viewed the hired help. While the state-of-the-art classrooms and campus grounds were so impeccable that they could have been plucked straight from a wholesome propaganda film relaying the benefits of staying in school, the faculty offices were contrastingly bleak: small windows (if any), worn carpet, creaky old furniture, faded paint a shade Eric thought of as "prison cell gray." He probably could have insisted on a nicer office with his list of demands, but he'd figured that he'd pushed them enough and he, being the new guy, hadn't wanted to alienate himself from other professors in the department by rubbing their noses in a flashy office.

Jake had once joked that, at Lamount, they were like commoners shoveling coal down below on the *Titanic* while the wealthy reaped all the benefits at the top. A British professor in Eric's department had also provided a cheeky idiom on the topic, stating that the private university was all fur coat and no knickers. Met with confusion from Eric, he went on to explain that LU took great pains to remind attendees (their parents, more pointedly) and patrons of its greatness while the many unsavory occurrences on campus that might have contradicted the sentiment—violent outbursts in the classroom, illicit student-teacher affairs, athlete doping—had been quickly swept under the rug. Case in point: Eric had absolutely no formal credentials that qualified him to teach the subject his employment was centered on, yet there he was, the university's so-called celebrity expert on crime. Though Eric had no business thinking this way—he was a knowledgeable and widely liked professor—some days he believed himself a fraud, and he frequently felt guilty knowing that his students (or their parents) had paid good money to hear him lecture despite him having nary a single law- or criminal-justice-related certification to his name.

Lamount had reached its heyday in the nineties, when it had given nearby Stanford and prestigious Ivy League universities on the opposite side of the country like Harvard, Columbia, and Yale a run for their money. While the LU campus was undoubtedly lovely and the professors perfectly competent, what had catapulted the university into overnight popularity was that it had been used as the setting for *Away*, a popular dramatic television show about a group of beautiful young people leaving home for the first time to attend college. Though the dialogue of the cast and the situations they found themselves in were impossibly sophisticated and had obviously been dreamed up by middle-aged screenwriters, teenagers and twentysomethings—and many aged beyond that—couldn't get enough of the show. Lamount soon became The Place where the who's who of West Coast status and wealth sent their children. Politicians, tech millionaires, movie stars, and vintners alike fought tooth and nail to get their offspring admitted to the once-obscure Bay Area institution.

But nothing good lasts forever, as the saying goes, and the cast of *Away* grew too old to pose as college students, which was probably for the best, as the show had become trite and excruciatingly formulaic. Enrollment numbers swiftly fell at Lamount once the show went off the air. The university would receive a bump in applications every so often when a cable network ran a marathon of reruns, but it had been some time since that had happened. Though higher-ups would vehemently deny it if ever pressed, and though they'd done an excellent job hiding the fact, the university couldn't afford any further decreases in attendance. They were desperate to be placed back in the limelight.

Enter one Professor Eric Evans.

The particular class he and Jake were discussing now had an enrollment of about two hundred, though Eric taught three separate courses per week, all on the same subject. In total, he had about six hundred students. It was a lot, more than he'd thought he'd ever be able to handle, but the university had furnished him with three other assistants in addition to Jake. And, of course, his shabby office notwithstanding, he was being paid handsomely. He had very little cause to complain.

The essay prompt for his class had been to find unusual crimes that had taken place throughout history and then delve into the methods law enforcement had used to investigate or solve the case. Students were encouraged to give the paper a persuasive slant—to argue why or why not they believed the actions the authorities had taken were effective. They were also to state whether they believed the crime had occurred as it was reported in the media and, if they didn't, to expand on what they thought had really happened. The assignment was straightforward enough, yet there was always a student or two who missed the mark.

As if on cue, Jake plucked an essay from the pile and said, "Look, here's one on alien abduction."

Eric couldn't help but laugh. He ran a hand through the cropped, thick brown hair that he'd worn chin length and floppy not so long ago, before he'd separated from his girlfriend, Susan. Upset by the breakup, he'd had it chopped off on impulse. He couldn't say why he'd done it, but what he did know was that he didn't miss having strands of wild, curly hair tickling his face constantly.

Not like how he missed Susan, which he did every day.

He said, "Not exactly the sort of nontraditional crime I had in mind." Fraudulence aside, it surprised him how much he'd been enjoying teaching the course, which he'd been doing for the better part of eight months, for two separate semesters. "Though, I guess it does technically fulfill the prompt, so I'll let it fly."

"At the very least, you'll get a different perspective . . ." Jake's words trailed off as a student came barging into the office.

The kid hadn't knocked and had flung the door open so roughly that it hit the wall with a bang and then bounced off his backpack as it juddered forward. He wore sunglasses, a light-blue hoodie pulled up around his skull, and the lower half of his face hinted at the whisper of an incoming beard. Eric recalled the sketch he'd seen many years ago during the manhunt for Unabomber Ted Kaczynski, thinking that the two bore a striking resemblance.

"Um, can I help you?" he asked, more amused by the kid's gall than angry. He wouldn't have had the nerve to do the same when he was his age. He probably wouldn't have the nerve to do such a thing even now.

The kid took off his sunglasses and pulled down his hood. "I need your help."

"Okay," Eric said slowly. "But, as you can see, we're right in the middle of somethi—"

"*Er-ic*," Jake sang, giving him an urgent look. He seemed distressed by the intrusion.

"No, it needs to be now," the kid said. With his eyes pinned on the two men, he quickly shut the door and then reached around his back and locked it. He had the textbook wild-eyed, disheveled-haired appearance of a human on the brink of a nervous breakdown. This did not cause Eric alarm, as it was nothing extraordinary. Most undergrads looked that way around exam time.

Eric, who had so many students in his class that he had trouble even remembering them by appearance (and forget about names), didn't recognize the kid. The classroom he taught in was massive to boot, with movie theater–style seating that sloped downward. He couldn't always get a clear view of the students who sat at the far end of the room. As he'd discovered in his years of teaching, there was a direct correlation between grade average and where a student positioned themselves in class: those who sat in the first two rows typically scored As and high Bs. As the rows descended, so did the student's grade. He'd also learned that those who started the semester in the back of the room rarely took it upon themselves to move forward. Therefore, if he had no idea who the pushy kid was, it was probably because he hid out in the last rows and never raised his hand.

Which meant that he was probably looking to argue his way out of a bad grade.

Eric sighed. "If this is about your essay, we haven't finished grading them yet."

The kid frowned, shook his head. "Essay? What . . . no."

"He's not in your class," Jake commented in a voice that was full of meaning. "This is Bryan Mc—"

"Don't even think about it," Bryan told Jake, who'd been slowly easing his cell phone out of his pocket.

Finally, Eric was understanding what was happening. However, had he still been lost, Bryan offered plenty of clarification via the gun he brought out from the waistband of his jeans. He aimed it in the general direction of the two men. "Hand me your phone," he said to Jake, who immediately complied. "Where's yours?"

Eric brought his hands up, using his index finger to point at his desk. "In the top drawer. Look, there's no need for this. If you want, we can go to the police together."

Bryan shook his head. "No police."

Jake, hands also raised, said in a reasonable voice, "Come on, man—you murdered your ex. They're going to find you no matter where—"

"I didn't do it," Bryan told the two men as he broke down in sobs. "I swear I didn't murder Samantha. I loved her."

CHAPTER 2

Though it seemed that the authorities had been trying to keep the story quiet, news of Samantha's murder had spread over campus like wildfire in the two days since it had taken place. The name Bryan McDougal was on everyone's lips, including Jake's and Eric's. Before turning their attention to the student papers, they'd been discussing how gossip was painting him as guilty beyond a shadow of a doubt. While Eric didn't endorse the way his students were so quick to condemn—he'd reminded them in class that even murder suspects deserved the right to a fair trial—Bryan wasn't instilling a lot of confidence in him now by sticking a gun in their faces.

"I can try to help, but I don't understand what it is that you want from me, or why you feel it necessary to point a gun at us," Eric explained to Bryan in a voice he hoped was disarming. This wasn't the first time his life had been threatened, but the situation with the gun-toting kid was entirely different from in the past, when he'd genuinely believed that he was in real danger of being shot. While he didn't relish having a firearm brandished in his office, instinct told him that the kid had no real intention of using it. That was the thing about the desperate and the unstable: sometimes they just wanted to be heard out.

Bryan had made Eric move from behind his desk so that he was sitting next to Jake. He positioned himself above the two men, giving himself a physical advantage. He said, "The police are convinced I murdered Samantha."

"It's all people are talking about on campus," Jake interjected. "And social media. Your photo is everywhere."

Eric gave Jake a hard look: *You're not helping.*

"Is that true?" Bryan asked, looking about as panicked as a person on the lam could be. He began to pace in front of the door like a caged animal.

Eric nodded, figuring that there was no need to lie. Still, he didn't want to cause further unrest, because chaos tended to incite unnecessary violence. "I don't know about the social media stuff, since I deleted all my accounts some time ago. But, yes, word has been put out all over campus, which is why I didn't recognize you initially—I know you only by name. The police are actively searching for you, Bryan. That's why it would be better if you turned yourself in. It's going to be far worse for you in the long run if they have to continue using manpower. Sometimes, showing an act of good faith goes a long way in the eyes of the police and the public."

"Plus, hiding out makes you look guilty," Jake added.

Bryan shook his head. His gaze was bloodshot and exhausted. "But I'm *not* guilty! That's why I came to you, Professor Evans."

"I'm not trained as a lawyer, if you're looking for representation—"

"No. Nothing like that." The kid was shifting the gun from hand to hand as he spoke, making Eric anxious. Jake didn't seem too happy about it either. "I want you to do your thing."

Eric was getting a fair idea where the conversation was going. "My thing?" he asked nevertheless, as if he didn't know.

"Yah, I want you to read my mind or whatever you've done to solve crimes. Then you'll know I'm telling you the truth. Maybe you could, uh, talk to Sam's spirit—she can tell you who killed her? You're a famous person, so if you say that I'm innocent, the police'll have to believe me."

Eric didn't want to set Bryan off by denying the impossible request, so he deflected. "How about you start by telling me the story from the beginning, from your side of things?"

Bryan shrugged and, thankfully, stopped pacing. Eric had started to get nervous. "There's not much to tell. The police came to my apartment yesterday morning to talk to me about Sam's . . . you know." He broke off, cleared his throat. "I wasn't home—"

"Where were you?" Jake asked.

"I was on my morning run—well, morning for me; it was a little past ten. If I don't do it first thing, then it never gets done," Bryan explained. "Anyway, I was about a mile in when my roommate called me on my cell and said that the police were there to take me in for questioning. Sam had been found dead in her condo by her cleaning lady. She'd . . ."

Bryan, on the verge of breaking into sobs again, stopped to collect himself. He was either genuinely upset or one hell of an actor. He made a fist with his free hand, closed his eyes, and took a deep breath.

Eyebrows raised and head tilted, Jake glanced at Eric meaningfully, as if to ask if they should try to rush their captor. Standing four foot three, Jake was a dwarf, but Eric had no doubt that he could hold his own in a scuffle. He was fierce that way. Still, no need to escalate things and make the situation turn ugly. Besides, despite the gun, Bryan didn't seem to pose a threat.

Eric slowly shook his head, mouthing to Jake to *relax*. He let his breath out when he was sure his friend was going to stay put in his chair. His eyes drifted to the wall clock above the door. His office was located off one of the quieter hallways in the Social Sciences faculty buildings, so it could be well over an hour before another student or professor came knocking. He wondered if any visitor would manage to overhear what was happening and then sneak away and get help, or if they'd be taken hostage as well. He said, "It's okay, Bryan. Continue when you're ready."

Bryan's throat made a clicking sound when he swallowed. "Sam had been stabbed. Multiple times. They said there were also signs of an attempted sexual assault—attempted, because the police think the attack had been interrupted, you know, before it started . . ." He looked sick. "They also found opiates in her system."

Jake frowned. "Like what?"

"*High levels of opioids* was what the cops told my roommate. Like she'd been drugged or something, or had gone on a bender," Bryan said. "And before you ask, Samantha wasn't a druggie. She'd get hammered off one peach daiquiri, so the idea of her shooting up or, I don't know, smoking opium is beyond ridiculous. She's never even puffed on a cigarette."

"But you've also been broken up with her for some time, right?" Jake asked. "Maybe she'd started using and you didn't know it."

"You know that popular saying 'Peach daiquiris are the gateway to heroin'?" Bryan asked. Before Eric or Jake could speak he answered, "No, you don't, because it's *not* a saying. Samantha wouldn't just suddenly start experimenting with hard-core drugs. I'm telling you, never, ever in a million years would she do *any* kind of drug. And, you know what? I'd try to convince you otherwise if I *were* guilty, since it'd take some of the suspicion off me—the police think *I* might have drugged her. But I have no reason to lie."

Eric asked, "Why do the police think you're responsible for her death? Because of the drugs in her system?"

"It's mostly because I was the last one seen with her," Bryan answered. "They believe she was murdered the night before last, shortly after I took her home from the bar."

Thinking of Susan, Eric said, "My ex will hardly talk to me. I'm sure she'd rather walk a thousand miles than ask me for a lift. If you two were broken up, why'd you give her a ride home?"

"Word on the street is that you two had a nasty breakup. She dumped you hard," Jake chimed in.

Bryan flapped a hand dismissively. "It's not like that with us. We still cared about each other—just because I didn't want to be with her anymore didn't mean I didn't still love her. And, for the record, I was the one who ended things with *her*, in case you're thinking I've got a chip on my shoulder about the whole thing. She just likes everyone to think she was the one doing the leaving. I honestly could give a shit what people think, especially around here, so I let her claim what she wants. I gave her a ride home because she was acting weird, that's all."

"Weird?" Jake asked.

Bryan said, "Like I mentioned before, she's not big on the booze. She hardly ever drinks. Honestly, I don't think she's been drunk in her entire life—not *really* drunk, anyway. She'll have a cocktail occasionally, but she'll nurse it all night, until even the ice is melted. It was weird, though, because that last night I saw her at the bar, she ordered three drinks from me in the span of about an hour."

"You made her drinks?" Eric asked.

"He's a bartender down at Salty's," Jake said. "It's where all the kids on campus go. I don't, though. I'm too old."

"I've seen you in the bar a couple times," Bryan said to Jake off-handedly, and Eric noticed the color rising in Jake's cheeks. "And, sure, I made her drinks—I'm a bartender; it's my job—but I didn't put any opiates in them, if that's what you're implying. I don't even know if it's possible to drink heroin or opium or whatever, and I wouldn't know where to get something like that. And, even if I did, I wouldn't have a need to use it on my ex-girlfriend to incapacitate her."

"Oh, I don't know about that, Bryan," Eric said, playing devil's advocate. "Might you have been regretting the breakup, feeling lonely?"

"I'm the one who ended things with her, remember? She'd made it pretty clear that she'd like to get back together."

"So you say," Jake commented.

"Look, I'm not some kind of creep. I'm hit on by at least a half dozen coeds during my shifts. These rich girls love bartenders, for whatever reason—maybe it's some working-class fantasy they harbor. So I could go home with a different girl every night, if I wanted to. But it's not my style." Quickly, Bryan added, "But, even if girls *didn't* hit on me, I'd never do something like that, drug someone. I swear, I took Samantha home, put her in bed, placed a glass of water on her nightstand for her to drink when she got up, and then I left. The *only* things I took off her were her keys, to let us in, and her boots, so she wouldn't get her bed dirty. That's it. It was whoever that came in after me that tried to undress her."

Eric nodded neutrally. He supposed that, even if Bryan were a predator, he'd hardly admit it, would he?

Bryan paused, perhaps sensing their doubt. "Look, my sister, back in high school . . . she was at a party, and some guys . . ." He shook his head, plainly disgusted. "You'll just have to believe me. I would never, ever, force myself on a woman. Not in a million years. It takes an extra-evil type of a person to do something like that, and I'm not. *Evil.*"

"Tell me more about her acting weird," Eric prompted. "Was she scared, maybe behaving as if she was being threatened? Did she say that she thought someone might be after her?" He had an ulterior motive behind the questions. Naturally, the guilty often tried to pin their crimes on others. That had, in fact, been the focus of one of Eric's classes, where he'd presented various ways notorious criminals through-out history had tried to frame the innocent. He wanted to see if Bryan would do the same.

Bryan did no such thing, which, Eric realized, didn't surprise him. Call it a gut feeling, but he wasn't getting guilty signals from the kid. "No, it was nothing like that. Sam had arrived at Salty's with a bunch of doters, though, and it was like she was trying to avoid them. Usually, it's *me* she tries to avoid—she'll order a drink and then walk off the second I give it to her. No *Hello, how are you?* But, when I served her the third drink that night, she stayed at the bar."

"A bunch of what?" Eric asked. "Did you say *doters?*"

Bryan nodded. "That's right. They're these fanatics who run an environmentalist club here on campus. DOTE stands for *Defenders of the Earth*, so they call themselves doters for short."

"I think I've heard of them," Jake said, nodding. "You've had run-ins with the group personally?"

"No, but they know I don't like them, and the feeling is mutual on their end. They're actually one of the major reasons I broke things off with Sam. After she joined up, she got all preachy."

"Preachy like how?" Jake asked.

That's good, Jake, Eric thought. *Keep the exchange conversational. Easy breezy.*

Bryan considered the question. "With Sam, there was always something I was doing wrong. If I bought a mass-produced bar of chocolate, I was somehow personally exploiting migrant workers. Sam has *her* 'ethical' chocolate shipped in all the way from Africa at twenty bucks a bar. Her parents buy it for her by the case."

"You've got to be shitting me! Twenty bucks?" Jake scoffed. Eric might have thought he was merely feigning outrage because he was being held at gunpoint, had he not known how frugal his friend was. Jake was likely so outraged that he'd probably forgotten all about the gun. "That had better be some amazing damn chocolate."

"It's not, trust me. I've had it. Even weirder, it's shaped like a baby—part of the proceeds from each bar sold go to a local orphanage on the Ivory Coast. Want to know what that part is? Ten percent. So, the orphanage is getting a measly two bucks for every eighteen dollars the corporation pockets. Real ethical, right? Sam didn't like it too much when I pointed *that* out." Bryan shook his head. "But the lunacy didn't stop there. She'd go through my closets, telling me that the clothes I'd been wearing for years were all made by five-year-old sweatshop workers, when she never had a problem with them before. It was that sort of stuff, always putting me down and making me feel like I was destroying the world just by being alive."

"That would be hard to deal with," Eric said, trying to gauge how deep Bryan's resentment ran. Had he gotten so fed up with his ex-girlfriend's haranguing that he'd committed murder?

"It was," Bryan agreed. "One time, she berated me for a solid half hour because I'd bought a premade sandwich at a grocery store on my way home from class."

"What was the issue with the sandwich?" both Eric and Jake asked.

"She said that I should've bought local. There was a little independent café next door to the grocery store, and they sold sandwiches there—for over *twice* the price of the one I'd gotten. Which, of course, someone like Sam can afford, having rich parents and a trust fund. But I can barely afford near-expired clearance food as it is working two jobs and paying my own way through school. I have a partial academic scholarship, but it's just not enough.

"That was what bothered me most about her joining DOTE, the hypocrisy of it all. There she was lecturing me, a low-income individual, about how I was exploiting the poor, when the only reason she could afford to buy her 'ethical' ten-dollar organic-bread sandwiches was because of the real estate money she got from her money-grubbing capitalist parents, who are about as close to slumlords as you can get. She is awfully judgmental for someone who's never had a paying job."

Eric noted Bryan's use of wording in present terms: *Someone like Sam can afford. She is awfully judgmental.* He remembered a class lecture he'd taught about a missing persons case, where a husband had spoken about his wife in the past tense during television interviews long before her body had been found, her throat slashed so deeply that she'd practically been decapitated: *She was so kind. She was such a caring person,* he'd said. It was what had tipped investigators off about the husband's guilt, his slip of the tongue over acknowledging that his wife was already dead, which the guilty often do about those they've murdered. The innocent—those who are truly devastated about the loss of a loved one—are reluctant to accept that the victim is gone. They will continue speaking about the deceased as if they are still living long after it has been confirmed that they are not.

Was that the reason Bryan was speaking this way now, because he was being truthful in his claims of innocence? Eric had, of course, revealed these facts during the lecture, and Bryan could have easily gotten notes from other students. Had he been studying up on the right things to say, knowing that the professor might be looking for key phrases? Could he be that diabolical?

"You said the Nevilles were slumlords?" Eric asked. He was hoping Bryan would continue to remain relaxed if they showed that they were listening and interested in what he had to say.

"Pretty much," Bryan said with a grunt. "Well, some of the time. Most of the mega, multimillion-dollar commercial deals they do are aboveboard; they go out of their way to promote those in a big public way. If there's one thing the Nevilles love, it's celebrating their own grandness. But they also do these shady side deals with mobile home parks that you wouldn't believe. *Those* they don't talk about. Not ever. And, if you try to bring them up, they'll shut you down quickly."

"Seriously, trailer parks?" Jake asked. "I thought the Nevilles were highfalutin kind of people?"

Bryan said, "Oh, they are. I don't mean to give the impression that they're dealing directly with residents. I'm sure they wouldn't be caught dead doing *that*. They have a management staff for that sort of thing. I don't know the nitty-gritty specifics of it, but from what Samantha told me way back when, here's what they do: They'll seek out a larger park that is either struggling financially or maybe has an owner who's let the property become run down and wants out. So, they buy it at a steal, with a hundred or so mobile homes included in the package. And, here's where the shady part comes in. Once the ink is dry on the deed, they'll send out notices to the current residents, informing them that the park is changing policies and will now house solely felons, and that they've got sixty days to vacate. Some of these people have been living in these parks for years or even decades, and then suddenly they're told they're out on their asses."

"Why on earth would they do that, seek out criminals as renters?" Jake asked.

"Because, a lot of apartment complexes won't rent to felons," Bryan answered. "And, everyone, including felons, needs somewhere to live, right? So, the Nevilles, after kicking everyone out, will build a huge fence around the park, jack the rent prices way up, and then start moving in the criminals. They know felons will be desperate for housing and will pay whatever they charge. And they do. Still, even at the inflated rate, the rent on a trailer is cheaper than an apartment, so, in a way, the new residents think they're getting a bargain. And, once the felons move in, they're on the hook—where else are they going to go, right?—so the Nevilles will then start raising the rents even more, but they'll spread it out over the course of the year, so it's less glaring.

"As strange as it sounds, there's big bucks in owning a trailer park. The Nevilles are renting each of those ratty little trailers out for well over a grand a month—and they're on a property that requires very little upkeep and that they've done zero renovations to, other than the giant fence. Multiply that by a hundred, and you're talking over a million a year in revenue. And they own several of these parks all over California. Half a dozen, at least. Maybe a dozen. You can do the math on how much they're raking in. And I'm sure they're probably also getting some kind of tax break from the state for housing ex-cons."

"They sound pretty ruthless," Jake said. "Rich, but ruthless."

Bryan said, "You have no idea. And what's *really* shady is what they're doing to these communities. Imagine owning a house in the same area as the original mobile home park, which has probably given you very little grief or concern throughout the years, and then suddenly learning that you're about to have a horde of felons as your new neighbors. And I know for a fact that they're running at least one park that caters to—and you're not going to believe this—*pedophiles*. How would you like living by a hundred or so child molesters?"

"We don't have kids, but I see your point," Jake said, making a face. "They wouldn't just stay in the park, so you'd see them around. They'd be shopping at your local hangouts, like your grocery store, where you'd probably take your kid."

"How is that even legal, what they're doing to residents living near the park?" Eric asked. "I can't imagine what that would do to home values in the area."

"Maybe you haven't heard, but the Nevilles are loaded," Bryan replied with a thin smile. "The amount of money they've got is scary, and they've got powerful connections. Any problem that can be solved with money is no problem at all when you're rich. I know the Nevilles have been sued by a few people over all this—moving felons and pedophiles into a neighborhood—but you can imagine the sort of attorneys they can afford with their kind of wealth. But what's a few fines or paid-out lawsuits when you've got cash to burn? Oh, and the police *love* them for what they're doing, which is keeping the criminals all rounded up in a single place. All these criminals at the park are on some kind of registry, so the police can find them any time they please."

"I'm surprised nobody knows about them being involved in this trailer park business," Eric said. He was happy to note that Bryan was lowering his gun. He hadn't put it away, but he'd stopped pointing it at them, and that was something.

"They operate under a generic business name with partners, and they—well, their lawyers—make it extremely difficult to track them down. Oh, they're great at putting up a good front. Guess that's how Samantha learned how to lie so smoothly about our breakup. That whole family, right down to Samantha's psycho, cat-killing seventeen-year-old brother, are good at keeping up appearances."

Jake asked, "Her brother killed a cat?"

Bryan nodded. "It was the neighbor's. Nobody was ever able to prove it, but Samantha was convinced her brother did it, especially after she found Dexter's—that was the cat—collar in his room when she was snooping around looking for proof. The kid has major problems—he should be locked away in an institution—but of course her parents tried to gaslight Samantha and suggest she was overreacting when she told them about the collar."

Eric said, "You think he's capable of hurting Samantha?"

Bryan shrugged. "I don't think anyone can really say what another person is capable of until they do it."

You're not really helping your cause with comments like that, Eric wanted to say.

Jake asked, "Who else would have access to her apartment? Does she have a roommate?"

Bryan shook his head. "She did have a roommate a while back, some writer flake named Tori Blakenwell, but she took off last semester after she was given a grant to go and live in some creative arts community. *The Greater Collective*, it was called, if you've ever heard of anything so pretentious."

"Is there any chance she might have come back to hurt Samantha? Was there bad blood between the two?" Eric asked Bryan.

"Oh, there was *definitely* bad blood happening there. It was actually Tori who got Samantha interested in DOTE. She was doing a story on them for the school paper or her blog or something; I can't remember. The crazy thing is that it was Tori's criticizing of the group that drove her to join. Samantha's always been contrary like that. I think it's her way of rebelling against her parents." Bryan shook his head. "But, no, Tori wouldn't hurt Sam. She was an artsy-fartsy, pacifist type. She was far too snooty to commit murder; she'd find that beneath her intellect. She was very self-righteous, which didn't earn her a lot of friends. "

Jake said, "Okay, so besides the cat-killing brother, who else do you think could be responsible?"

"It could be anyone," Bryan replied with an aggressive shrug. "All I know is that it wasn't me. This is San Francisco—the city's not exactly known for its safety. This place seems to breed the crazies. I mean, take your pick. You've got thousands of homeless transients roaming the streets—even in Sam's swanky neighborhood, they're sleeping on the sidewalk right outside her building. There's her nutty DOTE friends. There's who knows how many people pissed off at her parents for moving criminals into their neighborhood—maybe it has nothing to do with Sam at all, and it's a revenge thing. Oh, and then there was this old creeper hanging at the bar."

"The night Samantha was killed?" Jake asked, and Bryan nodded. "Who was he?"

"I have no idea. I'd never seen him in there before, and he came in alone. He was totally out of place, though. He was real skeevy looking—like, at least twice as old as everyone in there." Bryan ran a hand down his cheek. "His face was all pockmarked, like he was no stranger to drugs—bad teeth too. Ratty clothes, but not so ratty that he seemed homeless. Just worn, you know. I didn't get close to him, but he *looked* like he probably smelled of farts and nicotine. He had food smeared all down his front, like he'd been using his shirt as a napkin. He didn't order a single drink while he was there, but Keira— that's the bartender I was working with—said she thought she'd seen him pinching leftovers off tables. He must've gotten a couple, because he was acting like a drunk, or like he was on something. That's why he was on my radar, at least at first, because I wanted to make sure he wasn't stealing drinks from customers—or their wallets or backpacks or whatever. I try not to be judgmental, but I could tell there was something up with this guy from the moment I saw him. Come to think of it . . ."

Bryan paused while he rooted through his back pocket and extracted his phone. "I took a photo of him as he was hitting on a few girls. He wasn't grabbing on them or anything, and, really, I was more worried about what they'd do to *him*. Some of those girls, man, they can be kind of mean when they want to be. He was keeping his distance, but acting the fool, like doing little dances and then bowing. He hit on Sam too—you should've seen her shut him down. I don't know what she said, but it must have embarrassed him because he got away from her fast. She likes to think that she's all sugar and spice, but her tongue can be sharp when the occasion calls for it.

"At first I thought it was kind of *amusing*, I guess you could say, because he was so ridiculous. I do what I can to keep humor about the job, or else I'd probably just end up hating everyone—it doesn't matter how fancy the booze; all drunks are disgusting in their own way to a jaded bartender, and I can't afford to get fired over a bad attitude. Anyway, this all went down in the time span of maybe, hmm, five minutes? Probably less. I was actually about to throw the guy out when Keira beat me to it. Guess this dude hit on some frat guy's girlfriend, and they were getting into a brawl over it. I texted the pic to my roommate."

Bryan brought up his text log and handed the cell to Eric. Along with the photo, Bryan had included the message: If I'm ever this pathetic, please kill me. His roommate had messaged back: Yikes. That's embarrassing. Eric handed the phone over to Jake, so that he could get a look at the man.

Jake enlarged the photo on the screen and nodded. "Oh yah, this dude's way too old to be hitting on college girls. I see what you mean about him looking like a junkie. And like he smells." He handed the phone back to Bryan.

After a silence fell over the room, Eric suggested, "Why don't you tell us more about her doter friends?"

Bryan nodded. "These doters, they became her life. They're like members of a cult, always recruiting. They're not just here on campus; they've got chapters everywhere. They encouraged Sam to cut ties with anyone in her life who might not agree with their viewpoint. I know she stopped hanging out with her best friend since kindergarten because of them."

"Harsh," Jake said.

"You have no idea. It wouldn't surprise me if they were the ones convincing everyone I killed Sam. I'd tried talking her into quitting the group from pretty much the moment she joined, which they knew because Sam told them everything about us."

"What do you mean?" Eric asked.

"I mean she told them all the things I said about them. *And* about the places we went, what we did on our dates, the people we talked to, the arguments we had . . . let's just say our private life was no longer private, which I'm not okay with," Bryan answered. "And, although I have no proof of this, I think they're dangerous. They have a fanatical air that never sat right with me, which is the biggest reason I wanted Sam to get away from them. They're like a ticking time bomb about to go off."

Eric asked, "Okay, so if you're innocent, why haven't you just turned yourself in to the police?"

Bryan didn't have to think long about the answer. "Samantha's parents, they're pretty influential people here in San Francisco. They've donated *a lot* of money to law enforcement over the years—this, on top of the cops already loving them for their felony trailer parks. They also never liked me, even when Sam and I were in high school—and they'd never approve of Sam slumming it with a bartender if we were still together now. I'm worried that they might be fueling my manhunt. For all I know, they're even telling cops that it'd be great if I could 'accidentally' fall down some stairs and hit my head on the way in to the station; they're not the kind of people you want to mess with. I'm sure they've already got a long list of district attorney friends calling them up to offer their services, just itching to fry me." To Eric, he added helplessly, "This is why I need you. If you clear my name, I'll happily turn myself in to the police. I'll go anywhere you want."

Eric could no longer avoid answering. "I'm really sorry, Bryan, but my brain doesn't work that way. What I do, it's not like a television that I can tune in to a specific channel. I don't know why I see and hear the things I do, but I have zero control over it." *Which is why I wanted to write a book to set the record straight,* Eric thought. *But then the idea made Susan so mad that she suggested that we take a break from each other.*

"But, if you're innocent, you're innocent," Jake cut in quickly. "With the amount of scrutiny the police are under these days, they're not just going to rough you up. Unless there's something else you're not telling us?"

Eric was sensing, too, that maybe the whole story wasn't being provided.

Bryan let out a long sigh. "Okay, the knife that stabbed Samantha? It had my prints all over it. That's what the police told my roommate when he wouldn't give me up. They were trying to use it as proof of my guilt, so that he'd tell them where I was."

"You might have led with *that* bit of information," Jake said, casting an incredulous look at Eric.

Bryan looked sheepish. "Sorry, but I knew if I did, you'd immediately think I'd done it. But it wasn't my knife. It belonged to the bar, so *of course* my prints were all over it. I must cut up a dozen lemons a night. Sometimes, too, I'll use a knife to open beer cases when I can't find the box cutter, which always seems to walk off on its own. Literally anyone could have taken it right off the bar—it's not like I went out of my way to hide it. These knives, they're just cheap things that the owner buys in bulk, and we've got a ton of them scattered all over behind the bar because they get dull pretty quickly and are always getting lost or accidentally thrown out. If Sam had been murdered with the end of a broken-off beer bottle or a corkscrew, my prints would be on those too. Pretty much everything there my prints would be on: glasses, barstools, other people's credit cards that had been handed me to charge . . . everything."

"Anything else?" Jake asked, his eyebrows raised. "Besides you being the last person seen with her and your prints being all over the murder weapon?"

"I kind of had an incident with the police a while back," Bryan finally admitted.

"Go on," Eric prompted.

"I . . ." Bryan went silent.

Somebody had come knocking. Eric and Jake exchanged a panicked look, both unsure of what to do. Spooked, Bryan ran toward the window, yanked it open with a screech, and began to climb out. Lucky for him, Eric's office was on the first floor.

"Wait!" Jake called, but Bryan was nearly out of sight. Just before he disappeared completely, he turned back to the two men, their mouths agape, and hurled the gun straight at Eric's head. Bryan was halfway across the quad before Jake gingerly picked up the gun and determined it was fake.

CHAPTER 3

Frowning, Susan Marlan flipped through the file on her desk, which pertained to a missing person named Chung Nguygen—frowning, because this sort of situation, a lone civilian's disappearance, was usually not cause for federal concern. The cases she focused on as a part of a special unit team at the San Francisco Field Office of the FBI were typically larger in scale and required a fair amount of urgency; something to the tune of a child snatched from a schoolyard, or a drug-addled lunatic holding a bank full of hostages at gunpoint, was usually what it took for their small but efficient squad to get involved.

Most of the time, her job had her chained to her desk doing research on suspects. She'd look into their backgrounds, check their financial and travel activity, and interview known associates, so that she might get a better clue where and how to track them down. There was, however, occasionally some action that took her out into the field, and she liked the mix. Her instincts were keen, she was good at what she did, and certainly she saw a hell of a lot more crime than when she'd worked in Perrick as a police officer. There, she'd investigated such gripping cases as oranges stolen from fruit stands, noisy burnouts in parking lots, and toilet-papered front yards. This was, of course, barring the events at Death Farm, which had shaken her and her tiny little community to the core.

Susan's position at the FBI, which she'd acquired about a year ago, had come with the benefit of an assistant-slash-budding agent named Keith Haines. She'd never had anyone working under her before, and it secretly gave her job an extra feeling of importance. Thanks to Keith's neat, efficient comments on the page margins, she was able to ascertain that it was actually *two* individuals who'd gone missing, Nguygen and another man named Dov Amsel. While the disappearances had piqued her interest, she still couldn't understand the need for federal attention; the files of wanted persons and suspected terrorists were typically denoted as such, and these were not.

Further inspection of the notes (thank you, Keith) revealed that Nguygen and Amsel were both employed at Gruben Dam, which instantly cleared things up. Given the sensitive information the two men had been privy to—Nguygen was an engineer and Amsel an armed guard—their jobs would have required a high level of security clearance. Susan was unfamiliar with how, exactly, dams operated on a micro level, but it took very little effort to imagine the sort of havoc the two men could wreak on the area if they were disgruntled and looking to settle a score. Nguygen would have intimate knowledge of the inner workings of the dam itself: knowing how to release water being the most critical skill he'd possess. Amsel would know the ins and outs of the building and how to get them to high-security areas. Scary stuff.

She grabbed the small pad of Post-its she kept on her desk and made a note to ask the HR department at the dam if they'd had any issues with either employee: complaints from coworkers, frequent tardiness, or a generally bad attitude. It was a basic and obvious query, but a good place to start in order to learn about what sort of people the two men were. Friends and family could always be counted on to lie, but Human Resources would have no reason to fudge the truth.

Susan ran a quick internet search, Google Earth specifically, to see how the dam was situated in relation to the surrounding area. It sat right above a residential neighborhood of a hundred or so single-story homes. Beyond that was a major highway that moved a lot of traffic. She thought of a gigantic wall of water crashing down over the top of it all—roofs crushed like soda cans, cars floating away like small insects in the rain—and shivered. It was unlikely that anyone could live through such a disaster. Suddenly, locating the two missing men was feeling a lot more urgent.

Deeper in the file, she learned that the two men had gone on a lunch break together the day prior and never returned to work. She sat back in her office chair, the bones in her lower spine popping softly, and tried to think of any logical reason why a security guard and an engineer would disappear together in the middle of the day—something other than foul play. Could they have possibly been friends outside of work? If so, perhaps they'd complained about their jobs over sandwiches or tacos or whatever and then made the hasty decision not to return—a type of "sticking it to the man" sentiment.

But she didn't think this likely. Abruptly walking away from a job would make a lot more sense if the two men were in their late teens or early twenties, single and childless, or if the job in question was menial and easy to replace. Yet both men had specialized skills for their occupations, and she imagined Gruben Dam must've paid well enough.

She checked their ages next. Nguygen was nearing fifty and Amsel was thirty-one. Both were married. These were men who had people in their lives they'd have to answer to if they'd abruptly made the choice to cut out a major source of income. They'd have bills, mortgages, mouths to feed.

Okay, so what could be the other possible implications of their disappearances?

As if to make her think faster, Special Agent in Charge Denton Howell, a brusque, no-nonsense man who'd acted as a mentor of sorts to Susan, materialized in front of her desk. He had a habit of doing that. "Where are we with Gruben Dam?" he asked as a way of greeting. He wasn't being unkind; that was just his manner. He wasn't much for chitchat, and Susan would've been more alarmed if he'd inquired about any fun plans she might have for the weekend.

Howell had been pivotal in Susan's move from Perrick PD to the FBI—he had, in fact, been the one who'd sanctioned it. She held a great deal of respect for her boss, and his opinion meant the world to her. She'd never voiced as much, but she imagined he knew anyhow.

Susan continually felt pressure to perform at a maximum level on the job, for fear of disappointing Howell. Maybe some paranoid part of her supposed that she was punching above her weight, that she really wasn't as qualified as everyone thought for the big title she held. The step up from small-town cop to member of a specialized team at the FBI had been massive, and she'd been thrown straight into the deep end. Half the time, she felt as if she didn't know what she was doing and that it was only a matter of time before someone found out.

She'd poured all her energy into the job, sacrificing a personal life— her relationship with Eric, most notably—normalcy, and a whole lot of sleep. She'd always abided by the "fake it until you make it" mentality, so while she'd presented herself to the world as hardworking, collected, and confident, inwardly she was terrified of screwing up, letting the rest of the team down, and making Howell regret ever bringing her onboard. In a recent performance review, he'd told her that she'd exceeded his expectations by always thinking quickly on her feet. So, perhaps there was some merit to being a faker after all.

"I've just started looking into Nguygen's and Amsel's backgrounds," she told Howell. "But there's something else I've been thinking about. I have a distant cousin, Josh, in the national guard, and I remember him talking a few years back about how a local dam—he's in South Dakota—had been on their watch list during a high terror alert. Since the dam was a major source of power, the concern was that the area would be severely crippled and vulnerable to an attack should that dam be damaged by enemies of the state. Take out the dam, and you're essentially taking out an area's ability to function on a basic level."

"Are you thinking their disappearances might be linked to terrorism?"

Susan shrugged. "I haven't gotten that far yet, but I think it might be an angle worth exploring."

"Could be. It's best not to rule anything out at this stage," Howell said.

"My gut is telling me there's more behind this than two guys suddenly deciding that they don't want to go back to work after lunch, though it could be something completely unrelated to the dam. I'm going to dig into everything I can find."

"Any theories on the terrorism angle?" Howell asked. That was one of the traits she admired most about him, that he was always open to suggestions and out-of-the-box ideas. It was the primary reason he headed up their unit, which handled a lot of cases that required unorthodox measures. For such a stern individual, he was extremely open minded. He'd taken a chance on her in the past by listening to her hunches, even when he had no reason to, and they had paid off. That was the thing about Howell; agents had to prove their competency to earn his trust, but he was always willing to give them a chance.

Susan shrugged. "It's a stretch, but if they hold foreign passports, there's the possibility their government might have sent them here to gather intel at the dam. I'm going to look into their residency statuses, see if anything raises a red flag." Even after nearly a year on the job, she was stunned (if not a little tickled) that she was investigating such matters. Had she uttered anything close to the same statement back at Perrick PD, she would have been laughed straight out of the station. The closest thing they'd ever had to a terrorist situation in their small town was the time a few vendors at the farmers market had been suspected of advertising pesticide-sprayed fruit as organic. The clean-living shoppers had been outraged over what they'd deemed a mass poisoning of the public.

Here at the FBI, however, she was taken seriously, and her opinion counted. She'd be forever grateful to Howell for it. After being forced by higher-ups at Perrick PD to take a leave of absence because of a traumatic incident at Death Farm, and then subsequently becoming embroiled in a multiple-murder investigation in Clancy, Washington, while on vacation, she'd been questioning what she *really, truly* wanted to do with her life.

But now she knew. This was it.

She said, "I'll check with the airlines, too, to see if either of them have attempted to book tickets to leave the country."

Keith suddenly appeared next to Howell, holding a mug of coffee so fresh that there was steam coiling out the top of it. With a suppressed smile, Susan wondered if he'd dumped the last cup he'd gotten only a short time ago into the wastebasket at his desk so as to have an excuse to happen upon them on his way back from the break room. He had the tendency to magically appear whenever Howell was nearby discussing a new case. She could hardly begrudge her assistant's eagerness to make an impression and prove that he had what it takes to handle cases on his own, having been in similar shoes herself once upon a time as a rookie police officer.

Offhandedly, as if just thinking of it, Keith said, "Oh, by the way, I've taken the liberty of calling all the major hospitals in the area."

Despite his nonchalance, Susan suspected that he'd practiced the statement in his head at least twenty times before saying it. "That's great, Keith; thank you. Any luck?"

"Not a single hospital has had either man check in, so I'm thinking we can rule out that they were involved in an accident." Howell frowned, and Keith's cheeks reddened. Quickly, he added, "Er, if *you* think that it should be ruled out, I mean."

Susan could have sworn that Howell was trying hard not to laugh.

"I've also touched base with the police and sheriffs' departments," Keith said. "They don't have either man in custody."

"Good work," Howell praised, and Keith seemed to grow taller by about a foot.

Once Keith finished with his enthusiastic thanking of their boss, Susan said to Howell, "I'd like to have a look at their bank statements as well, to see if there's any unusual activity. It's hard to believe that anyone would be stupid enough to use their personal bank accounts to commit a federal crime, but you never know."

Howell nodded. "I'll contact IT and see what they can dig up."

Howell and Keith left Susan at her desk so that she could get to work. Although she could sense she was in for a long day, she was content. Not as happy as she'd be knowing that Eric was at home waiting for her, but happy enough. And that would have to do for the time being.

CHAPTER 4

Pompous ass were the first words that came to Jake's mind after Dean of Students Alan Williams entered Eric's office and uttered but a few simple words. He'd wasted no time making it evident that he was unhappy about the wait he'd suffered while he'd futilely knocked for a time period that spanned, by Jake's estimate, no more than twenty seconds. Given the way he'd followed up his grumbling by declaring *and I can't imagine any good reason why your door was locked*, Eric might as well have killed someone.

Eric had stashed the gun before allowing his snippy visitor to enter, providing a look to Jake that suggested it was probably best if they stayed quiet about Bryan's intrusion. Jake briefly wondered if Williams had overheard the exchange between them and Bryan, but it was evident that he hadn't; if he had, he would have been screaming his head off for every available law enforcement officer in the greater Bay Area to come and deliver them from evil, self-important as he was.

While Jake wasn't sure *why* Eric was loath to spill the beans, he was okay keeping mum for the time being. Even if he wasn't, Alan Williams would be one of the last people on earth he'd confide in. The guy had a major stick up his ass about everything, and Jake suspected that he was still bent out of shape over having to let him slide through admissions because of Eric's job conditions.

And here was Williams now, staring down at Jake disdainfully, as if he was wishing he'd evaporate. Whatever he needed from Eric, it must have been urgent—or at least urgent in *his* mind, which, really, could amount to something as trivial as him needing a jump on the dead battery in his car so that he could make it to a racquetball lesson on time, or whatever the hell it was guys like him did for recreation.

Jake told Eric, "I'll just be outside," acting as if he hadn't been held hostage by a wanted murder suspect only moments ago—never mind the embarrassment that a gun a child could probably identify as a prop was what it had taken to scare them into submission. He took the papers that needed grading with him, the insinuation being that he was going to work while he waited for them to have a conversation.

Jake got to work outside in the hall, all right, but it wasn't on the papers. Quickly, he set about finding a good position to eavesdrop, first checking to see if the coast was clear. He found the old-fashioned way worked best, pressing his ear against the door, which was potato chip thin and made out of cheap plywood. For as much as LU students paid for tuition, the university could have sprung for a nicer door, though it was par for the course.

"I'm sure you've heard the news by now about Samantha Neville's murder," Williams said. He let out a long-suffering sigh, as if the poor girl had gotten herself murdered just to spite him and eat up time on his already jam-packed schedule. "Anyway," he continued, so Eric must have nodded, "I have just spoken with her parents, who are understandably upset. We actually talked for a great deal of time." Another sigh. Then, reluctantly, "Much of it was about you."

"About me?" Eric asked. There was a hint of caution in his voice, and probably for good reason, Jake thought. Williams never would have come to this side of the campus unless he absolutely had to. The dean avoided most social science and liberal arts faculty offices like the plague—word on the street was that he shunned any professor who didn't teach a high-dollar subject like those under the STEM blanket—science, technology, engineering, and mathematics.

Putz.

Williams cleared his throat so loudly that Jake had to take his ear away from the door momentarily. That must be some mucus buildup; it sounded like he was churning cement in there. Yuck. "You know my feelings about your . . . clairvoyance."

"I don't call myself a clairvoyant, never have. But I understand what you're getting at. You think I'm a fraud," Eric replied dryly, and Jake thought: *Go, Eric!* He imagined few professors had the gall to speak to Williams with such bluntness. Then again, most professors weren't as impervious to firing as Eric was, which must have incensed the dean to no end.

Jake anticipated an outburst of denial from Williams, but it never came. He might have been compelled to employ Eric at the university, but he was under no obligation to be kind about it. Civil, it seemed, was the best he could manage. "Regardless of what *I* think, the Nevilles seem to believe you're legitimate," he said in the cynical tone of a staunch atheist dismissing the authenticity of Jesus's face appearing on a slice of charred toast.

If Williams had been expecting a reply from Eric, he was about to be disappointed. Eric, who Jake knew had little respect or use for Williams, said nothing. Jake considered this a greater slight than a nasty retort. To speak would have taken energy, but by remaining silent Eric was telling the dean that his opinion of him mattered so little that he wouldn't waste even one breath defending himself. Sometimes, saying nothing communicated volumes more than shouting did.

After a moment of silence that was awkward even for Jake, the dean said, "They—*we*—would appreciate it if you could help them in their time of need." Jake could almost hear him gagging on the words as they came out, like little pieces of rotten fish.

"Help them do what?"

"Well, since there are *some* who seem to believe you're credible in your claims, the Nevilles feel it would go a long way with the authorities if you could go down to the station with them and make a statement."

That's funny, because Bryan wanted us to do the same thing only a minute ago! Jake wanted to burst in and shout. He could just imagine the hilarious look on Williams's face if he did just that, though he doubted *Eric* would find humor in the interruption.

Eric said, "I don't understand."

Williams sighed impatiently. "It should be obvious. You'd tell whomever is in charge at the police that they need to find this Bryan McDougal character and put him behind bars!"

"Why would I do that?" Eric asked, his voice contrastingly calm to the dean's shrillness.

"Because! The Nevilles are generous patrons of the university!" Williams sputtered, sounding as if he was struggling to keep his temper under control. Then, as if realizing his gaffe, he added, "But that's hardly the point. A young woman has been murdered, and her killer needs to be brought to justice."

Eric said, "I misspoke. What I meant was *how* could I do that? I have no idea if Bryan is guilty or not."

"You *know* because he's the most obvious culprit. It's *usually* the boyfriend who does it."

"And here I thought I was the one teaching lessons about crime," Eric said mildly, and Williams made an aggravated *hmph* sound.

Jake put a hand over his mouth so a giggle wouldn't escape.

"Look, according to Samantha's parents, Bryan was jealous of her relationships with other students. He wanted her attention only on him, and he was angry when she ended their relationship. He did not take kindly to rejection." Williams's tone indicated he felt his time was being wasted with these ludicrous debates and Eric's dismissal of his opinion—ironic, then, that he should be the one criticizing Bryan for not taking rejection well. It was clear the dean was accustomed to other

professors at the university bowing to his bullying and had not anticipated Eric putting up a fight. "*Of course* he did it. Who else could it
be, if not him?"

Smoothly, Eric remarked, "You're basing your assumptions on what
the grieving parents of a murdered girl are telling you. For all we know,
they didn't like their daughter's choice of the now ex-boyfriend, and so
they're pinning the murder on him because he's low-hanging fruit." Had
he not known better, Jake wouldn't have had a clue that Eric had just
spoken with the ex-boyfriend in question about the very matter. "And
it's probably safe to assume that Bryan's parents aren't also generous
benefactors to the university?"

"I'm not sure what you're insinuating with *that* remark—"

"Have you considered the possibility that the Nevilles could just
be angry about their loss and are looking for someone to blame?" Eric
interjected. "It's quite common."

"Are you going to help or not?" Williams asked abruptly. Jake imagined he was probably making a show of checking his wristwatch. With
what was undoubtedly a smarmy smile, he added, "I would consider it
a personal favor if you did."

As if he's tripping over himself to do you *a favor,* Jake thought with
a roll of the eyes.

Eric sounded sincere as he said, "I *am* sorry about the loss of
Samantha, and I *do* want to help in any way I can. But I can't go to the
police and pin a murder on someone when I don't know the full story.
That would be unethical. Part of the reason people find me, as you earlier pointed out, *legitimate*, is because I don't go off half-cocked to the
police accusing potentially innocent people of murder."

"Do you understand how admissions work at our university,
Professor Evans?" the dean said, apropos of nothing.

"I have a fair grasp, yes," Eric replied humorlessly. The subtext
being: *I'm not a moron, you moron.*

The dean continued, as if Eric hadn't answered. "One of the major reasons parents feel . . . *righteous* about sending their children to our institution is because of our upstanding reputation."

"I don't understand what that has to do with—"

"If I may finish," Williams cut in tersely.

"By all means."

"As I was saying, Lamount is a place of high moral standing. We don't just let *anyone* in, contrary to what your employment ultimatums may have ordained when you joined us. Your friend got lucky. As you are aware, that was a special circumstance, and I can guarantee you something like *that* will never happen again, not as long as I am running this institution."

Jake could feel the heat rise up the back of his neck. The dean was clearly speaking about him. He wondered if he might somehow have been aware that he was eavesdropping and was being spiteful for his benefit. He quickly checked to see if his feet might be casting a shadow under the door. He was in the clear, as the door hovered mere centimeters above the old navy-blue carpet that ran along the hallway. Spite just must come natural to the man, then.

"Is there a point to all this?" Eric, it seemed, no longer cared about making nice.

Jake couldn't help feeling a little guilty about the whole thing since his interest in the university and his studies had been lacking as of late. If he were to really dig deep down within himself, he might even find that he wouldn't have cared all too much had the dean angrily declared that his teacher's assistant position had been revoked and he was being thrown out of Lamount. He might have even welcomed such a thing.

The dean cleared his throat. It sounded as if it was all he could do to keep himself from shouting. "My *point* is that the last thing this university needs is some tacky media scandal. How do you think that will make us look? We've got a would-be rapist that *we* gave a little free tuition to and a girl from a high-profile family found stabbed to death, and *doped up* no less—despite what the Nevilles think, their daughter was no angel. *Obviously*," he quipped with a snort. "What do you think it would do to our reputation if the story got out?"

"I guess I haven't thought about it," Eric said with blandness that must have irritated the dean to no end, because the next thing Jake heard was him mutter something about it being clear that he was not getting through to the professor—that God forbid he should do anything to help the university.

Like a ridiculous parody of an old Hitchcock film, Williams said darkly, "You're going to regret this. I'm not a person you want as your enemy."

Hearing footsteps, Jake scrambled back from the door, and not a moment too soon. Seconds later, the dean was skulking out into the hallway. He glared at Jake when he saw him, as if to say: *Try talking some sense into that idiot in there, would you?*

"Have a nice day," Jake sang with the widest grin he could muster. The pleasantry was not reciprocated.

CHAPTER 5

Jake went into the office and plopped down on his butt-ugly chair, which was done up in a loud red plaid from the seventies and uncomfortable as all get-out. "What an asshole."

"Listening in, hmm?" Eric smirked. It was good to see that the dean hadn't robbed him of his humor.

"You'd better believe it, though I'd hardly need to, to determine such a thing," Jake said with a guilty laugh. "I don't know how you managed not to lose it on the guy."

"Him? That's nothing. You should read some of the things reporters have written about me."

"I have—no wonder you're writing a book. It'd piss me off like crazy, having people essentially calling me a liar to my face."

"Tell that to Susan," Eric said with a grunt. "She's still mad about it."

"Hardly the same thing. You're only trying to clear your name."

"Again, tell that to Susan. She said I'm just like her father, trying to make a buck off tragedy."

Jake frowned. He was aware that Susan's father had badgered her to sell her story about her involvement in the events at Death Farm and Clancy to a media agency known for producing salacious (if not exaggerated) narratives. Although she would have made a shocking amount of money, she'd said to do such a thing would have made her feel smarmy, since she'd have to break the confidentiality oath she'd pledged to victims as a law enforcement officer.

However, what *Eric* was trying to do with a respected publisher, Jake knew, was reveal how he'd gotten involved in two famous cases and clarify how his so-called psychic visions worked.

Jake had always thought that Eric and Susan had made a sweet and complementary couple, like salt and pepper, with him being imaginative and a little out there and her being responsible and grounded. So, it had disappointed him when he'd learned of their split. He'd made it known to both parties that he thought that their ending a relationship over a book was ridiculous; however, they'd both later confided in him that it wasn't *just* the book. There had been other issues at play. He hadn't pressed too much on what those issues were, since it really wasn't his business. Besides, no matter what "he said, she said" conversations might reveal, the only two people who could genuinely know what happened were Eric and Susan.

After a moment of thoughtful silence, Jake asked, "You think you'll call her—Susan?"

"About Bryan?"

"Yah."

"I wanted to talk to you about that, actually," Eric said, and then he made a move to give them some extra privacy.

"I don't think he did it," Jake said as soon as the door was closed.

"Why do you say that? I'm inclined to agree with you, but I'd like to hear your reasoning."

"I've seen how Bryan behaves at work. He isn't a creeper. If anything, he's the opposite. I was in the bar one time, and this drunk basketball player started getting into this girl's personal space. He was cornering her, grabbing on her waist, asking what the hurry was—that sort of thing. It was gross. Anyway, Bryan was there in a heartbeat, telling the prick to get the hell out of the bar, even though the guy was twice his size. He seemed pretty furious. He was so concerned about the girl being okay that she actually got a little embarrassed by the kerfuffle. Then, another time—"

"I thought you were *too old* for that place?" Eric cut in with concern that put Jake on edge. "How often are you actually going there?"

"I'm not drinking too much, if that's what you're worried about," he said, defensive, and even a little heated, not particularly relishing having his actions policed. He was also worried about potential eavesdroppers, being one himself. The last thing he needed was for people on campus to start quizzing him about his trauma and his band again. They'd finally, for the most part, lost interest in his tragedy. While he'd loathed the unwanted attention, what had irked him most was the entitlement they exhibited when meddling in his personal affairs.

"Of course I worry. You lost two of your closest friends and your band in one fell swoop. A year is not that long ago. It's okay for you to still be upset."

Thanks for the permission, Jake thought indignantly and then checked himself. Why was he getting so irate, and at Eric of all people? His friend's concern was coming from a good place, and a sincere one. Unlike the countless others who'd offered their condolences, Eric had been right by his side in Washington when he'd lost his friends. If anyone on earth could truly understand his anguish, it was the professor.

"I'm all right," Jake assured Eric with words he did not feel. *Was* he all right? Some days he wasn't so sure. But what could Eric do about it—what could he? His friends were gone, and dead was dead. The killer had been apprehended as well, which was supposed to have made him feel better. It didn't. Nothing did.

"You don't sound all right. You sound annoyed," Eric said with a disarming chuckle that teased a reluctant smile from Jake. "I just don't want you filling your spare time up with booze, since you're not playing shows anymore. You can't only do homework and grade papers—you'll go mental. You know, if you're ever feeling lonely, I'm always up to jam. Can't remember the last time I even saw drums."

"Thanks, I appreciate it." It also had been a while since *he'd* played his new violin, but this was mainly because making music made him feel sick to his stomach. Steering them back on topic, Jake said, "From what I've seen, Bryan has always acted more like a protector of women, not someone out to prey on them. And I believe him about him being the one who did the dumping. I've seen him interacting with Sam—at the time I didn't know she was his ex, but I do now that I've seen her photo plastered all over the place—and it seemed like he was done with her, even if he still cared about her well-being. *She* was the one who always looked moony eyed over *him*; before I'd learned who she was, I'd always assumed she was just one of his groupies. He wasn't lying; he *does* get a lot of attention as a bartender. He certainly has no shortage of offers."

"Who do you think committed the murder, then? And what about the opiates?" Eric asked.

"I was thinking about that. Just because Bryan was the one who served her the drinks, it doesn't mean that someone else couldn't have tampered with them once they were in her possession. It'd only take a second or two of her looking away for someone to drop something in her glass. Maybe she left it on the bar while she went to use the bathroom." Jake shrugged. "Or maybe she really was a closeted heroin user."

"I don't know about that. A heroin addiction would be hard to disguise," Eric countered. "Shooting up is not like sneaking a cigarette out the window when nobody's looking."

"Okay, I have to agree with you on that one. When we were on the road, we saw our fair share of junkies backstage—believe you me, there's no such thing as a casual user. You're either a heroin user or you're not."

Eric nodded. "You think someone broke in and killed her after Bryan left, then?"

"I don't see why it wouldn't be possible. Bryan said he used her keys to let them in, but he said nothing about making sure the door was locked when he left. And, even if he did, it's doubtful he would have locked the door *and* set an alarm, which means the locks could have been picked or a window could have been jimmied open. Maybe some creep spiked her drink at the bar, followed Samantha and Bryan home, and then broke in after he left, knowing she'd be blacked out. Or, maybe one person drugged her drink at the bar, and then an entirely unrelated person broke in and tried to assault her. I mean, stranger things have happened."

Eric said, "Or, maybe Bryan has played us both, and he's guilty on all counts."

"Maybe. But I really don't think so. What about this DOTE group? If she'd been hanging around with them as often as Bryan said, they might know something."

"It's very late 1990s or early 2000s, isn't it—the idea of ecoterrorism?" Eric commented. "You don't hear much about it anymore."

"You're forgetting, I was born in the nineties."

"Oh, right. Way to make a guy feel old," Eric said with a laugh. "When *I* was a kid, though, it was all over the news. What did they call it, when hard-core groups sabotaged companies they thought were bad for the environment? *Ecotage.*"

"Like setting test animals loose in labs, that sort of stuff?"

"Exactly. There was a big story in the early 2000s about a firebombing down in San Diego—I remember because I'd studied it in one of my classes as an undergrad. An 'ecoterror' group was angry that a housing development was being built, so they torched the whole thing. Caused something like fifty million dollars in fire damage. They even left a note saying they'd do it again if more developments went up. The FBI was involved in that one, since it was classified as an act of terrorism; they later offered a twenty-five-thousand-dollar reward to anyone with information that would lead to the capture of the individuals who did it. I'm not sure if anyone ever came forward, though. With a group like that, you'd almost be afraid to."

"They sound like a far cry from the Sierra Club," Jake said.

"It was a popular thing to do in the media back then, label any environmental group that leaned toward zealous as 'ecoterrorists'—though the arsonist group in San Diego was obviously dangerous. The whole notion became widespread overnight, it seemed, kind of like how 'satanic panic' got heat in the eighties. Everyone was talking about it, and it was the subject line for a lot of TV shows—I want to say that there was even an *X-Files* episode about ecoterrorists—until it just sort of fizzled out and people moved on to something else to obsess over."

"You think these doters are like that—terrorist types?"

Eric lifted his shoulders. "I have no idea. You'd probably know more about them than I do. I'd never heard about the group until today. None of the students really talk to me about that sort of stuff. I think they see me more like a parent they're afraid of judging them."

"Those doters do sound a little nutty," Jake said. "Though it could just be Bryan's sour grapes talking. I'd still like to check out the group, maybe talk to some of the members."

"You sure you want to get involved in this or with them? You might be causing yourself a whole lot of unnecessary grief."

"I'm intrigued. And weren't you just saying that I needed to find myself a hobby?"

Eric's frown exasperated Jake. "I guess I should have clarified. I meant a hobby that would take your mind off doom and gloom, not immerse you in it. After all that you've been through . . ."

Jake gave Eric a warning look. "I don't need to be reminded about what happened. I was there—and, unlike you and Susan, I was taken hostage and mangled in a plane crash. Head bashed. Bones crushed. Try forgetting *that*."

Eric sighed. "I'm not downplaying your tragedy. That's the last thing I'm trying to do. I just think it's best that you sit this one out."

"Why? You act as if I'm a child, like I need to go to the corner." Jake was perplexed and caught off guard by his own flaring anger, yet he felt it anyway. His emotions as of late were like quicksand: peaceful on the surface, yet perilous underneath. Once he allowed them to take over and pull him down-down-down, he was no longer in control, as if they were an entity separate from himself. While his heart occasionally suggested that he might need to speak with a professional to help him deal with his trauma, his head—the naughty voice that spoke loudest and meanest of all—told him to forget such nonsense, that what he really needed was a drink. He listened to his head more often than he'd realized until now.

Or, at least, more often than he cared to admit.

"I understand, Jake, that you're a grown, capable man. If I didn't, I wouldn't have suggested that you work with me here at the university."

"So, what's the issue?"

Eric shrugged, blew the air out of his puffed cheeks. "Honestly, I don't *know* why you should back off, but I have a strong sense that you should. Maybe it's because these doters sound like trouble waiting to happen. Also, with Sir Ass of Hole Williams getting involved, you might be rocking the boat unnecessarily. If you think he's a pain now, try getting on his bad side."

"Really? Because a couple minutes ago, you were acting as if you didn't care what he thought," Jake said, though he supposed Eric had a point. While he could care less if the dean was unhappy, he didn't want to take on the aggravation of having to deal with him. "But, fine, okay? I'll leave the doters alone."

And Jake meant what he said too. But then that naughty voice in his head was speaking up again, asking when he'd started answering to other people. Wouldn't it be more fun to do what *he* wanted?

CHAPTER 6

Susan jumped like a bomb had gone off as her personal cell phone started ringing on her desk. When she saw who it was, she mused that one might as well have. "Hello, Eric," she said formally, if not a trifle frostily, once she picked up after letting it ring a couple times.

She nearly followed up with a polite question after she was met with a brief moment of silence—*How are you?*—but she decided against it. Although she'd been quite busy tracking down leads on Dov Amsel and Chung Nguygen, she was having a good day—a great one, in fact—and she didn't want it potentially ruined by Eric telling her that he'd met someone new and things were just fine and dandy. To hear that would indeed make a bomb go off, all right, inside her head. And her heart.

"Hi, Suze," he said and then laughed uncertainly. This made her feel a little better, knowing he was nervous too. "Hope you're doing well."

It wasn't really a *question* about the state of her well-being, but at least he was making an effort. "Thanks, you too. What's up?" Best cut to the chase, she thought, in case he was calling to argue about their breakup. Although, if she were to be honest with herself, some small part of her was hoping that he was. She missed him every day, though her pride would not allow her to acknowledge it.

No such luck. "I've got a question for you—legal stuff. Maybe it's more like advice that I'm after."

"Uh-oh, did you do something bad?" she asked in a tone that was . . . *flirty*, she realized with alarm. She instantly checked her emotions, telling herself to cool it. Not only was her flirting completely left field and weirdly misplaced, but she was also at work. Now was no time to be gushing over her ex like a love-struck teenager.

At any rate, he laughed, which lifted her spirits. "No, not me. I had a kid come into my office just a short while ago—Bryan McDougal. Are you familiar with the name?"

"Should I be?"

"I guess not. You probably investigate so many delinquents that the names all run together."

"So he's a criminal, then?"

"Maybe," Eric said. "He's suspected of murdering his ex-girlfriend during an attempted sexual assault. They found opiates in her system, and she was stabbed multiple times. He's kind of . . ."

"What?"

"Hiding out from the police," he confessed.

"God, and he was just in your office? Eric!"

"He, um, held Jake and me at gunpoint—"

"Seriously?"

"Don't worry, it was a fake gun."

"What the hell?"

He laughed dryly. "He wanted me to use my psychic mojo to see that he was telling the truth about being innocent. I told him my mind doesn't work that way."

Susan was wondering where it was all going, and why he'd decided to call her. She no longer entertained even the possibility that it was because he was missing old times. "Then what happened?"

"He jumped out the window when someone started knocking on my door. That's how we discovered the gun was fake—he threw it at us before he took off running. I haven't seen him since," Eric said, sounding strangely calm for a man whose life had just been threatened—well, *sort of* threatened. She wondered if the fake gun fired fake bullets, perhaps made of candy. "So, now I'm calling you for guidance."

"And you still haven't reported seeing him?"

"No."

"No?" Susan scoffed. "Then my advice is to hang up with me and call campus police immediately. Come on—you understand enough about the law to know that not reporting the incident could be viewed as obstruction of justice."

He sighed. "I know, I know. I'll call as soon as I hang up, all right?"

"An attempted rapist and a murderer—why are you even protecting this cretin? That's not like you." And it wasn't. Eric was the smartest, most sensitive man she knew.

"Because, I think he might be telling the truth about being innocent. So does Jake."

Susan trusted both Jake's and Eric's judgment, so she decided to hear him out. There were few people in her life she would have extended the same courtesy to. She listened as Eric outlined the conversation he and Jake had had with Bryan. At gunpoint.

"Bryan believes Samantha's parents might be convincing the police that he's guilty—he says they've always had it out for him. According to him, they're extremely wealthy and have got a fair bit of political pull. He comes from a poor background, so he's worried that he won't have the financial resources to defend himself properly."

"Still, it'll look a hell of a lot worse if he continues hiding out."

"That's exactly what I told him. But then he had to go and jump out the window. Before you ask, I have no idea where he is." Eric paused to take a sip of water. This, Susan knew, since he made a soft *aaahhh* sound at the end of his drink. It was one of the many idiosyncrasies of his she'd picked up on unconsciously. "The dean here at Lamount is also pressuring me to go to the police."

"To tell them about Bryan holding you at gunpoint?"

"No, he has no idea about that. The guy's a major jerk. Seems Samantha's parents are pressuring *him* to get me to go to the police and tell them Bryan's guilty. They want me to claim that I know he did it *psychically*. Funny, right, since Bryan wanted me to do the same thing, except with a claim that he was innocent. I told the dean that I wasn't interested in doing his bidding, and he made some weird threat about me becoming his enemy."

"Are you concerned about the threat?"

"Physically?"

"Yes."

Eric snorted. "Not at all. The guy's half my size and nearly twice my age. I doubt he could fight his way out of a wet paper bag. I don't think he was threatening me that way, but more with what he could do to my career at the university. Petty politics."

She asked, "So, this Bryan, he thought that you offering up a psychic defense would help his cause?"

"I guess so."

To put a face to the murdered girl's name, Susan ran a quick internet search on Samantha Neville as they carried on their conversation. She didn't see too many results for her, barring a couple of social media accounts, but her parents were all over the place, mainly for their high-dollar business deals and involvement with nonprofit organizations. She clicked on a news article from a couple years back that had linked all three names, and then there on her screen was a photograph of the family that had been taken at a black-tie charity event benefitting cancer research.

Mr. and Mrs. Neville were close to how she imagined a wealthy San Francisco power couple would look. Though he was about ten years his wife's senior and nowhere as attractive, Mr. Neville, in a crisp, impeccably tailored tux, was handsome in a bland, white-bread sort of way. What he lacked in good looks he compensated for in charisma; shoulders squared and chin held high, he exuded the type of confidence that might be attributed to arrogance. Mrs. Neville, her strikingly pale skin and wheat-colored hair a stark contrast to her plunging deep-red ball gown, was a porcelain doll come to life. Her smile was tight, unnatural, and didn't reach her eyes. Near them, but not quite at their sides, stood Samantha, her arms folded across her chest and her expression stoic. She seemed ill at ease in her matronly pale-pink gown, which would have been better suited for a woman three times her age.

Susan imagined that if she were to be trapped in an elevator with the trio, she'd struggle to find something to talk about with them.

Eric said, "Hey, here's something a little off topic, but still related. Have you ever heard of an environmentalist group who call themselves Defenders of the Earth?"

Susan was surprised that he knew the name. "Sure, DOTE for short, right?"

"That's the one."

"Why do you want to know about them?" Susan was in full work mode now, her frustration over their breakup temporarily forgotten. While it was true that she was perpetually fearful of letting her boss and colleagues down, it was still behind her desk that she felt most empowered. Here, she was in control—she wasn't just run-of-the-mill Susan; she was *Special Agent* Susan Marlan.

"Bryan said Samantha went a little screwy after she joined the group. He also said they might be dangerous."

"I haven't personally worked on a case with them, but someone on my team has," Susan said. "He—Johnathan—and I have actually talked a lot about DOTE, since he came onboard around the same time I did, and they were the focus of his first cases. Doters have been becoming increasingly active in the community."

"Which means more of a nuisance and a federal concern," Eric deduced.

"Right."

"And here I was thinking that ecoterrorism was a thing of the past."

"Well, yes and no. The old-school methods are still being used by a lot of groups—arson, vandalism, etcetera—but the game has changed because of technology, the internet, and the dark web. They're definitely not the hippy-dippy tree huggers of the days of old, chaining themselves to logs in forests and throwing red paint on women wearing fur coats. Now, you can see a very fixed distinction between *activist* and *terrorist*, though a lot of the terrorists would like the world to believe that the government is simply rebranding them as such. In the beginning—back in the sixties and seventies, I'm talking about—the lines got a little blurred, since environmental activism was a fairly new construct in America. Anyone who spoke out against the government was deemed a radical. Now, though, there are actual textbook definitions to the terms and specific actions we look for as red flags. You start setting off bombs or threatening to kill CEOs, you're going to be called a terrorist, which a lot of them don't seem to understand."

"So, it must be a 'thing' again, then? Ecoterrorism?"

"I wouldn't say it *exactly* that way," Susan said, "since it never fully went away. It's more like the activity of radical environmental groups comes and goes in waves. A lot of individuals get riled up; then someone makes a very public grand gesture. Things go quiet for a while, until another incident happens and people once again take notice."

"It's strange, though, the extremism? It seems like these environmental groups are either sane and aboveboard, or they are completely nutty and dangerous. It's unfortunate, because the shady ones are giving the good ones an undeserved bad rep."

Susan said, "And the scary groups are also a lot more covert now and organized. Militarized in a way that hasn't previously been seen. Again, because of the internet. Back in the day, they'd have to photocopy newsletters and then hit the street, hoping to get them distributed to even a couple hundred people. Now, with a click of a few keys, they can reach millions of people all over the world. It's frightening, when you think about it, how quickly a group can spread their doctrine. They can create an army of followers without even leaving their homes."

"This is the sort of stuff you hear about and you start to think that maybe moving to the middle of nowhere and living off the grid isn't such a bad idea."

"After some of the things I've seen working here, I'd have to agree," Susan said with a laugh. "But DOTE, they're an odd one."

"Odd how?"

Susan went quiet as she considered the question.

"It's okay if you can't tell me—if it's FBI confidential. I don't want to get you into any kind of trouble for leaking information," Eric said. While he'd unofficially worked with her and Howell on a case previously, he'd always respected her boundaries and took her professional limitations into consideration, which Susan appreciated.

Always, except for his plans of writing a tell-all book, she reminded herself.

He added, "I don't want you thinking that I feel as if I'm entitled to the FBI's database. I know I never would have even met Howell or have access to confidential information if it weren't for you."

"Thanks, but it's nothing like that. I was just trying to figure out how to phrase it. DOTE, as a group . . ." Susan shook her head, even though he couldn't see her. "They're almost like Jekyll and Hyde."

"How so?"

"Again, I'm basing this on what Johnathan encountered during his dealings with them," she said. "On the one hand, you've got the members who are so cliché and phony that they might as well be cardboard cutouts of themselves. Remember those—what did Jake call them—*trustafarians* we met up in Clancy?" The recollection stung Susan as soon as the words came out of her mouth. She and Eric had been on vacation at the time, and still a couple. They'd traveled up to Washington together in the same car from California; they'd gone out to eat, hiked through the lush Pacific Northwestern forest, toured the dying little downtown. And, at night, they'd shared the same bed. She squeezed her eyes shut, pushed the sweetest memories from her mind.

Eric laughed. "I remember. Those two wannabe hippy kids in that beat-up, spray-painted RV, 'roughing it' with their brand-new smartphones, laptops, and purebred dog—"

"Drinking lattes, bitching about how they couldn't get their nature photos to upload on Instagram." Susan chuckled through the hurt.

"Don't forget their shiny road bikes that cost more than our cars."

"Right! Anyway, there's one side of DOTE that is the Dr. Jekyll side. While they're bothersome to those they target, they're generally harmless and they mean well—like the trustafarian couple. They're your garden-variety young, impressionable college kids looking for a cause to rebel on behalf of. They're typically in their early twenties and come from fairly well-off backgrounds. Idealists who have yet to be *really* hurt by the world."

"Sounds just like Samantha—or at least how Bryan described her."

"I'm not surprised," Susan said. "Anyway, these are the members who do things like go to protests and take their grievances out on social media. Wear shirts with slogans."

"Pretty standard stuff."

"Right. Then, though, you've got the Mr. Hyde side of DOTE. These are the scary members, the ones we try to keep an eye on, although it's difficult to pin down the perpetrators. They never put a name to their work—criminal activity, I mean, not protests—not the way a group like Earth Liberation Front did when they were most active."

Eric asked, "What do they do?"

"I'll give you an example, which will help explain the two-sidedness. The first DOTE case Johnathan worked involved the Art Modern Museum of San Francisco and Neal Proctor. Proctor's this ultramodern artist who makes 'art' I don't really get—installations with crying, naked people throwing chess pieces at each other and giant boxes of cigarettes painted with squid ink. Cuckoo stuff that sells for a couple million bucks."

"Hey, whatever floats, right?" Eric said with a chuckle.

"I guess rich people need frivolous things to spend their money on too," Susan commented. "Anyway, Proctor did this one installation that involved stuffed fox carcasses with pig's blood dripping from their eyes. There were also live orchids sticking out the foxes' butts. The pieces were suspended from the ceiling by old telephone cords."

"Naturally," Eric joked.

"The doters were furious about the dead animals, so they picketed the museum day and night for weeks, even when it was closed. They set up tents on the sidewalk, sprayed with the DOTE emblem, which is a red capital *D* with a triangle around it. They also dressed up in fox costumes—like those big mascot outfits with googly eyes—and called customers names as they bought tickets. Some covered themselves in fake blood and sprawled in front of the museum, screaming their heads off. Johnathan showed me footage; it was quite a show."

"Don't these people have jobs they have to go to? How do they afford to take so much time off work?" Eric asked.

"Funny, I asked Johnathan the same thing. Guess you can always tell a person who didn't grow up rich, because having enough money is a constant concern."

"True that."

"Most of these wealthy DOTE kids don't work—it's their parents who are footing the bill, half of whom probably don't know what their kids are up to," Susan explained. "Of course, the media started showing up at the museum, and then the whole exhibition became more about the war between Proctor and the doters than the art itself. Eventually, they had to shut the exhibit down because it was affecting road traffic near the museum, not that Proctor minded. He made millions from the publicity that his pieces had gotten. It actually made him more famous than he already was."

"I'm sure DOTE were livid. Talk about a backfire."

"I'm sure of it, too, because here's where the Mr. Hyde side comes in. A couple nights after the exhibit closed, Proctor was sleeping up in his loft when a fire broke out in his studio below. It was where some of his new paintings were being stored—his works in progress."

"Arson?"

"Absolutely. Molotov cocktails," Susan said. "He barely made it out alive, since the doors had been nailed shut. He had to throw a chair through a window and jump down about fifteen feet. He got all cut up from the glass and broke his ankle."

"Jeez!" Eric breathed. "So, DOTE wasn't just trying to send a message. They were genuinely trying to kill him."

"That's the thing—DOTE never takes credit for the really bad, illegal stuff, but Johnathan is sure they're behind the attack."

"How?"

Susan said, "He brought a suspect in for questioning that he knew was affiliated with the group. Kid started bawling his eyes out the moment they sat him down in interrogation. Just as he was about to crack and roll on those responsible for the arson, the parents—wealthy, that goes without saying—came in with some big-time lawyer they keep on retainer and got him to clam up. Seems this wasn't the first time the little shit had gotten himself into trouble."

"That's just gross."

"The kid later recanted everything he said. The lawyer made it out that he had given confused testimony because he was under duress. It's like whoever is calling the shots at DOTE is using impressionable college kids as a smoke screen to conceal the truly nefarious activity. It's like they want people to look at the group—the Dr. Jekyll side—and say, 'Oh, look at those silly kids, wearing their costumes and making spectacles of themselves.' Meanwhile, the Mr. Hyde side is committing the truly heinous acts."

"So, the Dr. Jekyll kids are basically a diversion," Eric said. "But every military has a leader, so then who is DOTE's?"

"That's what makes the group so clever. Because they never take credit for the really bad stuff, it's difficult to pin down who's in charge. They're not a registered charity the way other environmental groups are, and they stay out of trouble with the IRS by not collecting any monetary dues. Instead, members pay dues through direct action: protests, writing blog posts, etcetera—although, Johnathan suspects that the rich kids are funneling funds to the group through stealthy means. And, as far as the illegal activity, they're almost like a gang in this respect: they get members to commit crimes so that they never have to worry about the members turning on each other."

"You're not going to rat on someone for committing a crime if you've committed one yourself," Eric said, and Susan agreed.

"Anyway, DOTE are on the FBI's watch list, but near the bottom." Susan moved her mouse around on her desk to wake up her computer after it had gone into sleep mode. "Remind me again of Bryan's full name."

She used the FBI database to run a search, immediately seeing that he was flagged as being wanted in connection with Samantha's murder. Her parents had political pull, indeed, if both the police and the FBI were on the lookout for him. She delved further, finding information that seemed to refute Eric's claims about the kid being innocent. "This is *not* good," she said darkly. "Your boy Bryan is a registered sex offender."

CHAPTER 7

Spotting Howell swiftly approaching her desk, Susan didn't get to further explore Bryan's charges. She would have liked to see specifics on the sex crime, since the conviction contradicted Eric's earlier stance that Bryan was a morally upstanding human being with the unfortunate luck of having himself set up as a fall guy. Eric's insight was typically keen when it came to crime, so she was surprised that a college student who seemed a far cry from a criminal mastermind had managed to bamboozle both him and Jake.

She quickly hung up, secretly hoping that she could later find a reason to call Eric back. It had felt good to hear his voice, but it had also made her wistful. She wondered if he might be feeling the same.

She was on the brink of asking Howell what was happening, but, like always, he beat her to the punch. "Just got word that Chung Nguygen's body was found," he said.

"Where?"

"A couple hikers discovered it washed up onshore two miles downstream from the dam."

"And what about Dov Amsel?"

Howell shook his head. "Still at large."

"Are we thinking that he's looking good for the murder?"

"Seems like it. The working theory is that Amsel went to lunch with the intention of murdering Nguygen, though the motive remains unclear."

"Are we still thinking this has something to do with Gruben Dam, or is it personal?" Susan asked. Reflecting out loud, she added, "There's always the possibility that it was *not* premeditated. Maybe the two went to a bar, had a couple drinks over lunch, and things got heated during an argument. Although, the fact that Nguygen's body was found so close to the dam might suggest otherwise. I'll check the bank statements to see where they ate, once I hear back from IT."

"Only time will tell on that one, but it would be premature to rule out a potential security threat to the dam." Howell glanced at his watch. "IT probably won't have anything for you until tomorrow morning. There was a delay down there because of a possible mainframe breach. They shut down for a few hours."

Susan made a move for her jacket and bag. "I'll go to the dam now, then, and talk to some of Amsel and Nguygen's coworkers to see what I can dig up. Their jobs are entirely unrelated, so I'm curious as to how the two became close enough friends that they'd take a lunch break together. I wonder how much cause an engineer and armed guard would have to interact on the job, especially at a location as vast as a dam. Maybe they met at a company picnic or something. Or maybe they knew each other before they started working at Gruben."

"Those are good questions to ask while you're there," Howell said, and then he and Susan parted ways.

On the way to the dam, Susan placed a call to Dr. Mikael Abbonzio, the medical examiner in charge of Nguygen's autopsy. Like Howell, she was polite but brusque, which Susan didn't mind too much. Between the conversations she'd had with Eric and Howell, she was feeling rather talked out.

"Cause of death is blunt-force trauma," Abbonzio said. "Back of the skull. One solid hit was what seems to have done it."

"So, this indicates that the murder was more out of necessity than passion—or else you might see more injuries, right? Could this indicate that it was premeditated, because, if it wasn't, the attack might have been sloppier?" Susan asked the doctor.

"I'm no psychologist, so I can't comment on that. All I can tell you is what I see," she said blandly, and Susan started to miss Salvador Martinez, the ME she'd always worked with at Perrick PD. *He* would have commented, being a huge true-crime buff in his private time. Hell, he probably would have had a whole theory cooked up, complete with diagrams, and he would have shared them with her and concluded the conversation by giving her a recipe for a grilled fish marinade. She missed that about working in a small town, the personalized touch. At the San Francisco FBI, the specialists she interacted with were often rotating, so it was difficult to build rapport. They were mostly all business, which had its perks when she was in a hurry.

Sometimes, though, it was a reminder of how alone she really was.

Susan, while outgoing, didn't have a lot of close friends. She'd never been a "go out with the ladies for cocktails" kind of gal; she preferred a one-on-one setting. Her family unit was virtually nil; she was an only child, so no siblings. She was close with her mother in a vague sort of way, polite and warm on the surface, yet their conversations (usually by text message as of late) were typically about superficial topics: work, crime news, weather. And her father, well, the only thing she really had in common with him was the youthful looks they shared. With the same chocolatey brown hair, deep-blue eyes, and athletic build, they looked closer to brother and sister than father and daughter. She hadn't spoken to him in almost a year, when he'd berated her for not wanting to sell her story to a salacious publisher, which she'd learned would have given him a hefty finder's fee for convincing her to work with them.

She never thought she'd become the sort of person who could say her job was her life, yet here she was. The median price of a home in San Francisco was over $1.2 million, so she'd given up the idea of owning her own place in the area some time ago. But that didn't mean she wasn't craving *a little* stability and hominess.

Her homelife wasn't much of a life at all. She couldn't remember the last time she'd made herself a sit-down meal—she didn't really have "meals." She merely scavenged scraps of food from the refrigerator whenever she became aware that her stomach was growling. With Eric—*here you go, fixating on Eric again,* she thought with some disdain—she'd had a taste of domestic bliss. Now that it was gone, she was wondering how she'd ever functioned so long without it, much the same way a person who's walked all their life on sore feet feels once they've been blessed with an automobile. Being with him had made everything feel so effortless. A single person again, she'd thought about hitting the dating scene *in theory.* It was the actual practice part that made her stomach do flip-flops.

She sighed away from the phone, so the doctor wouldn't hear her losing her patience. "Right. Is there any possibility that this could have been an accident? He worked at a dam, so is it possible that he could have fallen into the water somehow and hit his head on a rock, or something to that effect?"

"I don't really like to speculate . . ."

The doctor was about as pliable as cold titanium. "Oh, go on—I won't arrest you if you're mistaken," she said in her cheeriest voice.

Abbonzio cleared her throat. "If I had to make an educated guess, I'd say, no, he didn't fall into the water. The wound is far too concentrated for it to be accidental, at least from my experience." Susan got the impression that she was answering just to speed things along.

"What do you think did it, then? The weapon, I mean."

"Again, if I had to—"

"Yes," Susan said, "make an educated guess." She tacked on "please" after she heard how annoyed she was beginning to sound.

"I'd say it was probably a hammer."

"How about toxicology?"

The ME laughed incredulously, as if Susan had asked her for a topless photo. "Oh no, *that* won't come back for a while."

Susan thanked Dr. Abbonzio for her time and focused her attention on the navigation screen on her dashboard. She was nearing the dam, which was set back from the city at the top of a long, winding road. The guard at the gate disappointed her by staring back at her badge, unimpressed, when she flashed it. It had become a point of pride for her, and she liked showing it off, since it was something she had earned through hard work and proving her competency.

It was peculiar; she'd found her credentials prompted two very different reactions. People either glanced at her badge in a disinterested fashion, the way the guard had done, or they gushed like she was a superhero, pummeling her with questions: *Is it like what you see on TV? Is it true you take over police investigations? How can I become a special agent?* She probably got asked the last question the most by the general public, which was odd since the FBI had application information right on their website for the whole world to see. Maybe they were hoping she'd give them a recommendation that would help them skip to the front of the line—because that would be a responsible thing to do, provide a personal reference to a federal agency for someone she'd met on the street and had known for all of twenty seconds.

"We had someone from the Department of Homeland Security here earlier," the guard said haughtily, as if the visit had lessened the impressiveness of her job. "He said he was from the Dams Sector."

She nodded, pretending it wasn't news to her. She wasn't surprised, though, given the high security of Gruben Dam. Still, it would have been nice to have been told that other government agents were on-site.

Susan figured HR was a good place to start asking questions; however, when she arrived, the office was closed for an unnamed reason. She put her badge away and went into the break room, which she'd always found to be a good source of gossip. The space was rather large, as far as break rooms went, with a few long laminate tables, benches attached, set up in orderly rows. It reminded her of a high school cafeteria, minus the pimples, food fights, and overall air of despondency.

Employees sat scattered in small groups, drinking coffee mostly, but a few were eating sandwiches and munching on the sort of snacks that had obviously come from a vending machine. Unlike when she'd been a police officer in uniform, which had made her stick out like a sore thumb no matter where she went, here, in business casual attire, she blended right in. She ambled over to the sink and rinsed out a coffee cup, as if she belonged there, trying to get a sense of the general atmosphere of the place. Most of the employees seemed happy enough, and their conversations were innocuous. They talked about what they'd seen on television the night prior, a cute thing their toddler had done, the annoyance of lawn upkeep.

There was one table, however, where three men and two women were speaking in hushed tones. *Bingo,* she thought. She tilted her head a fraction in their direction, which did absolutely nothing to help her hear better. Not wanting to spook them with her stillness, she quietly rooted through the cabinet above the sink, as if searching for a particular mug. Because other people were talking in the room, she was able to make out only snatches of words in their conversation.

" . . . I wonder what they were doing . . ."

" . . . I bet they killed each other . . ."

" . . . lying in a ditch somewhere . . ."

They stopped talking when somebody new came up to their table and sat down. Susan figured it was as good a time as any to make her approach. She pulled her badge and flashed it at them. "May I?" she asked in regard to sitting down next to them. From experience, she knew it would put them more at ease if she were at eye level, opposed to looming down from above. She also knew better than to ask for their names, which would give the chat a sense of formality. It was always best to keep it casual.

They seemed stunned to see an FBI agent, and one of the women looked worried. Susan assumed it was because she was the one who'd seemed to be gossiping most. Susan quickly explained why she was there, stating that she'd like to ask them some questions about Amsel and Nguygen. They seemed willing enough to talk, though what they knew didn't get her any closer to tracking them down.

"They hated each other—just hated," a doughy, sunburned man with copper-colored hair and a beard to match said dramatically. Susan imagined him lounging in his backyard the weekend prior with a happy, hairy dog and an ice chest filled with cheap beer, the radio blasting. He looked as if he'd dozed off in the sun for about eight hours. His singed skin appeared hot enough to fry an egg on, Susan mused, thinking that he must be in a great deal of pain.

"Why?" Susan asked the group, who suddenly didn't seem so chatty.

A tiny mouse of a woman with a frizzy bob haircut and large wire-frame glasses that gave her an owlish appearance raised her hand, as if she were in a class. Susan told her to speak freely, and she said, "Maybe it was because Chung was a square, and Dov was . . ." She clamped her lips tightly closed.

"Dov was what?" Susan asked, and the group exchanged guilty looks.

The gossipy woman eventually said, "We're not trying to get anyone in trouble."

Susan gave them what she was hoping was a disarming smile. "I'm not here to stir up trouble. I'm only looking for clues that may help me locate your two missing coworkers."

After a moment, the mousy woman said, "Dov was, how should I put it . . . ?"

"Useless," the sunburned man cut in. "There, I said it."

Susan asked, "How so?"

"He didn't do shit, pardon my French," the gossipy woman said. "I've seen rent-a-cop security guards at the mall take their jobs more seriously than Dov did. He was lazy as all get-out. I can't imagine what would have happened if we'd actually had a real security threat while he was on the clock."

"That's because he was always . . ." The mousy woman clamped a hand over her mouth. She behaved as if she'd stopped maturing around age sixteen. Susan gave her an encouraging nod, and she added, "I, well, a lot of us, we kind of suspected that he might have been, though we don't *really* know, since we have no actual proof—"

"Jesus, Jeanine, just spit it out," the sunburned man said. "High. A lot of people around here thought he was high. Which is awesome, right, since he carried a loaded gun? That's just the sort of person you want to see armed."

"High on what?" Susan asked.

"Do *we* look like drug addicts?" the gossipy woman quipped. Susan raised an eyebrow at her, and she sunk down in her seat. She spoke quieter as she said, "I mean, we're not experts on the subject. Nobody really *knew* what he was on, but most people suspected it was nothing good."

"Is this true?" Susan asked the table, and everyone nodded. "So, Dov was a terrible worker and possibly on drugs. How was he able to keep his job?"

The mousy woman said, "That's what we could never figure out. He must have had some serious dirt on some big boss in the company— that's the best we could come up with, anyway."

"And what about Chung?" Susan asked, and the table erupted in incredulous laughter.

Shaking his head, the sunburned man said, "Chung taking drugs? No, just no. Not a chance in hell."

"And what was he like on the job?" Susan asked.

"Anal. Don't get me wrong; he was perfectly nice. Nobody ever had a problem with him, other than Dov, of course. But Chung followed rules to a T, which set some people on edge. He never ratted anyone out for breaking the rules, but you could tell he was judging you," the gossipy woman said and then pursed her lips. If the crisp tone of her voice was anything to go by, she was speaking from personal experience; she was a part of the "some people" group.

Sunburned said, "He actually set an alarm on his phone when he went on his breaks. If he came back even one minute late, he'd make up for that time by staying one minute later at the end of the day. He never took so much as a pen home from the office, and he kept his desk immaculate."

Susan frowned. "So, you've got one worker who's lazy and potentially taking drugs, and you've got another who's essentially a walking employee manual. Why did they leave here together to go to lunch?"

"That's what we're trying to figure out. It just makes no sense," the sunburned man said.

The gossip seconded the statement. "No sense whatsoever."

Susan distributed her business card to the group and thanked them for their time. She asked them to call her should they think of anything else, reminding them that sometimes seemingly insignificant tips led to big discoveries. She returned to the HR department, frowning to find it still closed. She pulled out one of her cards, planning to leave it with a note for the HR rep to call her. Reconsidering, she returned it to her wallet. It was always best to approach, in person, with the element of surprise.

CHAPTER 8

Although he couldn't help thinking that it would have enriched the lecture (and his day) a whole lot more if Susan were there, Eric was nailing his talk on the myths and misconceptions of FBI protocols. He could always tell when he held the students' attention and when they were bored. This was not so much about their behavior, but because of the overall energy he felt coming off the room—a notion he would have scoffed at before his otherworldly quirk had made itself known.

When they were bored, he felt and heard a dull hum bouncing off the walls, like a fly dying a slow death after being swatted. When they were interested, as they were now, he had their full, undivided attention as a collective unit, pens moving along paper fluidly and fingers tapping at keyboards at a synchronized pace. Strange as it was, his brain interpreted the scene as a song coming from a beautifully tuned violin, like something Jake would play, though he doubted anyone could hear the melody but him.

He was smack-dab in the middle of explaining that, no, the FBI did not simply *take over* investigations from local law enforcement like how it was depicted on television, when his class began to stir. It started as clusters of whispering scattered throughout the room, accompanied by the restless *bzz-bzz-bzz* of cell phones vibrating. Fingers tap-danced along keyboards, sounding like rainfall, as instant messages flowed in. Hands flew to mouths, students gasping in unison.

Strangely, the emotions were mixed. Some faces grinned while others teared up, and then there were the three boys in the back high-fiving one another. Two students on opposite sides of the room leaped up from their chairs and bolted out the exit.

"Okay, what's going on?" Eric demanded. The class looked back at him in a deer-in-the-headlights fashion, too timid to answer after he'd used such an exasperated tone. His hands flew to his hips identical to how his mother would have done. It was a quirk he was wholly unaware of. His brother, Jim, who Eric had not spoken with since discovering that he'd been sleeping with Maggie, the woman who was now Eric's ex-wife and Jim's current one, did the exact same thing and was as equally unaware. "No, really. Someone tell me, *please*."

Finally, Nate Boyle, a beanpole-thin kid in the front row who typically scored perfectly on tests, slowly raised his hand. "It's that guy everyone is looking for—the one who killed his girlfriend. He's dead."

"Seriously?" Eric asked, too stunned to articulate a better question. Then came a series of murmurs. A group of girls in the second row: *He deserved it.* A voice near the back: *Good.* A sobbing young man: *I can't believe it!*

Jake hurried up to the desk as the room erupted in chatter. "I think we should call the class."

Eric did just that. As books and laptops were crammed in backpacks, he provided a reminder that everyone, including Bryan McDougal, was innocent until proven guilty. That netted him a few eye rolls.

Once everyone was gone, he asked, "Was it the police who killed him?"

Jake shook his head. "They're saying it was suicide. Took a header off the top floor of the parking garage here on campus."

"Which one?" LU had several, located on four corners of the campus.

"West lot."

"That's the lot *I* park in—my car's there right now!" Eric had so many questions it was difficult to choose which to ask first. "How did you find out so fast?"

Jake said, "Come on—you know how quickly news travels around here. Remember how *everyone* was looking for him yesterday *everywhere*, and word of the murder had only just gotten out? Bryan's suicide is all over Facebook, and while you were talking to the class about the FBI, I had about a dozen texts come in about it."

"When did he do it—jump off the roof?"

"Like twenty minutes ago, while we were here in class. It's peak attendance time, so I'm sure a few students had to have seen him hit the ground. Imagine carrying *that* image with you for the rest of your life. I wonder if anyone saw him actually jump." Jake went quiet for a moment. "Do you think he did it, then? Killed Samantha?"

Eric said, "Although there is evidence to the contrary, I still don't think so."

"Weird he'd commit suicide, then, don't you think? I mean, if it were me, I'd want to clear my name first. Or at least *try*."

Eric grimaced. "I think that's what he was attempting to do in my office yesterday."

"Idiot dean barging in on us," Jake muttered.

"He *is* an idiot," Eric agreed. "I wonder if things would have gone differently if we hadn't been interrupted."

"How do you explain Bryan's sex offense that Susan told you about?"

Eric shook his head. "I still don't know. I've been racking my brain about it. I can't explain it, but it's one of those weird feelings I get. I'd like to know more about the actual charges, because something feels . . . hinky."

"Yesterday, I thought he was innocent too. But, now, I just don't know anymore. Given how determined he was to fight for his innocence when we talked to him, it seems odd that he'd give up twenty-four hours later and commit suicide. Makes me wonder if he decided that fighting was pointless since he'd actually done what he's being accused of."

Eric shook his head. "Who knows what goes on in a person's brain before they take their own life? He obviously wasn't of sound mind. And we know he was scared and exhausted—I can't imagine where he was hiding out, with his face being all over social media and the news. Probably under a bridge somewhere, with little to no food, given that he couldn't go out in public to get supplies. Imagine being him with all that going on. Plus, there's a campus full of students—people you thought were your *friends*—the police, and your ex-girlfriend's politically powerful parents thinking you murdered a promising young woman while you were attempting to sexually assault her."

"That *would* suck."

"And you and I know from personal experience how news and gossip get twisted. You should have heard all the things kids on campus were saying about Bryan this morning."

"Oh, I heard," Jake said, nodding emphatically. "They've got him stabbing, not just Samantha, but *other* women—like Ted Bundy–style serial killing—and spiking drinks, selling drugs, and embezzling from the bar. Everyone's got a friend of a friend who was either harassed or attacked or drugged by Bryan. So, sure, I guess it's no wonder he killed himself."

Eric said, "Trust me—considering the heinousness of what Bryan's being accused of, if I had even a *whisper* of doubt that he was guilty, I would never defend him. And I certainly wouldn't have gone to Susan about him."

"I feel bad, you know? *Guilty.* Do you think there's a chance Bryan killed himself because of us?"

"You mean because we didn't do more to help him?"

"Right."

"Well, he *did* jump out the window."

"I know," Jake said, his shoulders slumped in a manner that was almost childlike. "But, if he really *is* innocent, I'd like to help clear his name, because I'm guessing there's not a lot of people out there lining up to do the job. And, this goes without saying, I'd like to do the most important thing, which would be to catch the person who is actually responsible. Just think, if Bryan *is* innocent, there's a drink-spiking, murdering, would-be rapist on the loose."

Eric shuddered. "I know. I look at all these young girls in my classes, and they seem so vulnerable. I want to go out and buy a canister of pepper spray for every one of them. I know it's not fair—women being put in a position where they should even *need* to protect themselves in the first place. And, in a perfect world, men would be taught from birth to be gentlemen and not hurt these girls the way they do. I try not to scare students with my lectures, but, unfortunately, I think some of them *should* be a little more scared and not so trusting. Especially being in a big city like San Francisco. Some of these young kids, they come from the middle-of-nowhere towns with like a few thousand people—"

"Or affluent gated neighborhoods with around-the-clock security guards," Jake cut in.

"Exactly. They expect the same level of safety and courtesy living in a city with nearly a million strangers in it."

"Unfortunately, Samantha's murder is a reminder that nobody is untouchable by violence." Jake paused and then ventured, "I suppose I could always talk to that DOTE club."

Eric shook his head. "I still don't think that's such a good idea. Susan made them sound as if they might be dangerous."

Jake flapped a hand and made a *pffft* sound. "I think I can handle a group of tree-hugging college kids."

"It's not the college kids I'm worried about. It's the ones who are hiding behind them like cowards."

Jake nodded, though Eric suspected he was going to do whatever it was he wanted to, anyway. His friend was stubborn like that, which he supposed was one of the reasons he liked him so much. Jake had a good sense of self and always behaved in a manner that was true to his core belief system—which was to treat others how he wished to be treated. Eric supposed one would have to be that way to stay sane, being born a dwarf. He'd witnessed the harassment, sideways glances, and giggles Jake had to contend with every day of his life. Unlike Eric's schizophrenia, dwarfism was something that could never be concealed. He admired his friend for never cowering and always keeping his chin held high.

Jake was simply too good for the world he lived in.

Still, he couldn't help worrying. His friend's display of solidness, for want of a better term, had been fading during the past few months. Between his grief over the loss of his friends, his teacher's assistant duties, and his dropping grades (this, Jake had inadvertently let slip one day in idle conversation), he seemed to have enough on his plate. Going off on some half-cocked investigative mission was probably the last thing he needed. No, not even *probably*; he didn't need any potential negativity, and that seemed to be what any association with DOTE would bring.

"I wonder how word got out about him being accused of the attempted rape?" Jake asked. "Everyone knew about the murder, but I thought only the police knew about the other part."

"Like you said, word travels. I'm sure the police told the roommate to stay quiet about what they suspected just as I'm equally sure the roommate then told his closest friend just to get it off his chest, and then that one friend told someone else, and on and on. Gossip is, after all, the currency of academics."

◆ ◆ ◆

By the time Eric headed out to his car, the campus was void of students, with all classes being canceled for the rest of the day. He'd opted to stay in his office and catch up on some papers that had needed grading while he waited for the parking garage to be opened back up. He'd been working at a rapid pace until the ape-grinning Alan Williams decided to make an appearance in his doorway to the tune of, *Well, I guess we can consider the case of Samantha's death good and closed!* Leaving was the only thing he could do to stop himself from punching the dean's lights out.

Eric had parked on the third floor up, which was a far enough climb to rationalize taking the elevator, yet still close enough that he felt guilty for not taking the stairs. "To hell with it," he muttered, and then he pushed the button to call the elevator. It had been a rough day, to say the least, so he figured he could allow himself a small luxury.

He crinkled his nose when he entered the elevator; someone had been smoking clove cigarettes, a scent so distinct that it was hard to confuse with anything else. He'd always found the smell nauseating, so he was grateful when the doors to his floor opened and let in a gust of fresh air. He'd only made it a few steps outside the elevator when he knew something wasn't right.

He was being followed, as if someone had been lying in wait for him.

Turning in a full circle so that it was obvious he was aware he was being tailed, he scanned the parking lot. From what he could see, he was the only person on the floor, although there were still plenty of vehicles—perhaps a few other professors had gotten the same idea as him to catch up on work. "Hello?"

In the distance, behind a tall black truck, came a series of snickers. Given that he was on a university campus, this wouldn't have bothered him in the slightest on a normal day. But tonight, the hairs on his arms were rising and his flesh was sprouting goose bumps. He cleared his bone-dry throat. "Is somebody there?"

A car alarm bleeped to life in the same row as the truck. He opened his mouth to shout at the pranksters that any practical joke was in poor taste given recent events, but then something at the back of his mind told him that to do so would not be a wise idea—that the smart thing to do instead would be to run, *run!*

So he did.

He jammed his hand in his pocket and frantically fished for his keys as he navigated the U-shaped lot, nearly tripping over his own feet as he rounded the corner. His neck popped as he snapped his head around and peered behind him. He could hear the pounding of footsteps on pavement—multiple individuals, it sounded like—yet there was nobody there.

Still, he kept running.

He let out a breath of relief when he spotted his Jeep. He was in such a frenzy that he hit the panic alarm on his key fob instead of the unlock button. Finally, finally he made the doors unlock. Yet, as his hand closed over the door handle, a cloth was forced over his head, and his view went dark.

CHAPTER 9

Susan had gotten the background checks on Dov Amsel and Chung Nguygen back from IT that morning. Sipping her third cup of coffee of the day, she'd flipped through them to see if there was any additional information she could use to her advantage during her questioning of Anne, Dov's wife. The gossips at the dam had given her a great understanding of their characters and work ethic, and now she was going to get down to the nitty-gritty.

Nguygen's file had been quick and easy to navigate, since he was near squeaky clean. Given what she'd learned at the dam, this wasn't surprising. Barring a couple parking tickets he'd gotten down in the city, which was hardly a federal crime and actually normal for the area (if anything, it was more remarkable that he had so few), his record was devoid of any infractions. He also had an excellent credit score and had paid his taxes early every year from the time he'd had a job. *He must have lived the life of a saint,* she'd mused going through the file, lamenting that it made his death all the more tragic. The world could use more people like him.

The one blip, if it could be called that, she found on Nguygen's file was in regard to his bank account. Just like with his taxes, Nguygen had been well organized with his money. Every time he'd gotten a paycheck, he'd immediately paid all his bills. He'd then placed 30 percent of the remainder into savings, another 10 percent into an emergency fund, and dedicated another 10 percent to investments. He left the rest in checking. Since he was such an orderly man with a high level of formal education, Susan was surprised he didn't also have college funds designated for his children, but then she saw in the file that he didn't have any offspring.

Nguygen's bank account reflected the organized pattern for as far back as his records went, like clockwork, his paycheck always coming from Gruben Dam. It was unusual, then, that he'd received a onetime check from a company called Zelman Industries a little over a week prior. She made a note to herself to check on it later.

In contrast to Chung Nguygen, Dov Amsel was quite the disaster. Again, not too surprising. Throughout his adult life, he'd had multiple run-ins with the law, mostly over drugs: cocaine possession in 2009, 2010, and 2015, with a couple charges of heroin possession thrown in for variety in 2013. He'd also gotten a DUI in 2010. In 2014, he was busted for writing bad checks. His credit score was a shocking 352; she didn't know it was possible it could be that low. How had someone with a background like Dov Amsel's been able to land a job at a high-security dam—and not just any old job, but one where he'd carry a gun?

With the arsenal of information from the background check, Susan went to the Amsel household to speak with his wife, Anne, with the intent of turning the screws on her. If anyone ever knew anything about where a fugitive might be hiding out, it was typically the significant other. But, not surprisingly, it was often the same person who knew the most that was willing to offer up the least, since helping law enforcement would hurt their lover. Human nature stuff, really.

Susan had been expecting to be greeted with hostility at the Amsel house, but what she hadn't expected was to be met at the door by a *very* pregnant Anne, who looked like she could give birth any day. Susan liked to think she was impartial to witness appearances, yet even she understood that she was not going to relish having to badger a woman who was with child. As she stepped over the threshold of the modest one-story home, she quickly decided to change her approach to one that better suited the witness.

Anne reluctantly offered Susan a seat on a well-worn beige sofa that was of the popular plump-cushioned style of the 1980s. She wore sweatpants that were baggy in the seat, a faded sweatshirt that fit her like a parachute, and thick wooly socks that scrunched around her ankles like two flat tires. She looked on the verge of drowning with all that fabric she was swimming in. She was clearly not happy to have an FBI agent in her home, yet she still maintained her manners. "Can I offer you something to drink? I was just making myself some chamomile tea. It's supposed to be good for nerves."

Ordinarily, Susan would have countered with, "Do you have something to be nervous about, Anne?" However, she decided to approach this particular situation with a little more finesse. She smiled pleasantly. "That would be wonderful, thank you. It's a chilly one outside today, so my bones could use some warming."

Anne went into the kitchen without another word. She looked dog tired, Susan noted, as if she hadn't slept a wink since Dov's disappearance. Though she appeared uncomfortable—and who wouldn't be with an FBI agent sitting in their living room, waiting to question them about a potentially murderous husband—she didn't seem as squirrelly as one would if they were hiding a fugitive in their home. Perhaps Dov's whereabouts were as big a mystery to Anne as they were to everyone else. *Perhaps.*

Still, Susan kept her hand close to her gun.

As Anne puttered around the kitchen, Susan extracted herself from the squishy sofa cushions that had enveloped her like rising dough and had a look out the large square window that faced the front yard. Like Anne, the yard looked tired and as if it had seen better days. It seemed the Amsels were not fans of mowing and had thus opted for the easy route, which was to pave over everything in sight with either concrete or large mismatched rocks that looked as if they'd been pilfered from a local creek. There wasn't a hint of living nature to be seen, unless a birdhouse counted, though she could see no birds near it. It was a pretty little thing, though, done up in a midcentury modern style, with a bright orange-red pop of color peeping out from the underside of the roof. Susan frowned at its peculiar placement, which was at a height more suitable for a mailbox. Weren't birdhouses supposed to be high up? Maybe they'd kept it low because it was the only attractive feature of the yard.

She turned back to the living room. While the surroundings were shabby and uninspired in here as well, the household showed pride of ownership: surfaces dusted, wood polished, floors vacuumed. Artwork, while generic, had been hung. Bookcases held mystery novels, home-made scrapbooks, and how-to guides that focused on woodworking and home repairs. Framed photos were scattered along shelves: Dov and Anne dressed as a pirate and wench for Halloween; Anne laughing on the back of a horse; Dov waving at the camera from behind the hood of a vintage car he was tinkering on.

Dov looked as if he'd lived a hard life. His weathered complexion made his age appear closer to forty-five than thirty-one, though his bald head might have also had something to do with it. Still, had she not seen Dov's file, she never would have believed that he'd had a history of drug-related legal offenses. Despite his battered appearance, there was something within his features that hinted at a boyish outlook on the world. Perhaps it was immaturity that had gotten him into trouble.

"How far along are you?" Susan asked as Anne returned to the living room. She accepted the tea graciously and then placed it atop a beaded coaster on the coffee table. After learning of a bad experience Eric had had with his drink being drugged in a killer's home, she made it a rule to never consume anything offered to her during a formal house call.

Anne placed her own mug down, eased back into a recliner, and cupped her belly. The burden she carried was physical as well as mental, and Susan felt a twinge of pity for the woman, who looked like she was barely out of diapers herself. *What an absolutely awful time to have your husband take off on you,* she thought.

Anne surprised her by saying, "He didn't do it, you know. Kill Chung. That's why you're really here, isn't it? You don't care that I'm just a few weeks away from giving birth, or that with Dov being gone I have no idea what I'm going to do for money, or that nobody is willing to help me now that everyone thinks I'm married to a killer—you just want to know where my husband is so you can arrest him." She put her face into her hands and started to sob.

Susan waited patiently while Anne cried herself out, discreetly passing her the box of tissues from a side table next to the sofa. She didn't bother denying that there was a possibility that she'd arrest Dov—or, at a minimum, bring him in for questioning. She also didn't lie and tell her that everything was going to be okay. It wasn't okay and probably never would be for Anne ever again. The man Dov had left for lunch with had turned up dead, which meant that he'd probably done it. And, if not, there was a good possibility that he might also be dead himself.

To give herself something to do, Susan went into the kitchen and fetched Anne a glass of water, though she already had a warm mug of tea. When she returned from the kitchen, she said to Anne, "Why don't you just tell me what you know, okay?"

Anne honked her nose into a tissue. She seemed to be getting herself under control. "Well, I know Dov didn't kill Chung."

"Okay, how do you know?"

"Because, he wouldn't do something like that!" she screeched. And then, a little quieter, "I know him."

Susan felt it would be pedantic to point out that people rarely knew their spouse was capable of murder until they committed it. "Word at the dam was that your husband and Chung Nguygen despised each other."

Anne nodded. "That's true; they did."

"Yet they went to lunch together? Help me understand this, Anne," Susan said, leaning forward.

Anne let out a long sigh, a little hiccup escaping her at the end. "It was childish, really—I actually feel a little embarrassed talking about it, since it involves the man I'm married to."

"You have nothing to be embarrassed about, Anne. Trust me when I tell you that I've heard it all." Susan smiled reassuringly.

"It all started when Chung's lunch was stolen from the break room. There had been an ongoing problem with food theft, and people were pretty riled up about it. You wouldn't believe how territorial some of these guys down at the dam are about their lunches."

This is good; she's relaxing, Susan thought. *Keep her talking.* She peered at Anne warmly. "Oh, I can believe it. Someone pinched my coworker's blackberry yogurt from the break-room fridge and he acted like someone had killed his dog."

Anne laughed softly. "Sounds a lot like what's going on at the dam. Anyway, Chung was convinced that Dov had taken his lunch. It was some kind of special rice dish that his wife had made, and Chung said Dov had a piece of the same rice stuck to his scarf, which was hanging on a shared employee coatrack. Chung had actually gone from department to department throughout the building, searching for remnants of his lunch. Dov said he even sifted through a couple garbage cans."

"He really went full *Columbo*, didn't he?"

"What's *Columbo*?"

"Never mind," Susan said. "Please, continue."

"Chung brought the scarf to Dov as proof, and then Dov called him crazy. He essentially laughed in his face, which wasn't very nice. So, the next day, Dov goes in to work and finds that Chung had stolen his parking space. They don't actually have assigned spots, but it's the kind of deal where everyone always parks in the same space and everyone knows each other's cars. So, to retaliate, Dov put a dead mouse in Chung's locker. Then, Chung broke Dov's coffee mug in the break room . . . it really does sound so juvenile, like little petty children fighting in the schoolyard," Anne said, shaking her head.

"Boys will be boys," Susan said with a roll of the eyes, further establishing rapport. Anne chuckled softly, though to Susan's ears it was the sound of glass breaking. Here was a woman who hadn't had a genuine laugh in some time.

"It went back and forth like that for a while, until one day Dov finally decided to come clean."

"You mean he actually stole the lunch?"

"He did," Anne said, taking a sip of tea. "Why, I don't even think he knows. Guess he didn't like what I'd packed for his lunch that day."

Susan asked, "Why do you think he finally admitted what he'd done?"

Anne hesitated, twisting a tissue in her hands. "It was a step in his program. Making amends."

"Narcotics Anonymous?"

"That's right. He's been clean and sober now for about a year and a half. I'm so proud of him. He quit drugs for good because we'd been trying to get pregnant, and he's done right by his word."

Not according to what everyone at the dam seems to think, Susan thought, though she said nothing on the topic. It was never wise to play all her cards at once. It was interesting, though, the two conflicting stories. Could Anne be that much in denial, or were the gossips at the dam just that conniving? Perhaps Anne had been preoccupied with other matters, being pregnant. She asked, "How did Chung take it when Dov came to him about the stolen lunch?"

"Dov said he was surprisingly gracious about it. He thanked him for admitting his mistake and even promised to keep Dov's NA activity quiet without Dov even asking him to."

Could Dov have been going to NA while taking drugs, living a double life? It wasn't too much of a stretch to imagine other addicts had done something similar. But how could people who hardly knew Dov at the dam be aware of his drug use yet his own wife be oblivious? Perhaps Anne was suffering an old-fashioned bout of selective blindness. Susan asked, "And so then what happened?"

Anne shrugged. "That's pretty much it. Dov offered to take Chung to lunch to make up for the one he stole. He said he'd take him anywhere he wanted. Chung told him that he didn't have to do that, but Dov insisted. And, when Dov left for work the morning he disappeared, he was excited. He said making things right with Chung put him one step closer to being a better man."

The picture Anne had painted of Dov was entirely different from the one Susan had fabricated inside her head before her arrival. Not only did she have the off-the-cuff testimony of the dam employees but also Dov's rap sheet, which had read like a menu of drug and petty-crime charges. She'd also been speculating that Anne's pregnancy could have played a major role in Dov's disappearance, but now she wasn't so sure. Even if he was doing drugs behind her back, he cared enough about his wife that he was willing to live a double life for her, regardless of how twisted the logic. If he didn't care whatsoever, his attitude may have been closer to *deal with it*.

Then again, according to rumors around the dam about Dov being lazy, he hadn't seemed too concerned about keeping his job. Which was odd, with him having a pregnant wife—it seemed the Amsels could use all the money they could get. And, on that front, how had he been able to afford all the drugs he'd allegedly been taking? Maybe he'd been pressing his luck with the intent of self-destruction, whether deliberately or not, his hope being that everything would blow up in his face if he continued abusing drugs and neglecting his job and his pregnant wife. Maybe he was hoping the universe would step in and take everything he had and destroy him, since he was too cowardly to do it himself: freedom through annihilation. It wasn't too much of a stretch, given how he'd been conducting himself most of his life.

There was, of course, the possibility that Anne was lying about being in the dark about Dov's activities and whereabouts, but her gut was telling her no. She didn't strike Susan as the sort of woman who'd be okay living on the streets with a newborn, should Dov succeed at wrecking the life they'd managed to build for themselves despite his shaky past.

Susan asked, "Before Dov disappeared, do you remember anything strange happening?"

"Strange? Like what?"

"Cars you didn't recognize sitting out on the street for extended periods of time, or maybe someone stopping by the house claiming to be a repairman or a census taker—something like that? Anything out of the ordinary?"

"There is something but . . ." Anne blushed. "I thought maybe Dov was having an affair for a little while there because we kept getting hang-up calls on our home line. We must be one of the few people left in America who still have one. Of course, he wasn't—having an affair, I mean."

"Any idea who it was?"

"The number was always blocked, but I eventually found out who it was. Dov was doing side jobs with one of his old contacts."

Susan asked, "What sort of side jobs?"

Anne shrugged. "It was mostly easy tasks that people didn't want to do for themselves: moving furniture, hauling trash to the dump, hanging Christmas lights."

"Someone paid your husband to hang Christmas lights?"

"He made a fair bit of cash doing it too. People want to show they have holiday spirit, you know, but they don't want to do the work. He'd also take them down once the holiday was over as part of the deal. But the money didn't matter to me, once I found out who Dov was working with. After that, I put an end to those side jobs."

"And who was that?"

"It was one of Dov's old drug contacts. He'd told me that he'd cut ties with all of them—the druggies from his past, I mean—once we found out I was pregnant. Some of them were pretty angry about it, according to my husband—he never said why, but I'm guessing he might have owed a couple of them money. But you know who was more pissed? *Me*, when I found out that he was still associating with them. I told him that I didn't care how much money he was making. I didn't want him hanging around with that crowd any longer."

"And did he stop?"

Anne looked down at her feet. She seemed reluctant to answer. "He *says* he did . . ."

Susan could tell there was more. "But what?"

Exasperated, Anne said, "But *look* at me. I'm the size of a whale. I can't follow him around twenty-four seven. He said he'd quit, and so I trusted that he did."

Maybe that was your first mistake, Susan thought. *Trusting Dov.* She made a move to pull out her pen and pad. "You got the name of the guy he was doing these jobs with?"

Anne shook her head. "I wasn't ever involved in that part of his life, so I never got to know his friends from back in the day. When Dov was on drugs, it was like he was a different person. *That* person I wanted nothing to do with."

"Sure, I understand."

"Look, I know Dov isn't perfect. But regardless of who he was in the past, I'm telling you, he isn't a killer."

Chapter 10

Eric was powerless as a series of hands tugged at his body and then seized his limbs. Because the cloth had been pulled over his head—he thought it might be an old pillowcase—he was unable to see his attackers. But he could hear them. They grunted and panted with effort as they dragged him away from his Jeep toward . . . *where?* he wondered, some small, deluded part of him still hoping that he was involuntarily partaking in a practical joke—though who the hell would find such a thing funny was beyond him.

His head throbbed as if he'd been struck, and it dawned on him that maybe he had been. They'd snuck up on him fast as lightning—so fast that he couldn't figure out where they might have come from—so it was very likely that he'd suffered a blow stealthy enough that he'd missed it. The warmth at the crown of his skull hinted that he'd been assaulted, that it was blood he was feeling raining down the back of his neck. He dug his heels into the pavement and then kicked out at them when it didn't work, but it was merely a futile attempt to slow their progress. They were dragging him away, and there was nothing he could do but let it happen.

"What do you want?" he demanded, but what he really meant was "Why me?" He couldn't imagine that any group of students would be so angry about a grade that they'd orchestrate such an elaborate ruse—which was the only motive he could think would spawn the attack.

But could he actually be sure it *was* students who were attacking him? The media attention he'd received during the past year had brought a few crackpots out of the woodwork—people who'd sought his "psychic services" to find missing loved ones or determine whether a partner was being unfaithful. What if this was some of them now, hoping to force his hand through kidnapping?

"Look, if you're wanting to hire me, we could sit down and talk—"

"Help me get him over the ledge," a gruff voice demanded.

Then, another voice, a female. "Whoa, wait. Hey—*ow!*"

A different male: "Take the hood off! They can't find him with it on!"

And, before Eric understood that they'd been planning to kill him all along, he was falling, falling.

◆ ◆ ◆

Wake up-wake up-wake up . . .

A voice whispering to him from behind.

Eric sat up with a start, a scream escaping his lungs. He patted himself down as the world came back into focus—

you're okay, you're okay

—realizing slowly that he was in the front seat of his Jeep. Safe, and very much not splattered on the sidewalk below.

But he was not alone.

His eyes slowly traveled to the rearview mirror, where he wasn't too surprised to catch sight of Bryan, mangled and bloody, staring back at him sadly. His mouth stretched into a wide, hideous grin, and Eric could see that only remnants of Bryan's teeth remained, jagged pearls peeping out from ruined lips. His skull was grotesquely misshapen, eyeballs looking off into separate directions, as if they belonged in two different skulls.

Eric commanded himself to pretend that everything was normal, to not launch from his car and run back to the safety of the bright lights in his office, like he so very much wanted to do.

The dead, he'd come to know, would find him anywhere.

I'm not the only one. Bryan's lips weren't moving, but it was like he was speaking nonetheless.

"The only one *what?*"

Professor . . . help . . .

But, of course, the kid was already starting to vanish, his sad, mangled silhouette dissolving until it was like he'd never been there at all.

A year ago, such an incident would have made Eric question whether he was having a schizophrenic episode. Now, he recognized the vision for what it was, the dead trying to communicate. And, although he was tired and desperately wanting to go home (never mind the trauma he felt after his trip off the roof), there was not a single doubt in his mind that Bryan would just keep coming back should he choose to behave as if nothing had happened.

He'd tried denial before with other visitors, and it had only made them angry and lash out. He shuddered as he recalled the time he'd awakened in his dark bedroom in the middle of the night to find a dead five-year-old boy named Lenny Lincoln staring back at him on the pillow, an insect squirming from his lips. He could live his whole life and be grateful to never see something like that again, thank you very much, so passivity was not going to be an option today.

Okay, so what did Bryan want? Well, that much was obvious. Although the dead Eric had encountered were often cryptic, Bryan's message, thankfully, had been clear. He had not committed suicide; he'd been murdered by people who'd gone out of their way to make it look like he'd taken his own life. But who'd benefit from such a thing?

The most obvious answer was rooted less in benefit and more in revenge.

Samantha's parents had the motive, money, and connections to orchestrate the murder in such a short time. Perhaps they'd been too impatient to wait for the courts to dole out justice. The act of violence had undoubtedly been premeditated; the attackers had the pillowcase on hand and ready to use. They'd been waiting for him in the parking lot, too, which meant they probably were aware of his schedule. But why use the pillowcase in the first place if they'd been planning to throw him off the ledge? Bryan could hardly identify his attackers if he was dead.

Ridiculous as the motive might be, Eric considered the possibility that Alan Williams, dean of students, might have done it with other members of the board. And why not? Once word got out that a salacious murder had tainted the campus's once-chaste reputation, parents might consider sending their precious offspring elsewhere. Benefactors, too, might feel that their donation dollars would be better utilized someplace where the students weren't killing one another. *But* if Samantha's murderer were to never stand trial—kind of difficult to go to court when you're wearing your brains on the outside of your skull—the hubbub surrounding the scandal might go away quietly.

There was always the third possibility, which was that an entirely unrelated group of vigilantes—men and women who did not even know, or had maybe never even met Samantha—wanted to send a message to would-be murderers and rapists: hurt a woman, and we're going to come out of the shadows to hurt you right back.

Of the three theories, the one where Samantha's parents were the perpetrators made the most sense. They were the ones most emotionally invested and the ones actively out for blood, given the way they'd been trashing Bryan. Additionally, they had never liked the kid, so the decision to end his life might not haunt their conscience the way it would another guilty party.

Eric made a move to start his car and then reconsidered. He pocketed his keys and exited the vehicle, retracing his steps to the elevator. From there, he walked the perimeter of the balcony, which was merely where builders had extended the concrete up about four feet, so that it made a blockade to the open air. He walked the whole third level, finding nothing, so he went up a floor. And then another.

About halfway around the fifth floor, he saw it: two distinct skid marks that ran up the front side of the blockade, as if someone had been dragged to the ledge. Eric was positive that the someone was Bryan. He scanned the lot behind him, finding the approximate area where he'd been grabbed in the vision two floors below, the area near where the black truck had been. He got down on his hands and knees and peered at the ground, finding a set of scuff marks here, too, where they'd begun to drag Bryan away. He rushed back down to the car, grabbed his cell phone, ran back up to the fifth floor, and began snapping pictures.

Exhausted from all the back and forth, he took the elevator down to the third floor. Once in his car, he looked up directions to the nearest police station. Before he had a chance to reconsider, he screeched out of the parking lot.

On the way to the station, he began to call Susan, but then thought better of it. She'd already advised him to go to the police, which he hadn't done, despite his assurance to her that he would. Besides, wouldn't calling her again be a little . . . ? "Stalkerish," he answered himself and then put down the phone. If he hoped to ever win her back, acting like a pest would be the last thing that would endear him to her.

CHAPTER 11

The waiting room at the police station was about as pleasant looking as Eric had anticipated, except it also had the added bonus of smelling like stale urine. He glanced at the scowling miscreants scattered about the room and then elected to take a seat next to a well-dressed woman in a tailored pantsuit who looked like she belonged there even less than he did. He gave her a polite smile as he sat down.

She leaned into him a couple minutes later and said, "Boy, do you look like—"

"What, like I've seen a ghost?" he said dryly and then had himself a private laugh. *Ho-ho-ho, so funny. Telling dad jokes when you're not even a dad.* And he never would be, thanks to the vasectomy he'd gotten when he was married to Maggie. Not unless he got it reversed. And with his love life being the way it was lately, he didn't see that happening any time soon. It had actually been Maggie's idea, and then after he'd had the procedure she'd gone and gotten herself pregnant by his brother, if you could believe it. *Ho-ho-ha-ha, isn't life funny?*

Smiling, the woman shook her head. "Well, no, I was going to say that you looked like you could use a piece of candy. I keep a bag of these in my purse for occasions like these." It was then that Eric saw that she was offering him a foil-wrapped lollipop from See's Candies. She studied him for a moment. "But, sure, the ghost thing works too."

Eric thanked her for the lollipop with a sheepish chuckle. "That's what I get for rudely interrupting people."

She dismissed the comment with a wave of her hand, which was sporting a wedding ring adorned with a diamond that could double as a bowling ball. She had matching stones in both earlobes, and a thick brushed-gold chain with a sizeable topaz pendant at her neck. Her handbag boasted a large French designer's emblem. "You're not a criminal, are you?" she asked, her immaculately penciled eyebrow arching.

"Why, because I interrupted you?"

"Cute." She flashed him a coy, pretty smile, and it was easy to imagine her being crowned homecoming queen back in the day. He placed her in her late-late-sixties, which in appearance-obsessed California was comparable to fifty everywhere else. The "mature aged" supposedly looked even younger down in Los Angeles, with all that access to cosmetic surgery clinics, but Eric didn't know this firsthand, having only moved to the state from Philadelphia a little more than a year ago. "I was only making small talk, because I'm nosy and wondering why you're here. I'm Greta, by the way. Greta Milstein."

Eric was quickly growing to like the woman, as her playful ribbing was a welcome respite after the day he'd just had. "I'm Eric, and, no, I'm not a criminal."

Her hand flew to her chest dramatically. "Phew! Because it'd break my old, dear heart to hear a boy as cute as you was out causing trouble. I might even have to make you give me the lollipop back. Like stealing candy from a baby!" She gave him a flirty wink.

Eric felt the color rise to his cheeks. He didn't know how to take this, sitting in a police station while being hit on by a senior citizen wearing a collection of jewelry that probably cost more than the house he grew up in. "I work at the university—LU. I'm here because of a suicide we had on campus. I knew the kid who did it, and I'm giving a statement."

"Oh, how awful—I'm so sorry for you! I heard about that on the news. Terrible stuff." Luckily, she didn't ask him probing questions, which he appreciated.

"Why are you here?" he asked. Then, to make her day, he added, "Been out stealing too many hearts?"

"Oh, you," she said, but he could tell she was pleased. "You ever hear of Grow Green?"

"Don't they do stuff with trees—paper products and whatnot? I'm always seeing their billboards and trucks going down the highway."

She nodded. "That's right. I own the company."

"Wow, that's unbelievable! You're a household name." Well, that explained the clothes and the jewelry. She must be worth millions upon millions.

Greta nodded proudly. "It was my daddy's company until 1987, and then my brother and I took over after he passed. Don joined Daddy in '07, so now it's just me."

"And who will you pass it to?" he asked before he could think better of it. Was that rude, asking an elderly person such a question?

She didn't seem offended, having laughed at his pained expression. "You mean once I kick the bucket?" She shrugged her bony shoulders. "I'm still deciding on that. Both my boys are lazy as all get-out—wouldn't know a hard day's work if it bit them on the butt. They'd run the company into the ground not six months after my passing, of that I have no doubt. I'm sure Daddy's rolling over in his grave right now with me just talking about it. You don't know anything about trees, do you?" she asked, giving him a once-over, as if considering him for the position.

He could only assume she was kidding. "Afraid not."

"Shoot. I guess I'll have to leave it up to the shareholders, then."

"So, why are you here at the station?" he asked, wondering if she was there to bail out one of the lazy sons, though he could better imagine her letting them stew in jail to teach them a lesson. Greta did not seem the type to brook anyone's bullshit, offspring or not.

She scowled. "A worker was attacked at one of my nurseries."

"By whom?"

"I can't prove it was them, but I know it was those DOTE creeps who did it."

Eric started. "Did you say DOTE—as in Defenders of the Earth?" She nodded, and he continued. "This is one crazy coincidence, because I was *just* talking about them to a, um, friend at the FBI." Eric was still uncomfortable mentioning Susan in conversation, and his speech usually stuttered whenever he spoke of her. She wasn't technically his friend, but it also felt just as strange saying *ex-girlfriend*.

Greta shook her head. "Oh, I don't think it's that coincidental at all. Those little bastards have been stirring up trouble all over Northern California. They're on a rampage."

"What have they done to you?"

She let out an angry grunt. "You name it. They've destroyed equipment, slashed tires on my delivery trucks, and set fire to storage sheds full of chemicals."

"Geez. That's nasty stuff."

"That's nothing. They've also driven metal spikes into my trees, so we can't harvest them, which I can't understand," she said. "We're not talking about centuries-old redwoods that are being ripped from a sacred forest; these are trees we've been growing for the sole purpose of harvesting. We're doing this on our own property—land that's been in our family for decades, since my daddy's daddy was around. I don't think these DOTE idiots even know who or what they're protesting against. Everyone is so addicted to outrage these days. Just watch the news for ten minutes. People can't seem to be happy unless they're angry about something."

"How do you know it's DOTE who's been harassing you?"

"I'll show you how," she said and then rooted around in her purse. She extracted a small flag and placed it in his hand. Printed on it was a red *D* enclosed within a triangle, just as Susan had described their emblem.

"I don't understand."

Greta explained, "See, if someone were to take a chain saw to a tree that had been spiked, the blade could hit the metal and they'd be injured by the shrapnel. That's exactly what happened to my guy. So, vandals mark their handiwork with these flags to warn loggers that the tree has a spike in it."

"Why did your logger cut into the tree if he knew it was spiked?"

Greta had started shaking her head before Eric finished his sentence. "That's the thing—he *didn't* know. For months these parasites have been spiking my trees, always, always leaving a flag. This last time, though, they didn't. It's like they wanted to get us accustomed to looking for their flags, and then as soon as we let our guard down, they came in and secretly spiked the trees. And now a man with a wife and two young children is in the hospital, fighting for his life. Doctors say that it's unlikely he'll live through the night . . ."

Eric looked away as Greta dabbed a tissue under her eye. When she turned her attention back to him, he asked, "Have you heard of them doing this to anyone else? Do you think they're capable of anything beyond passive violence?"

"Passive violence. Humph, that's an interesting way to put it," she said bitterly. "I think you're asking me if I know of any time they've attacked anyone outright, instead of setting traps like cowards?"

Eric nodded.

"I know a cattle rancher up in Salinas. They harassed him for months—spray-painted his buildings, overturned his tractors . . . same kind of BS they've been doing to me. They escalated things when they cut some of his fences near the highway—'liberating' the animals." She made a sputtering sound. "Naturally, his herd got out, and some poor pizza delivery kid hit one of the larger steers in his little beater car. It was dark, so he didn't see it; the dumb thing was just standing there, right in the middle of the road. It went through the windshield, pinned the kid until the paramedics came. Crushed his little plastic car like it was made of, well, *plastic*. Crushed the kid too. He did physical therapy, but he's always going to need a cane to walk. Roy, the rancher, was devastated because the boy was a friend of his son's—guess he'd even gone to his house a few times for dinner."

"That's so awful," Eric said. "It's so senseless, what they did. Crippling this poor kid, who wasn't even involved in ranching, for the rest of his life to, what, send a message? It could almost be viewed as attempted murder or something of that nature, couldn't it? They must have known the cattle would get out and that someone would get hurt. What else did they think would happen?"

"That's the thing—they *don't* think," Greta said. "So, Roy, after he'd been stewing a few days, getting good and riled, went to the ratty strip mall bar where he knew these little creeps congregated. And he confronted one of them. Words were exchanged, and then the guy provoked Roy by saying that *he*—Roy—caused the accident. He also said he wasn't at all sorry for what happened to the kid."

"Wow, that's just . . . wow."

"I know what you mean. Boy, would I love to get my hands on that little jerk," Greta said with her eyes narrowed viciously. "Anyway, Roy shoved the guy, which in the eyes of the law says that *he* was committing assault and that *he* was the one who instigated physical contact. According to Roy, the guy he shoved started howling, saying that his jaw had been broken."

"Had it?"

Greta gave him a look so incredulous that she might have just said, *Oh please.* "Roy had only shoved him on the shoulder. Don't get me wrong; he's a big, intimidating man—I certainly wouldn't want to tangle with him—but he didn't even come close to touching his face. But that didn't stop this guy's buddy from jumping in to 'defend' his 'injured' friend. The only thing is, once the new guy started swinging, the whole group of those lowlifes jumped in. Roy's face looked like hamburger meat after the attack. I saw him, and it was horrifying. His body was all bruised up too. He said they probably would have killed him, had a security guard not shown up."

"So, what happened after that? If Roy had been beaten badly, surely he could have pressed charges."

Greta shook her head. "If you were angry before, this part is *really* going to burn your britches. Roy hired himself an attorney and took them to court. He figured the kind of people they were, they'd cheap out on hiring a decent defense or might even be stupid enough to try to represent themselves. He couldn't believe it, then, when they showed up with an army of suits from one of the best law firms in the Bay Area. Those lawyers must have cost them tens of thousands of dollars for just the one day in court. Roy's attorney, while decent enough, simply couldn't compete."

"Poor Roy," Eric said, feeling a great deal of indignation on behalf of a man he'd never met. "How did those guys pull it off, getting all those lawyers?"

Greta shrugged. "Your guess is as good as mine. This group, from what Roy says, did not seem the sort to live in a world of high-dollar attorneys. He called them *ragtag*, said they looked like they might be living out of their cars and didn't have two nickels to rub together. They must have robbed a bank to pay for their defense. I wish I would have known what was going to happen in court, though, because I would have happily handed over every penny I had to Roy to hire the best lawyer in America, if it would have meant beating them."

"And what did happen?" Eric asked.

"Roy lost, of course. And the guy with the alleged broken jaw? He countersued Roy for a million dollars in damages." She provided Eric a disgusted look. "And he won."

CHAPTER 12

Although she hated intruding on a grief-stricken widow, Susan decided to take a detour to the Nguygen residence before heading back to the office. She figured speaking with Chung's wife, Lynda, would be the fastest—and likely the only—way to confirm Anne's claim about Dov taking Chung to lunch to make amends.

The Nguygens lived in a handsome two-story Victorian painted the color of clay. Susan didn't know architectural terminology, but there were areas of the house covered in what she'd describe as wooden fish scales that she found pretty. The yard was landscaped meticulously—which, given Chung's management of his bank account, wasn't unexpected—with a combination of succulents and dark, spiky shrubberies. It was a modern fairy tale she'd happily come home to every night, if she could ever dream to afford such a place.

In the driveway sat a long line of higher-end vehicles. Support for Lynda in her time of need. This made Susan feel both relieved and uneasy. While she felt better not being alone in a quiet, big house with a woman whose husband had just been murdered, she also wasn't looking forward to the accusing eyes that were likely to meet her—*Can't you see she's grieving? How could you show up like this?*

Lynda met her on the porch just as she'd begun to knock. Unlike Anne, who'd insisted on the informality of being called by her first name, Chung's wife seemed more like the *Mrs. Nguygen* type. It was a good guess too. When Susan addressed her as such, she did not make the offer to *Please, call me Lynda.*

Oddly, Mrs. Nguygen seemed less upset about her husband's murder than Anne had been about Dov's disappearance. Her eyes contained only the slightest tinge of pink. She was also, Susan saw, pinching a glass of red wine between her fingers, as if she were merely out on the porch enjoying some fresh air at a party. From inside, her guests erupted in a chorus of out-of-tune laughter—merriment with a manic edge.

Not quite what she had anticipated.

Despite the unexpected behavior, Susan knew there were no criteria for grieving, or for human reactions as a whole. Everyone handled adverse situations in their own unique way. Susan had seen a mother laugh hysterically until she broke down in frenetic moans after being informed that her child had been kidnapped. On another occasion, a white-collar embezzler audibly broke wind dozens of times throughout his interview and pretended not to hear it whenever it happened. They had to air out the room after he left, spraying down the seat with Lysol for good measure. Sometimes they became quiet as corpses; other times they screamed until they lost their voices. With humans, you just never knew.

Mrs. Nguygen offered Susan a glass of wine, which she declined.

Susan asked Mrs. Nguygen about Dov taking her husband to lunch, and she corroborated the story. "To tell you the truth, I don't think Chung was looking forward to it. He said he found the man obnoxious."

"So, why did he agree to go?"

"Not liking the man didn't mean that he wanted to hurt his feelings. Chung said he felt sorry for him—he said it was clear Dov had a lot of personal issues, and that the lunch seemed to mean a lot to him. He said he could sacrifice an hour of his life if it meant making someone so happy." Mrs. Nguygen shrugged. "But that was my husband. He always put others before himself, and now look where it got him. His problem was that he wanted people to behave the same way as he did. He was a good man, so he expected other men to be good, too, which is unfortunately not the way the world works."

Susan was struck by how incensed Mrs. Nguygen sounded, which might explain the lack of tears. Perhaps she was in the angry phase of grieving and looking for something to focus her rage on. "Do you think Dov had a reason to hurt your husband?"

Mrs. Nguygen took a long sip of wine. "Are you asking me if I think Dov killed Chung over something as trivial as a stolen parking space?"

"So you knew about their rivalry?"

"Oh yes, of course. Chung used to get so furious over the whole thing! If his anger was anything to go by, Dov was probably pretty upset too. I'd be lying if I said that Chung was completely innocent in the situation. He did plenty of things to antagonize Dov, I'm sure. He never told me specifically what they were, since he knew I didn't approve. But I could always tell when he'd been up to tomfoolery because he'd come home looking sheepish. I told him he was going to get himself written up or even fired, if he didn't watch himself."

"And what did he say to that?" Susan asked.

"He'd say, *Well, he started it.* So, I'd tell him that he could end it then, by not rising to such pettiness. Which, of course, he didn't." Mrs. Nguygen shook her head, her smile wistful. "Still, I refuse to believe that anyone would commit murder over such silly things . . . excuse me."

Now, the tears came. There were only a few, but they seemed authentic. Mrs. Nguygen was far from the theatrical type who'd fling herself on the ground, wailing. For her, crying in front of a stranger probably *was* a dramatic display of emotion. She dabbed the tears away with a cloth handkerchief she pulled from the pocket of her slacks, quietly apologizing for what she might have considered an outburst. Susan waited silently, wishing that she, too, had a glass of wine.

A petite woman with matching red-lacquered nails and lips peeked her head out the front door. "Everything okay out here?" Her eyes moved between the two women, her lips pursing.

Mrs. Nguygen gently waved the woman away. "Yes, I'm fine, thanks. I'll be in in a minute."

After the woman went back into the house, Susan said, "I'm sorry; I won't take up much more of your time."

Mrs. Nguygen gave her a thin smile. "Take all the time you need. That's Chung's family in there. Here to stake a claim on their dead brother's antiques, I have no doubt. Some of them are rather valuable. There's a painting in the bedroom worth about as much as this house. He inherited them after both his parents passed; he never gets rid of anything, so he's still got it all. His siblings were all pretty riled about it—they had a complex about their parents favoring my husband. They never considered that them being greedy and insufferable might have had something to do with them getting nothing. I'm sure they're in there right now, debating who is going to broach the subject with me first. I'm surprised one of them didn't show up with a moving van." She clicked her tongue and held up her glass of wine. "This is the only thing keeping me sane."

"Yes, family can be tricky," Susan said neutrally, thinking of her own. She also had to wonder if Chung's brothers and sisters might have wanted the antiques enough to kill for them. It seemed like a stretch. Why kill him now, and why do it while he was on a lunch break? If it was his family who'd plotted against him, they might have planned a little better. After a beat, she said, "Are you familiar with a company called Zelman Industries?"

"Sure, Chung did a job for them, oh, about a couple weeks back. Why? Do you think they had something to do with what happened to him?"

Susan smiled reassuringly. "No, we're just covering all our bases, making sure there's nothing we're missing."

"Well, we're missing *something*, all right: Dov," Mrs. Nguygen said, frowning. "If he's innocent, where is he? That's what I want to know."

"That's what we're trying to figure out," Susan answered quickly, not wanting the conversation to stray off topic. "What sort of job did your husband do for Zelman Industries?" Susan asked to keep the conversation rolling. Things would sour fast if Mrs. Nguygen began badgering her about why it was taking so long for Dov to be found. To anyone grieving over a crime committed against a loved one, it always took too long to find the person or persons responsible, regardless if it was a week or a year.

"I can't give you exact details about the job because I really don't know what he did for them. But I can tell you that someone named Marcus Zelman contracted him for a onetime job. Chung was an environmental engineer, which I'm sure you know, and this Zelman wanted him to conduct an environmental impact survey of the land surrounding the dam. He—Zelman—is some kind of land developer."

"Can you give me any other specifics?" Susan asked.

Mrs. Nguygen thought a moment and then shook her head. "I'm sorry; I'm afraid I can't. I wish I could be more helpful, but I just don't know anything else. I'd tell you if I did. Chung said the job was fast, easy money. He was paid a couple grand for a few hours' work. He submitted a report, and that was that."

The front door creaked open, and this time a teenage girl stepped out onto the porch. "My niece," Mrs. Nguygen told Susan, her eyes narrowing on the fragile-looking Chinese porcelain vase the girl clutched loosely in her left hand like it was an empty soda can she intended to toss in the trash. She was sending a text with her right, her eyes glued on her cell phone as her thumb tapped rapidly along on the screen.

"Please be careful with that, Sharice. It's very old."

The girl gave them an unenthused look that showed exactly how much interest she had in discussing her aunt's old junk. Susan was willing to bet the vase was worth a small fortune. She hadn't realized she'd been holding her breath until Mrs. Nguygen seized the antique.

"Mom says she wants to talk to you about it," the girl said. Judging by her lack of grief, she didn't seem too interested in mourning Uncle Chung's death either. Her attention was already back on her phone.

Susan resisted the urge to remind Sharice that a member of her family had just been murdered. She vowed that if she ever had children, she'd be damned if she'd let them get away with being so disrespectful. She felt for Mrs. Nguygen, having to deal with in-laws like hers. If the girl was this bad, what must the mother be like?

"Oh yes, I'd like to talk to your mother too," Mrs. Nguygen said with enough ice in her voice to cause the bratty girl to cease typing.

"I'll let you get inside. Thank you for your time, Mrs. Nguygen," Susan said. "And I'm very sorry for your loss. You're lucky to have such a caring family to help you in your time of need." While her voice had been void of even the slightest hint of sarcasm, she'd added the last part mostly to spite Sharice. It was petty, she knew, but it gave her pleasure to see the girl blush. Mrs. Nguygen gave her an appreciative smile that made it clear she'd enjoyed the shaming of her niece.

Susan made a move to leave.

As she started her car, she reflected how she sometimes longed for a big family. There were times, even, when being estranged from her father made her feel sad. However, it was interactions like the one she'd just witnessed at the Nguygen household that made her think that maybe she was better off on her own.

CHAPTER 13

Eric knew when he was fighting a losing battle. He'd honed his skills on that front during his divorce from the adulterous Maggie and the subsequent estrangement from his wife-stealing brother, Jim. As he'd learned during that very dark, very trying period of his life, sometimes, for the sake of your own sanity, you've just got to say to hell with it, cut your losses, and pack it in.

In his current situation, however, it was dogged optimism—or was it stubbornness?—that was stopping him from walking out the door, despite the frustration he was feeling. Part of this had to do with him being there on behalf of a person who was unable to speak for himself. Strange as it was, sometimes fighting another's battle was easier than fighting his own.

Officer Kravitz, who Eric was finally speaking with after a two-hour wait, could not have cared less about Eric's unsolicited theories about a crime authorities had already deemed solved. He had a stack of files on his desk about a foot thick, and every so often his eyes would drift to it, followed by a despondent shake of the head. He didn't seem to be doing it consciously, yet the young officer couldn't have made it clearer that he had far better things to do—actual *work*.

Eric began by quickly outlining the exchange between Bryan and him in his office, opting to leave Jake out of the narrative to skirt further complication. He finished with, "So, as I already said, he maintained his innocence throughout our conversation."

"A criminal maintaining innocence. Imagine that," Kravitz said dryly. "Next thing you're going to tell me is that he's being framed."

Though exasperated, Eric kept a neutral expression pasted on his face. "Well, no, not exactly—"

"Back up a second," Kravitz interrupted. "You had a fugitive in your office who held you hostage with a firearm. Did you report the incident?"

Eric shifted in his seat. *Oh, you idiot!* he thought, fighting the urge to bring a hand up and smack himself hard across the forehead. How had it not dawned on him to conceal this detail?

It hadn't dawned on him, he realized, because to do such a thing would have been impossible, since the timeline simply wouldn't have made sense. Bryan wouldn't have been in his office professing his innocence unless a murder had been committed. And Officer Kravitz here, while harried, did not seem stupid. Had Eric spun a different narrative, the officer would've realized that things weren't adding up—and once an officer of the law caught a witness in a lie, the remainder of anything they said fell on deaf ears.

"I'm reporting the incident right now," Eric said weakly. He was still debating whether he wanted to reveal that he'd spoken with an agent of the FBI about the matter, since he was fairly certain Susan had left it up to him to make contact with local police and had not done any reporting of her own.

The officer frowned. "A little late for that, isn't it? You ever think that if maybe you'd contacted the authorities like you should have done, this McDougal guy might not have gone and jumped off a building?"

Eric felt like he'd been punched in the gut. "I've been thinking that since I heard of Bryan's death. The only difference is that I don't believe he killed himself. I think his suicide was staged—"

"Whoa, whoa, whoa," Kravitz said, putting his hands up to silence Eric. He leaned back in his chair and let out a long-suffering sigh. "Look, Mr. Evans, I don't know why you're so invested in this case, but I'm sure in your own way you're trying to do what you think is helpful. I understand that you've assisted law enforcement in the past, and that's the *only* reason I'm not busting you for obstruction." His eyes traveled to the towering stack of files. "That, and I don't have time to fill out any more paperwork. I have enough as it is."

"I understand that; however—"

Kravitz put up a hand to silence Eric once more. Eric clamped his lips shut, not wanting to press his luck by antagonizing the officer. "I get that you think Bryan McDougal's death was staged, but let me tell you something that wasn't: he was a sex offender. He's even on the national registry, which is why I'm telling you. This is not privileged information; it's *public knowledge* that he had a history of not being able to keep it in his pants."

Eric folded his arms across his chest. "Could you tell me the nature of that offense?"

"Sure I could, if I had the time to look it up. But I don't," Kravitz said, shaking his head. Eric opened his mouth to interject, and the officer cut him off. "Look, the victim's family believes their daughter's killer is dead, and public opinion is also that justice has been served. Here at the station, we also believe there's one less bad guy on the street. So, I can't justify some flimsy attempt to exonerate a registered sex offender because you have what boils down to a hunch, especially not when there are other victims who are also in need of justice." He aimed his chin at the files pointedly. "Do you have any proof that substantiates your claim that the suicide was staged?"

"Actually, yes," Eric said, pulling out his cell phone. He brought up the photo he'd taken of the drag marks on the concrete blockade. He handed the phone to the officer, regretting it immediately.

Kravitz glanced at the photo and shrugged. "Want to tell me what I'm looking at?"

In the photo, the drag marks looked like nothing more than smudges of dirt. Even Eric could see that. "There," he said, trying not to sound like the crackpot he felt like. He enlarged the photo on the screen, though he wasn't expecting to change the officer's mind. "That's where he was dragged over."

"Right." The officer handed the phone back to Eric. He checked the time on his watch. "Have you got anything else?"

Eric didn't bother mentioning that he'd seen Bryan's spirit in the back seat of his vehicle. Officer Kravitz didn't seem the type to invest too much confidence in psychic visions. He shook his head.

Kravitz got to his feet. He opened the door for Eric and made a sweeping gesture with his arm. It was time to leave. "I'm afraid we're out of time. There are others waiting to speak with me."

Eric wasn't convinced that Kravitz was telling the truth about there being other people in the waiting room vying for his time, but it wasn't as if he had any grounds to argue. He quickly rose and walked out the door. He tried not to dwell on the fact that he'd spent two hours of his day waiting just to waste another ten minutes of his breath speaking with a man who'd already decided not to hear him out before he'd even opened his mouth.

"Oh, and Mr. Evans?" the officer called as he was making his way down the hall. "Next time a fugitive contacts you, remember, it's your civic duty to report it."

CHAPTER 14

Jake hadn't realized what a large portion of his life had previously been taken up by his band until the hours, nights, and weekends had started to free up, creating a black hole in his schedule where good times and love had once resided. He was lonely tonight, antsy and uncomfortable in his own skin. He didn't feel like himself, but that was nothing new.

It wasn't just the excess of free time that had gotten him down. It was that he longed for his lost friends and their camaraderie. With Madison, who'd been like a sister to him, he missed the good-natured banter they'd shared; with Chuck, it was the easy silences they immersed themselves in, sitting side by side in the van whenever they'd hit the road. He craved the comfort that only long-term friendship could provide, their inside jokes, the awareness that his history was contained within them, and they in him.

Jake was now the owner of a vintage houseboat that he planned to dock in Sausalito. However, it would be some time before he could move in, as the quaint little vessel required a few repairs to get it water ready. He'd rented himself a minuscule studio apartment near campus to live in during the meantime. It was about three hundred square feet and devoid of a kitchen. He stored his food in a bright-orange mini SMEG refrigerator, the one indulgence he'd allowed himself for the pad; besides his violin and computer, it was the priciest item in the place.

Based solely on how Jake lived, one would never guess that his bank account boasted a high seven figures, thanks to a familial inheritance he'd received a few years back. Having lived at home with his parents until recently, he had no furniture to speak of, which was just fine by him—he was commitment-phobic nearly to a fault and had the restless soul of a nomad. Also, less to move, he'd figured. He slept in a sleeping bag on an air mattress and kept his clothes in an old hand-me-down suitcase that he used as a makeshift dresser. Meals were cooked on a hot plate, and dishes were washed in the sink in the bathroom, which was the only other room the place offered. He showered almost directly over the toilet. But the view was great, and he considered it good practice for living on the boat, which would seem downright palatial by comparison.

View and fancy fridge aside, tonight he felt as if he'd been locked in the trunk of a car. The lack of space was suffocating, the walls closing in around him like an unwanted embrace from a greasy stranger. So was his grief, which often appeared ghostlike out of thin air, haunting him until he was good and terrified about spending his whole life living, and then dying, alone. The grief would eventually fade away as slyly as it had appeared, but not without taking a piece of his happiness with it.

He needed to get out.

Before he could change his mind, he grabbed his wallet, coat, and keys and strode out the door. He chose Salty's as his hangout by default, since it was the closest watering hole within walking distance. Once inside, he asked for a beer and then added a shot of tequila to the order, his logic being: in for a penny, in for a pound.

He had a look around the bar while he was waiting for his drinks, finding that he was already getting annoyed by the crowd, who seemed outrageously young for the setting. Or could it be that he was the one who was outrageously old? Deep down, he knew the answer.

The group of boys—and that's how he thought of them, as boys—nearest him was particularly irksome, with their boy-band looks and phony laughter, which they'd make a show of erupting into every couple of minutes. They came from money—that much was obvious—and there wasn't a shred of individuality among them. They dressed the same, laughed the same, and even had the same haircuts, as if one of them was planning on committing a heinous crime and needed decoys in his proximity so as to later trip up witnesses in a police lineup. *It was him . . . no, maybe it was* him *. . . um, now I'm not so sure.* Jake snorted to himself at the thought, and a few of the boys looked over at him curiously.

Jake opened his mouth to tell the busybodies exactly what they could do with their side-eyed glances, but then the bartender distracted him by returning with his drinks. Jake threw back the tequila as soon as it was set before him and immediately ordered another. "You know what, make it *two*," he grunted, and then he went about finishing his beer, trying to ignore the increasing rowdiness of the bar patrons. When had humans become so obnoxious? He'd encountered endless idiots while touring with his band, but he couldn't remember a time when bar goers had been this insufferable.

He was in a ratty mood, which might have had something to do with it. Few things in this world were more antagonizing to a depressed person than other people's joy. The crowd's laughter felt passive-aggressive, aimed at him as a reminder of his own unhappiness.

Oh, how he missed the lifestyle being in the band had provided.

His social life back then had been centered mainly on playing shows, and he'd been greatly disappointed by how many of his so-called friends had vanished along with his fame. Near the end of their touring, Augustine Grifters had garnered themselves a fair bit of notoriety, and their popularity had only increased once word of Chuck's and Madison's murders had spread. Initially, he'd appreciated the support from all the fans who'd reached out to him from around the world to offer their condolences. Over time, however, it started to seem as if that was all they wanted to talk about; the band's music became less important than the tragedy that had ended them. But then the story had become old news, and then no news at all. Everyone, it seemed, had moved on.

Everyone but Jake.

What he missed more than the friendships, albeit superficial, was female companionship. He'd met the majority of his girlfriends and lovers after shows, and lately he'd been finding the well of eligible bachelorettes running dry without the conversational opener of him having just played at his disposal. Despite his outgoing front, he was shy to ask women out on dates. As he imagined to be the case with most men, there was a hidden part of him that always feared they'd laugh in his face, which in his eyes would be far worse than any old punch. Rejection left far bigger scars than any physical assault could.

In the course of his angry ruminations, Jake had managed to get himself rather drunk. Surely all those empty shot glasses on the bar had not been consumed by him alone? He glared at the pseudo–boy band, incensed that they'd been setting their empties in front of him, and was not too startled when he saw that they were already looking his way. Guys like them never seemed to grasp that openly staring at a little person—at *anyone*, for that matter—was outrageously rude. They quickly looked away in unison, which only piqued his anger. Had they been laughing at him, making him the butt of their mean-spirited little-boy jokes?

Moments later, they broke apart, and a member from the group approached. "We going to have a problem, Skippy?" Jake sneered, causing the boy to stop in his tracks, his head jerking back. He seemed genuinely stunned. Wounded, even.

Wow, what an actor, Jake thought, unimpressed.

"Me?" the boy asked, pointing a finger at his own chest. "No. God, no."

"What do you want? As you can see, I'm busy here."

The boy nodded to his friend, who Jake saw was over by the jukebox. He squeezed his eyes shut as Madison's soulful voice and the strumming of a violin—*his* violin—filled the air. They'd put on "Until the Next," the second song of the Augustine Grifters' album *Painted Boneyard*. He bit down hard on the inside of his cheek to stop himself from screaming.

The boy held out his hand for Jake to shake, quickly lowering it when the gesture was not reciprocated. "I just wanted to tell you that I—all of us—are huge fans of yours! We weren't sure it was you, but it is, right? It's such an honor to meet—"

"What the fuck are you thinking?" Jake hissed, and the kid's mouth fell open. He slid off the barstool, so that he was facing him. "You think I want to hear my dead friend singing?"

"I . . . uh, no. I'm sorry. We thought—"

"You thought what? That you'd be a huge dipshit and get in my face? Well, now I'm going to get in yours." Jake shoved the kid with all his might, emasculated when he saw that the force had hardly moved him.

The kid looked around uncomfortably. They now had the attention of everyone in the bar, which had fallen pin-drop silent. Without any background chatter, the song had reached deafening proportions.

"*. . . wanted to say I loved you . . . ,*" Madison crooned. "*But instead I said so long . . .*"

"Come on, man—we didn't mean to upset you. I just wanted to buy you a drink," the kid said.

Jake shoved him once more. "I can buy my own drinks. I have *money*. What are all you looking at?" he yelled childishly at the rubberneckers. *Shove. Shove.* "Come on, motherfucker! Hit me! I dare you!"

"Come on, man—calm down. I'm not going to hit you," the boy said quietly. "You're like half my size."

Jake tripped over the stool's leg as he launched his attack. Adding insult to injury, the kid offered his hand to help get him back on his feet. Jake swatted him away and then shoved an uninvolved onlooker he could have sworn laughed when he'd fallen. He hadn't.

The man glanced down at him with a handsome face that was as sympathetic as it was unperturbed. "Let's get you some fresh air, buddy." He hooked an arm around Jake's back and led him from the bar. In an interaction Jake would later not remember, he gave the man his address, which the man then gave to a taxi driver, who, after a bit of convincing (and a twenty-dollar bill), was willing to drive Jake three blocks home.

Inside his apartment, Jake seized his violin and ran the bow across the strings violently, creating a sound that was reminiscent of an agonized woman screaming. He took a few deep breaths and tried again, nearly snapping his bow in half from the pressure he applied. He was only at it for a second or two before he was overwhelmed by the urge to vomit. He cast his violin aside and ran into the bathroom, where he heaved the contents of his stomach into the toilet.

Once he finished, he flopped down on his air mattress. While he'd expelled his dinner, his anger remained, as if it had burrowed itself into his bones and had become a permanent part of him. He extracted his cell from the back pocket of his jeans and made a call to Eric. He felt both angered and relieved when it went to voice mail.

"You maaaaaay be my bossssss at schooool, but you sure as shiiiiiit don't own me," he slurred into the phone. "I'm a grown man, you hear meeeee? I don't need your permissssssssion to live my life! If I wanna drink, I drink! If I wanna prooooovvve Bryan's innocent, I will!" There was more he wanted to say, but his guts had other plans for him.

CHAPTER 15

Jake's cell phone alarm might as well have been a bullhorn. He cupped his skull as he frantically patted his bed—well, air mattress—in search of the offending object. Finally, finally, he located it, and the room went blissfully silent. Had he been hit by a train last night? It certainly felt like it. How had he even gotten home?

He frowned and sat up with a start when he saw that he'd gotten a text from Eric that simply read: WTF????? His frown deepened as his brain conjured snatches of the voice mail he'd left for his friend—something about him being a grown man . . . and him not being the boss? He slapped a hand across his forehead and fell back on his air mattress with a groan. He couldn't stomach a call to Eric just yet. He was ashamed of himself and already wondering how he was ever going to be able to look him in the eye again.

It was time to face facts: He needed to get himself under control. He was drinking too much, had wasted hours and days and months of his life feeling sorry for himself . . . and then there was last night. He'd blacked out most of it, which, he suspected, might be something he'd done out of self-preservation. So, where would he begin?

He needed a distraction to help take his mind off things. He had school, of course, plus his teacher's assistant gig. But, really, those things didn't count. Those things were *jobs*. Which, truth be told, he really didn't need to have anyway, given that he had inheritance money he could live off for the rest of his life, should he choose. But that was the last thing he'd ever want, since he'd probably die of boredom.

Observing strangers like a secret agent, however, would be a blast, and the notion of going undercover gave him something to look forward to almost as soon as the idea struck him. He was so enthused that he forgot all about his pounding headache as he made a move to take a shower. After that, campus.

◆ ◆ ◆

Jake started to get into character as he crossed the campus quad toward where all the school clubs were setting up booths to promote their causes. His mission? To infiltrate DOTE, who might hold the key to uncovering what had really happened to Samantha Neville and Bryan McDougal, who may have been a victim of murder himself. While he was still "playing" Jake Bergman, his plan was to take on a slightly varied persona by mirroring the attitudes of the doters. It would be good to have a little escape from his life, if only for a minute.

Jake made a quick U-turn as he passed a coffee cart about a hundred yards out from the quad. He bought an eco-friendly, refillable bottle of water and two vegan cookies, then placed everything at the top of his backpack. Props for the encounter.

The DOTE booth was on point with his expectations. Fanned out across a couple fold-up tables were pamphlets promoting various environmental causes. Upon closer inspection, he saw that the depictions on the covers were gruesome in nature: bloody fox carcasses lined up like cigarettes, fur stripped from their bodies; emaciated children, clothes soiled and tattered, playing in a river of sewage; cute little bunnies locked in cages, eyes red and bloodied from chemicals that had been rubbed in them. Subtlety was clearly not the aim of the club.

Likewise, the doters that stood scattered around the tables were just as he'd anticipated. They were mostly clean cut with a rebellious, ecological edge: a stripe of blue hair here, a rip of designer jean there, trendy slip-on shoes made of natural fibers, bright woven bracelets. They snapped pictures with smartphones, exchanged social media information with new recruits. Jake was surprised to see an older student like himself seated behind one of the tables. He was also pleased to note that she was quite pretty—pleased, that was, until he reminded himself that he was there doing reconnaissance.

"Hi there," she called after she'd noticed him lurking. "It's okay; you can come closer. I won't bite."

Jake provided her with a warm smile. "No, I'm . . ." He hadn't really come up with an opening, which was a terrible start for someone who considered himself a budding secret agent. He gestured toward the pamphlets. "These are just, um, *wow* . . ." He shook his head, as if at a loss for words.

"Pretty full on," she finished for him.

"That's one way to put it. I used to have a pet bunny, so that one in particular makes me sad," he said, pointing at the pamphlet that called for putting an end to animal testing.

"Well, don't let them scare you off. I'm Kimmy," she said, extending a hand to him.

He took her hand in his. "I'm Jake, and those pamphlets don't scare me. They're just really—"

"Sad?"

He nodded. "Exactly. It's good there's people out there like you guys, who still care. Or else the world might be in trouble."

Kimmy got to her feet and came around the table so that she could talk more freely with Jake. "You make it sound as if anyone can't do what we do—we're not magical. You're always welcome to join us. That's why we're here, to reach out to like-minded people like yourself."

"But what if I don't have what it takes?"

Kimmy frowned. "What do you mean?"

Jake shrugged, his expression guilty. "A lot of this stuff is new to me, but I *do* know that I love animals and I care about the environment. I'm not really political. I mean, I'm not against talking about politics, but it's not something I know a lot about." While the part about him caring about animals and the environment was true, the claim that he knew nothing about politics was wildly incorrect. In truth, Jake knew a great deal about the subject. He had to, since it was a popular topic at the dinner table whenever he and his family got together. He needed to stay current to avoid being railroaded by his mother, who kept the news on in her home and car during most waking hours. It was a wonder they were from the same family, their worldviews so different.

"You don't have to be a poli-sci major to be in DOTE—though I am. Our members come from all kinds of backgrounds and ages. Obviously." Kimmy swept an arm out to indicate herself.

"Yah, it's great to see another older student here on campus." He smiled. "I usually give the other ones I see a little tip of the head, like, *I feel you.*"

Laughing, she gave him an enthusiastic nod. "That's too funny; I do the same thing! We're few and far between, that's for sure—students here are always confusing me for their instructor on the first day of school. But, even though it's a little embarrassing at times being the oldest person in class, it's no worse than what I had to deal with working in customer service. After a few years of taking other people's crap, I decided to go back to school and train to do something I was actually passionate about."

"Good for you." Jake grinned. He unzipped his bag, pulled out the bottle of water, and took a swig. When he returned the water to the bag, he pretended to be surprised by the two cookies as he drew them out. "Here, would you like one? I almost forgot about these. I was hungry this morning when I packed my lunch, so I grabbed two. Guess my eyes were bigger than my stomach. They're vegan."

"Thanks so much! I'm starving," Kimmy said, accepting the cookie gratefully. She tore into the package as if she hadn't eaten for days. "Vegan, huh? See, you're already on the right path."

He shrugged. "I do what I can."

She took a bite, chewed. "Yummy." He'd have to take her word for it. The thing had all the culinary appeal of a hockey puck. "Hey, speaking of doing things, what are your plans for tonight? You doing anything?"

Jake frowned, as if considering the question. "Nothing that I can think of. Why?"

"Want to come to a party? Well, it's more of a meet and greet."

Jake had to make a conscious effort to keep his voice neutral. "For DOTE, you mean? If so, count me in."

Perhaps he might make a great private investigator after all.

CHAPTER 16

Susan peeped down at her cell phone, saw that it was Eric, and sent the call to voice mail. She wasn't quite caffeinated enough to have a conversation with the ex, even though she missed him—maybe it was because she missed him, even, that she didn't want to talk. That, and she was on her way to Gruben Dam to speak with employees.

Moments later, her phone bleeped with a text. It was from Eric: Hi Suze. Hope you're having a good day. Wondering if we could talk later about Jake? He's okay, but he's struggling.

Susan knew what he meant by struggling, as she'd suspected the same thing. Jake was closer to Eric, but she still considered him a friend, so she was aware of the strain the deaths of his bandmates had put on him. She quickly replied that she was at work but they could talk later, hoping that Jake would be okay.

Now at Gruben Dam, she found that the HR office was open. That was just perfect, since that's exactly the department she needed to speak with. It had been niggling at her that a man with Dov's background had been able to obtain employment at a high-security facility like Gruben. It made her wonder what else might have slipped through the cracks, and whether their negligence might have played a part in Chung Nguygen's murder. If the rumors could be believed, many of the dam employees suspected Dov of using drugs, so it was astounding that Human Resources—a department created for the sole purpose of keeping tabs on employees—was completely in the dark.

Then again, Dov had fooled his own wife. And, on that note, what did that say about their marriage if his coworkers were aware of his drug use, yet Anne had no idea? Had *she* been that clueless with Eric? Were there signs that had indicated their relationship was faltering long before they both finally decided to throw in the towel? If so, what did that say about her as an investigator, being so blind?

She shook her head to clear it, setting her mind to complete the task at hand. Perhaps this was why she'd always avoided serious relationships, because they became distracting once they inevitably failed. Maybe solo was the only way she could roll.

She was surprised to see that there were two security guards in the HR office: a tall, lanky male and a short, muscular female. They watched as a lone woman cleaned out her desk, their expressions bored. The woman, scowling as she worked, avoided making eye contact with anyone in the room, passive-aggressively slamming doors and ripping drawers open.

"What's going on here?" Susan asked.

"That's none of your concern. Please move along," the small female guard said with an attitude Susan found unnecessary. She was an FBI agent, and she never treated the public that way. She took great pleasure in seeing the woman become flustered once she flashed her badge. "Sorry about giving you grief. We've just had a lot of pests come by asking questions, and we're not allowed to talk about what's happening with employees."

"And what is happening?" Susan asked.

"We were instructed to keep an eye on Ms. Jenkins here while she packs up her things," the lanky guard explained.

"Instructed by whom?"

"Department of Homeland Security," the female answered, and then she turned her attention back to the angry woman.

"Is Ms. Jenkins head of HR?" Susan asked, and both guards nodded. "Then I'll need to have a word with her. Alone." When they hesitated, she added, "Don't worry—I won't leave, and I'll be in here at all times."

The two guards left without any argument, probably happy to have an excuse to go and grab a quick cup of coffee. She couldn't imagine that watching an infuriated dam employee clearing out her office could be all that entertaining or comfortable, especially with all the noise she was making. The woman she'd come to know as Ms. Jenkins turned to her, and for the first time Susan could see that her anger was nothing more than bravado. The eyes don't lie, and hers were saying that she was fearful. She placed a hand on her hip and glared at Susan. "So, what, now I'm in trouble with the FBI too?"

Susan shook her head. "I'm only here to ask you a few questions about Dov."

"I already told those other guys I don't know where he is."

Susan frowned. "Why would you know where he is, Ms. Jenkins? You're not expected to know where all the employees are at all times, are you?"

"Of course not."

"Okay, let's start at the beginning," Susan said. "Why are you clearing out your desk?"

The woman seemed confused. "Because I lied about Dov," she said slowly, as if Susan might not be all there mentally.

Now Susan was starting to understand. Seems the Department of Homeland Security had scooped her. Again. "You mean about his criminal background?"

"That's right."

"So, you also must have known that he was using drugs on the job. Help me understand why you'd do something like that—hire Dov. I can see you've already lost your job, but do you understand the legal repercussions you'll now be facing because of what you did? You must be aware that you committed a very serious offense, Ms. Jenkins."

"I wasn't trying to do anything illegal! And what do you mean, using drugs on the job?" she asked, as if she'd never heard anything so ridiculous. She clamped her lips shut, lobbed a potted plant into a cardboard box, and then let out a long breath to get herself under control.

Susan saw that she was wearing a diamond-encrusted David Yurman watch that had set her back about $6,000. This, Susan knew with certainty, as Denton Howell had asked her opinion on the same piece as an anniversary present for his wife. The memory of the event had always stuck with her, given the rarity of her boss ever discussing personal topics. Seemed like kind of an expensive watch for someone who worked in HR to be wearing. She noted that Ms. Jenkins did not have on a wedding ring—rich lover, maybe? The massive dried-out bouquet of flowers on the edge of her desk indicated that it was a possibility.

Slam, bang! More objects lobbed into the box. "And could you please stop calling me *Ms. Jenkins*, like I'm forty years old? It's Cindy." *Forty years old*, like it was akin to being an old maid. Cindy appeared to be around twenty-eight, so she'd probably be singing a different tune in a few years. Oh, the arrogance of youth, Susan mused, though she wasn't much older than Cindy herself. "Look, what do you want me to say? He's family."

This, Susan had not known—of course she would *have* known if the Department of Homeland Security had touched base with her. Then again, she hadn't touched base with them either, and she was always free to do her own background searches. She tried to keep her voice neutral, so as not to betray her chagrin. "Right, he's . . ."

Cindy shook her head, exasperated. Susan wasn't fooling anyone. "You people really need to get on the same page."

Susan assumed "you people" signified anyone from a government security agency who'd taken umbrage with her lying. Susan agreed about the same-page thing, though she wasn't going to share this now.

"How is he related to you?" She hated having to ask, but she needed to know. And since she didn't want to spend all day at the dam, going directly to the source would be the fastest way to get information.

"Anne, Dov's wife, is my stepsister. But we grew up together, so we might as well be related."

"So, Dov is connected to you through marriage? Risking your job and getting into legal trouble for somebody else's husband seems—"

"What? Stupid? Crazy? Well, I can see that now," Cindy snapped. "But at the time Dov had come to me for a job, he was doing really well and had been clean for a long time. He and Anne were struggling hard for money, and they knew I was in charge of hiring here at the dam. Dov, you know, he's never been involved in any violent crimes—all the bad things he's ever done have always been when he was out of his head on drugs. He was willing to do almost anything for work—he said he'd even mop floors and clean toilets—but the only position we had open was for a security guard."

Susan already knew the end of the story. "So, you fudged his work experience, concealed his criminal background, and then gave him a high-security federal job, where he was required to carry a gun. And now he's wanted for the murder of a coworker." She shook her head. It never ceased to astound her, the asinine things people did for family. "What were you thinking?"

"It sounds worse when you say it like that!" Cindy threw up her hands. "I was thinking I could help out my sister in her time of need."

Susan was inclined to believe her, not finding any alternative motive that would explain why she'd lie. Still, she planned to run a background check on her later. The woman exuded shadiness.

"Were you really not aware that Dov was using again? Word around the dam was that he was sometimes high on the job."

Cindy hesitated. "Okay, I don't know about *that*. I tried to avoid him around here as much as possible, you know, since it would look strange if it seemed I had a personal relationship with Dov outside of work."

"But surely a few employees must have come to you about his poor job performance? It must have scared people, suspecting that he was on drugs and walking around with a loaded gun."

"Doesn't that sort of prove my point? If Dov was this big killer, like everyone seems to believe, then wouldn't he have shot someone around here when he was high?" Cindy probed, like she was a defense attorney nailing her closing argument.

Was the woman nuts or what? Susan wondered. "But Dov didn't have a problem with just anyone; he had a problem with Chung. And Chung is dead."

Cindy flapped a hand. "Regardless, I refuse to believe that Dov could kill anyone. He may have had his problems with drugs, but he's not a bad guy. You should have seen how excited he was about Anne's pregnancy. It's all he's been talking about for months. There has to be some other explanation . . . do you think I'll go to jail for this?" she asked abruptly, as if the thought had just occurred to her.

"I honestly don't know. But I can tell you that you'll probably receive more than a slap on the wrist." Susan called the two security guards back in. Now that she had her answer about how Dov had gotten his job, she wanted to move on to other areas of the dam.

She asked the two guards if they'd ever worked with Dov, and if she could ask a few questions while she searched his work space. "He worked with him most," the female said, gesturing to the lanky guard, who she discovered was named Howey.

Howey led Susan to the area where the guards kept their personal items while they worked. "We don't really hang out much back here, since we're always walking around during our shift. It's more like a locker room, except it's coed and nobody takes their clothes off," Howey explained with a perfectly straight face.

"Do you keep your things anywhere else? In an office?"

Howey shook his head. "Nope. This is it. Dov's locker is over here."

As Susan began to search through the locker, she asked Howey questions. "What did you think of Dov?"

"What do you mean?" he asked with a hint of caution in his voice.

"Was he pleasant to be around? Hostile?"

The guard thought a moment. "I wouldn't really say he was one or the other. He wasn't what I'd call friendly, but he wasn't a jerk either. He wasn't chatty, I mean. He mostly kept to himself. We'd make small talk about the weather or whatever when we were in here together, but he never talked to me about his personal life. I didn't even know he was having a baby until people around here started talking about it after he disappeared. Didn't surprise me, though, him taking off on his pregnant wife."

"Would you say he was secretive?" Susan asked.

Howey shook his head. "No, I wouldn't say that. He just was . . . hmm, *humorless*, I guess you could say. The other guards and I like to joke around and have a bit of fun—it makes the hours go by faster that way, if you ask me—but Dov was only here to get a paycheck. We're kind of family-like, the guards, and Dov . . . it was almost like he went out of his way to be excluded from the group. Like maybe he was too cool for us. Funny, I didn't know I'd gone back to high school." The guard sniffed.

Susan pulled a clear sandwich bag from the middle shelf of the locker. She held it up to the light, so she could examine the contents. "Is this birdseed?" She peered back inside the locker and saw that there were several other bags like it.

She'd been talking more to herself than to Howey, but he answered anyway. "Yep, it's birdseed, all right. We actually call him Bird Man, which he doesn't find too funny. See, I told you Dov was humorless."

"Does he eat it?"

Howey chuckled. "No, no, at least I don't think so. He likes to feed birds on his break. It's so weird, because the rest of us will grab a

Coke or something from the vending machine and go BS—or have a cigarette, there's a lot of guards at the dam who smoke, go figure—and Dov will be out there on his own, feeding the birds."

Hmm, seemed a little fishy. "Have you actually seen him do it?"

"I haven't seen him actually feed the birds, no. They're too far away. I do enough walking during my shift, so I don't need to be walking all over hell's half acre on my break," the guard said. "He always comes back without the bag, though, so there must be a few out there."

"Out where?"

"There's a birdhouse way out at the edge of the property. I think he might have even been the one who put it up."

"Nobody had a problem with that, him just putting up a birdhouse at the dam?" *What next,* she thought, *Christmas lights? Pink flamingo lawn ornaments? Lawn chairs?*

Howey shrugged. "It's just a birdhouse. And *we're* the security, so if anyone would have had a problem with it, it would have been us. We saw no harm in it, though. He likes to put seed in it and watch them eat, I guess, like a little old man in the park feeding pigeons. Frankly, once we realized that he wasn't a team player, we were happy to see him go off on his own." Howey grinned. "Man's strange enough, though, that it wouldn't surprise me if he actually was eating the seed himself."

The birdhouse continued to vex Susan. She'd found the placement of the lovely one strange enough at the exterior of Dov's house, which had been as warm and welcoming as a prison yard, yet to have one at a federal dam was downright irregular. She thought back to the photos and books she'd seen at the Amsel household. Had there been something there that indicated bird-watching was a hobby of Dov's? She couldn't recall seeing anything specifically, but she also hadn't been looking for it either.

A thought occurred to her.

She located the garbage can. Slowly, she dumped out the birdseed, using her fingers as a sieve. She'd considered that maybe Dov had been stashing whatever drugs he was on in the bags. It would be a clever way to smuggle them out on a break. But nothing.

She asked, "Could you take me to it?"

"The birdhouse? Sure, but it's a hike."

"That's okay; I've got my comfy shoes on." Susan wondered if Howey might be exaggerating, so as to spare himself from having to do some extra walking.

Soon, however, Susan realized that the guard wasn't kidding about the distance. She wondered if this might be where Dov went to do drugs when he was on shift. He'd certainly have privacy. Just when she was about to suggest that they go back and get her car, Howey pointed to a pole about a hundred yards away. "There."

"Well, that's weird," Susan muttered.

"What's that?"

She shook her head. "I was just thinking how strange it is that the birdhouse is so low." *Just like the one at the Amsel residence,* she thought—and it looked a lot like the one at the Amsel residence too. "Aren't those things supposed to be higher up, so that the birds can actually see it? That thing's like chest level."

Howey cocked his head. "Huh. You're right. I guess I never noticed that before, though I never come all the way out here." The radio on his hip blared to life, and a voice Susan recognized as the female guard asked what was taking so long. She also informed Howey that her shift was over, making it clear that she was not thrilled having to wait around.

"You know what—I got it from here," Susan said. "Why don't you head on out. I'll see myself back to the car."

Susan was more relaxed having Howey gone. Maybe it was the small-town cop in her that had gotten used to working on her own, but she found that she could think clearer without having someone looming at her side, distracting her. *Which is also probably why you're single,* a voice in her head chided. She promptly told the voice to shut up.

Susan's frown deepened as she neared the birdhouse. It wasn't *like* the one at the Amsel residence; it was an exact replica, right down to the orange-red paint on the underside of the roof. That had to be more than a mere coincidence. She found it odd that there was no sign that birds had ever used the house: no poop, no cracked seeds, no feathers. What was he doing with the seed, then? If he'd wanted to take a walk for his break, surely he didn't need to concoct a story about having to feed birds at the far end of the parking lot. It was his free time, so he could have used it how he'd wanted. And, as far as taking drugs went, he could have saved himself a journey and done them in a bathroom stall, unless he was smoking something.

She walked a few yards past the birdhouse, where the parking lot ended and a wide open field began. It was there she saw it, a small mound of sandwich bags full of seeds. *What had he been up to?* she wondered. She peered inside the birdhouse, finding it empty.

No, that wasn't quite right, she realized upon further inspection. On the far back wall of the house, there was a carving: a red *D* with a triangle around it.

DOTE?

CHAPTER 17

Eric didn't have to strain too hard to understand why Jake wasn't returning his numerous calls. He was probably embarrassed.

Or, what he thought was more likely, worrying about yet another reprimand for his drinking. Eric was now questioning whether he'd been presenting his concern in a fashion that had had the opposite effect of what he'd intended, which was to help. Obviously, it hadn't worked, or else he wouldn't have received the drunken voice mail from his friend in the middle of the night.

He also regretted discouraging him to further investigate DOTE. Defiant as Jake was, that was exactly what he would go and do now. After his conversation with Greta Milstein at the police station, he was worried his friend was feeding himself to the wolves.

But Jake was an adult, and he'd been in more than a few precarious situations in his day. Eric trusted that he'd keep his head cool in danger, despite his recent erratic behavior while intoxicated.

He was just about to call Jake again when his phone started ringing. "You must be psychic," he told Susan as he picked up.

"No, that's you, not me," she said dryly, but he knew she was kidding. "Look, I can't talk long because I've got a lot of other work to do, but I wanted to get back to you about a couple things."

Eric seized the opportunity. "Will you be free in a few hours? Want to come to my place for dinner?"

She hesitated so long that Eric thought she might have disengaged from the call. "Do you think it's a good idea?" she finally said.

Eric's casual tone was in direct contrast to the sting he felt from her words. "Well, we've both got to eat, right? And I'm sure it's been a long time since you've had a home-cooked meal."

"I actually can't remember the last home-cooked meal I had."

"There you go. It's long overdue, then." That was as far as he was going to push it, he decided, lest he sound desperate. Or, heaven forbid, like he was begging.

"Okay, okay!" she said with a light chuckle. "You've got a point there. What time are you thinking? I can't stay long, though, because I've got to work early in the morning."

◆ ◆ ◆

Four hours later, Eric was setting the table for dinner and trying to keep his hands from shaking. Though they'd occasionally spoken on the phone, he hadn't seen Susan in person since they'd "officially" called it quits. While he was aware that they were, in no uncertain terms, not having a date, he wanted to get the evening right. He'd felt uneasy about the way they'd left things, awkwardly, which he partially attributed to being clueless after a divorce.

He'd opted to keep the meal on the fun, casual side, for fear of looking like he was trying too hard by whipping up something elaborate. Funny enough, although he was now confident in his culinary skills (dare he even say a show-off), he'd been a disaster in the kitchen when he'd first moved to California. This he blamed on a coddled upbringing and his ex-wife's insistence on cooking everything—she'd said that it was more for herself than for him, since he frequently attempted to make up for his failings as a chef with enough salt to make one's mouth pucker. There was also the easy access to fast food and ready-made meals, as well as his sheer laziness. He used to consider the oven merely a place to store extra cookware, and *stovetop cooking* was a term he applied to anything edible he could heat straight from a can—really, the only food he could "cook." Being in a relationship with Susan had only intensified his laziness in the kitchen, since she cooked even less than he did. If he'd been under any illusion that she was going to prepare all his meals for him the way Maggie had—or at least the way she had in the beginning of their marriage, before she'd taken up sleeping with his brother—he'd been sorely mistaken. To Susan, "meal prep" was throwing some crackers and a block of cheese onto a plate.

After his relationship with Susan ended, Eric, who was a firm believer that idle hands were the devil's playthings, decided to sign up for some cooking classes to help take his mind off his heartache. He hadn't gone out of the way to find them; they'd just sort of popped up in his peripheral vision. Literally. He'd walked by a notice board at his local coffee shop and had seen the flyer. Had it been a similar advertisement for martial arts, he'd be tying on a karate gi now instead of an apron. He'd been skeptical when he'd met the instructor, Kent, who boasted a bowler hat, a beard long enough to tuck into the hem of his pants, should he choose, and a Japanese-style tattoo bodysuit that ran from his neck to his toes; Eric had opted to simply believe him on the full-coverage thing, though Kent had made numerous offers to show him intimate parts that weren't exposed—"No shame in my game," he'd said. Eric had to give credit where credit was due. The man could cook, and now so could he, though for tonight's fare, he'd decided to keep it simple.

His late father had been a master of the grill, so he was using his recipe for the hamburgers he'd touted as "world famous," though Eric could remember only his family ever having them. The key to the burgers was to use the freshest, highest-quality meat available, plus a dash of Worcestershire sauce, capers, and a few finely chopped fresh herbs. On the side, he would be serving homemade sweet potato fries with a chili blue-cheese sauce. It sounded like a whole lot of flavors going on, but, when Eric had made the meal for himself in the past, he'd found them complementary.

Susan arrived at eight o'clock sharp, looking, though a trifle on the thin side, as beautiful as he remembered her to be. "You cut your hair," she blurted when she saw him, and then they exchanged an awkward hug.

He ran a hand through his cropped mane. He'd worn it on the longer side most of his life, but the change felt nice. "You like it?"

"Handsome," she said, and then her cheeks became a little pinker.

They ran through the standard pleasantries of asking how their days went and made idle chitchat about work and life in general while Eric fried up their burgers. It felt natural enough, their conversation, as if only a day or two had passed since they'd last seen each other. She'd mentioned earlier that she couldn't stay too long, so he made a point not to dawdle. He handed her a cold beer and a plate of food, and then they took seats in his kitchen at the small rustic table he ate his meals on.

Eric felt compelled to get right down to it, to show her that he hadn't asked her over for dinner merely as a ploy to spend time in her company. "So, do you want to start with the Jake stuff or the murder stuff?"

Susan made a satisfied moaning sound and then dabbed her chin with a paper napkin. "Good God, I didn't know you could cook so well."

He shrugged modestly, though he was pleased she seemed to *really* like it. Susan had never been one to blow smoke, so if she said it was good, it was good. "I've been taking lessons."

She raised her eyebrows. "Really? Good for you. It shows. This is delicious. Let's start with Jake. You said you're worried about him?"

Eric swallowed down his bite, took a sip of beer. "I don't think he's fully processed the deaths of Chuck and Madison. Or, maybe he's processed it, but he doesn't know how to deal with it. His band, as you know, was his life. He told me he can't go near his violin now without getting sick to his stomach. He says the last time he played the thing was up in Clancy."

She nodded. "Makes sense. That's where their last show was, and where his friends were murdered. That's a shame. His talent is being wasted."

"His grades are also slipping. He tried to downplay it when I questioned him about it, but I'm buddies with a guy who works in admissions. He's not supposed to, but he let me see Jake's academic records. He went from As to barely passing. The school's actually about to send him a notice to let him know that he's been placed on academic probation. If he doesn't get his grades up, they're throwing him out."

"Yikes."

"That's not all. Worst of all, he's been drinking. *A lot.* He left me the most insane voice mail, telling me that I wasn't the boss of him, or something to that effect. It was hard to tell what he was saying because he was so wasted. I think he was mad at me because I told him not to investigate DOTE, which he's said he wanted to do."

Susan asked, "You think he's an alcoholic?"

"It's a weird one, Suze. I don't think he's drinking because he craves booze. My brother, Jim, now *he* had issues with alcohol, and his behavior was different from Jake's—though I imagine no two alcoholics are the same. But, with Jake, I get the feeling that he just needs something to occupy his time, because when he's on his own, he mopes. He needs to stop isolating himself. He's acting like I did right after I moved out here after my divorce. When you feel down like that, it's easy to get into your own head and forget that the world keeps moving without you. That was a train-wrecky time for me."

She smiled. "But, hey, you got through it."

"A lot of that was thanks to you," Eric said before he could think better of it. The comment hung in the air above them like the sky was about to fall. Their eyes met for a brief second, and then they both quickly looked away, as if trying to fool one another that they hadn't seen each other's reaction.

Susan cleared her throat and wiped a hand under her watery eyes. Was she on the verge of tears? "You'd said something earlier about him wanting to investigate DOTE?"

"He doesn't think Bryan is guilty, and, now that he's dead, he wants to investigate their group."

"Maybe he should." Eric frowned, and she clarified. "I'm not saying he should act like a secret agent and put himself in harm's way, but I don't see what it could hurt if he poked around and asked a few questions. He's one of them, after all, so they might be more inclined to confide in him."

"What do you mean, one of them?" he asked.

"Well, he goes to Lamount, where they've got a DOTE club on campus, right? And you've said before that students don't really tell you things because you're viewed as *the man*. So maybe Jake could get something out of them," Susan said.

She had a point. He said, "And, I suppose, it would give him something to focus his energy on, if only for the time being. Besides, something tells me he's going to do it anyway, if he hasn't already. Jake has a tendency to do what he wants, regardless of any advice given to him."

"He's certainly headstrong, our boy. But just keep an eye on him, would you? If he continues going downhill, we might have to stage an intervention," she said, and Eric nodded. "But, speaking of the DOTE situation, I looked further into Bryan McDougal's so-called sex offense."

Eric didn't miss her use of *so-called*. "Go on."

"Here's what I gathered: It relates to a campus stunt that involved streaking during his freshman year. Seems Bryan and a few idiot friends had gotten drunk one night and decided that it would be funny to run naked across the quad."

"Did anyone get hurt—assaulted?" he asked, his heart sinking.

"No one whatsoever. They actually made no physical contact with *anyone*."

"So . . . then, what? They scared some poor girl walking home from class? Or a mom with a carload full of kids drove by and saw?"

"Again, no. There was only a single security guard on campus who saw them, a man in his fifties. Real hard-ass. Bryan was the only one who got caught, since his buddies took off and left him in the lurch after they'd been spotted."

"Nice friends."

"Right," she said with a snort. "Anyway, though they threatened him with prosecution, Bryan protected his friends—the same ones who left him behind—and refused to give up their identities."

"So they made an example of him."

"That's exactly right. Put his name on the sex offender list because of the nudity."

Eric made a sputtering sound. "That's outrageous! He was a dumb kid doing a stupid, dumb-kid prank. And they thought a fair punishment would be to put him on the same list as pedophiles and rapists? For the rest of his life? When actual rapists his age can get away scot-free because their daddy knows the right judge?"

"I know, I know—it's disgusting," Susan agreed. "I have no doubt that if he'd had better legal representation, he probably would've only had to pay a fine, gotten a little slap on the wrist. It doesn't look like he fought too hard against it, though. He got caught and took his lumps without much fuss. Guess he thought the situation would go away on its own. Boy, was he wrong."

"So, what now?"

"Well, there's not much we can do about the sex offense thing, though I'm also starting to wonder if you and Jake might be right and he was wrongfully accused of his ex-girlfriend's murder."

"I can't find the connection," Eric said, "but I suspect DOTE might have played a part in the murders." He then went on to outline the conversation he'd had with Greta Milstein and the harried police officer who'd made it pretty clear that he intended to let sleeping dogs lie.

"I can't get into specifics now, but I'm going to investigate DOTE further. I think the group might be a lot more active in the Bay Area than the FBI previously gave them credit for." Susan glanced at her watch and made a face. "Oh man, I need to go. I had no idea it was so late—where did the time go? I've got to get up for work in just a few hours."

Eric wished she could stay longer. He missed hearing her voice and seeing her face light up when she smiled—he missed her in general. Still, he understood that she had obligations. "Agreed. I just want to mention one thing, and then I'll let you go. From the sound of it, DOTE is all about executing a series of smaller attacks and then going in for the kill with a grand gesture of all gestures."

"That seems about right," she agreed.

"This is just a hunch—"

"A hunch or one of those weird feelings you get about things?" she cut in.

"It's a little bit of both," he admitted. "Anyway, given DOTE's recent uptick in activity, I was thinking that, if they were going to make a grand statement, they might choose a day that has significance. Not so much to America as a whole, but to *them*."

"The way a serial killer might, but with an ecological edge," she said.

"Exactly. I had a look at a calendar, and do you know what holiday is coming up?"

She barked out a laugh. "Eric, I can hardly remember my own birthday most years."

He laughed too. "Arbor Day is coming up, Suze. Do you know what that is?"

"The celebration of trees," she said, her eyebrow arching.

CHAPTER 18

Jake was really getting into the whole undercover thing. He must've changed his outfit/disguise at least a half dozen times, though ultimately he opted to go as his usual self. Dressing like someone who was already a doter, as he'd initially done, would defeat the whole purpose of him having to attend a meet and greet for new members. His angle tonight would be to display enough ignorance to indicate that he was suggestive to new influences—he *hoped* that was how he'd be interpreted.

His jaw dropped when he pulled up at the party's location, an expansive Tudor-style house with a long, curved driveway. Multimillionaires lived here. He'd been anticipating a shack in the woods. Getting out of his car, he double-checked the address from the text Kimmy had sent him, confirming that he was in the right place. He sent Kimmy a message to let her know that he'd arrived and then headed up the gravel driveway toward the sound of happy-go-lucky indie music that was horn and banjo heavy.

Since he was thirty and his usual social hangout was a bar, it had been a while since he'd been to a gathering like this. He suddenly felt really old and a little like he was participating in the naughty teenage act of attending a friend's wild house party while the parents were out of town. As he'd soon find out, this was partially true.

Kimmy met him at the front door, looking even lovelier than she had on the quad. "Make yourself at home," she said as she ushered him in.

"Where *am* I right now?" he asked in astonishment as he stepped into the foyer. Off to his left was a grand staircase that curved along a wall decorated with highbrow art he wouldn't have even known how to price. Everything in the house screamed interior-designed opulence: sleek modern leather furniture mixed with carved wood antiques, a stunning blown-glass chandelier the size of a small sedan hovering above, abstract sculptures. His own family had a great deal of money, but not like this. This was what he'd call *gonzo rich*.

Kimmy laughed. "I know—it's embarrassing."

"That's not really the word I'd use," Jake said, thinking he'd give his eyeteeth to live in a place like this. "Is this house yours?"

She flapped a hand, rolled her eyes. "Please. It's my father's. Gross how much he likes to show off, isn't it? Hello, midlife crisis. But we needed a place that'd hold all of us for the party, and he'll be in the Bahamas for another month, so here we are." She smiled brightly. "Drink?"

Jake cast surreptitious glances at the partygoers as they made their way into the kitchen and Kimmy went to mix him a drink. He was perplexed by what he saw within the sixty or so people who were in attendance. While diverse in race and gender, the group could be classified into two categories, so distinct a line could be drawn between them.

The first group was younger, bright-eyed individuals who appeared a little ill at ease. Their demeanor was skittish; they were behaving as if, well, they didn't know *how* to behave. They fit the mold of what Jake had been expecting: the children of yuppies posing as Mother Earth types. To them, it seemed, the event was a novelty. They clung together awkwardly, gaped and giggled at Kimmy's father's antiques, snapped group photos, and drank as if the primary motivation was to get drunk.

Then there were the older, relaxed individuals who were dressed in an upscale, business casual manner. They spoke in quieter tones and were disinterested in the surroundings. A couple of them appeared to be making a list. In the few moments he watched them, he couldn't tell what for, but he could have sworn that they'd looked right at him and then quickly glanced away. As a dwarf, he was used to this happening. A lot.

These are the ones, Jake thought, *who I should keep an eye on. These are the ones who are running things.*

The atmosphere in the room changed when a handsome dark-haired individual Jake placed in his mid- to late thirties arrived at the party. The younger, Mother Earth group hushed their voices to murmurs as he confidently glided past. They tried to look at him without looking at him, which made them all the more obvious. He wore tailored blue jeans, an expensive-looking sweater, and glossy brown Chelsea boots that Jake assumed were vegan leather. His dark eyes were framed by a modern update of horn-rimmed glasses, and his smile was easy. Jake wondered if he was the leader.

"Who's that?" Jake asked as Kimmy handed him some kind of fruity drink. He took a sip, the scent of vodka and orange permeating his nostrils before the liquid hit his lips. Screwdriver. He hated screwdrivers. "Delicious. Thank you."

The newcomer tipped his head at Kimmy, and she smiled back. "That's Edward, but everyone calls him Rodent."

"Why?"

"His last name is Mowse—you know, like a *mouse,* but spelled M-o-w-s-e. Someone called him Rodent once, and it stuck."

"I'm going to assume the nickname is ironic," Jake said, glancing Rodent's way. The guy could be a model for his own cologne line, yet he also had the distinguished air of a well-respected classics author. Again, Jake was feeling chagrined at just how far off the mark he'd been. Where was the wild-eyed Jim Jones tyrant, the dazed cult-groupie followers? Could he and Eric have been wrong in their assessment of the organization? Had Bryan purposely led them astray? He felt like the sort of fool who'd believed every stereotype he'd seen on TV only to later find out it was all a lie—that real life was quite the opposite. Had he been blinded by his own personal biases?

Or were these wolves in sheeps' clothing?

"Not too hard on the eyes, is he?" Kimmy remarked in a manner that made Jake wonder if the two might have a romantic history. Maybe *she* was his groupie. He wasn't too bothered. She was giving him strong *friends only* vibes, and he was put off by her lack of gratitude toward her father's wealth, which had provided her a lifestyle—not to mention a place for DOTE meetings—she clearly took for granted.

Besides, he reminded himself, there was always the possibility that she was a budding extremist.

"He looks familiar," he said, tipping his head in Rodent's direction. "Do all these people go to LU? He's not a student, is he?"

"Oh no, not at all—Rodent graduated like ten or fifteen years ago." She squinted her eyes. "Or maybe he went to LU for a little bit but then dropped out. I can't remember."

And yet he's still hanging out with college kids, Jake thought. It was not lost on him that there wasn't a single person in the room who looked over the age of thirty, barring Rodent.

"There are some current students and other LU graduates, of course, but I'd say most of the people here are new recruits brought in by senior members." Rodent waved her his way. "That's my cue. Have fun, mingle," she said, and then she wandered off.

Rodent, Kimmy, and a few of the other older, well-dressed individuals gathered at the head of the living room. Rodent raised his palms in a quieting motion, and the room promptly fell silent. Jake wasn't sure how he felt about the power Rodent so obviously had over his disciples. It was evident these individuals looked up to him, but for what reasons? He noted that a few of the females had gone googly eyed over him, too, but that could have been simply because he was a heartthrob.

"Thank you all for coming." He smiled at the crowd. "I know you came here to meet some new faces and have some fun, so I'll cut to the chase so you can get back to it. We've picked you to join us tonight because we see potential in all of you. And we hope, in turn, you see potential in us. As I'm sure you know, not all of you will be invited to join our cause, but don't let that stop you from having a good time. Relax and be yourselves."

What did *that* mean? Not everyone could join DOTE? This was interesting news. He'd been under the impression that *doters* were the ones trying to convince *others* to join their cause. Could that have been what the list making was about—they'd been observing how new pledges behaved, documenting who was worthy in their eyes?

Rodent paused as the crowd whooped and hollered, raising his arms in acknowledgment, as if he were a messiah. *The crowd seems to be eating it up,* Jake thought with an internal snort. Praise and adoration were as addicting as an actual drug. Maybe more. This he knew unequivocally, having relished it when the crowd had cheered him on when he'd played with Augustine Grifters.

Rodent continued, "Just want to introduce some of my fellow foot soldiers who have been with me for the long haul, through thick and thin: Brice, Kimmy, Marty, Paige, Miguel, and that there down on the end is Jason. If you have questions, ask any one of us. And keep on fighting the good fight." He pumped his fist in the air like an illustrious political leader, and Jake had to stop himself from casting his eyes at the ceiling. The foot soldiers—Kimmy included—also raised their fists at the crowd, and then the group dispersed.

Jake went into the kitchen to find a beverage he actually wanted to consume, a beer, and then dumped the screwdriver down the sink when he was sure nobody was watching. He'd taken in about enough bullshit for one evening. Were DOTE participating in terrorist-like activities? He didn't know, but they sure were self-aggrandizing.

"Probably not what you were expecting, right?" a voice next to him asked.

Jake was surprised to see it was Rodent. He felt a twinge of guilt, as if he'd expressed his disdain about the group vocally. "I don't know what you mean," he answered vaguely.

"Most people come to our parties expecting to see a bunch of hippies gathered around in a drum circle, eating hummus and singing kumbaya earth songs or whatever," he said and laughed.

Jake was surprised to find that he was laughing along with him. Rodent's energy was infectious—he gave him that. "Okay, maybe that's a little of what I was expecting," he said, bringing his thumb and index finger together.

"You're Jake, right?" Rodent asked, holding his hand out for Jake to shake.

"That's right. Kimmy must've told you."

"Kimmy and a couple others here." Rodent turned to face him. "We know who you are, of course."

Jake's heart sank. "What do you mean?"

"You really don't know?" he asked, his eyebrow arched as if he were having a private laugh. "Your band. You were in Augustine Grifters."

"Oh, right." Jake took a sip of his drink.

"I've actually seen you guys play a couple times, back in the day. I used to go to a lot of shows, before I got too busy with this stuff." Rodent took a sip of his own beer. "Heard about what happened to you guys—your band members, I mean. I'm really sorry about that."

Maybe Rodent wasn't as bad as he'd been giving him credit for. At minimum, he sounded sincere. "Thanks, but I don't really like to talk about it," Jake said, and that was the truth. A memory tickled the back of his mind. He felt like he'd had this conversation with Rodent before.

"Completely understand. But I will say that I hope you keep playing, because what you do with your violin is beautiful. It would be a tragedy if you didn't, because if there's anything the world needs, it's more beauty like yours."

Jake reminded himself that he was not supposed to like the man. It was difficult, though. The way Rodent spoke to a person made them feel special, important. It was easy to understand how he'd garnered so many followers. While he was unquestionably charismatic, he was also kind. Of course, how could he truly know this, having only spoken to the man for a couple minutes?

And then, an image hit his brain with enough force to cause him to shake his head.

Jake said, "Wait a minute. You're that guy, the one from the bar. You . . ." He rubbed his forehead, his brain going fuzzy at the memory. "You're the one who took me outside and put me in a taxi. I tried to hit you, didn't I?"

Rodent shrugged. "Eh, who can remember these things?" he said good-naturedly, though Jake doubted that he'd already forgotten. What he thought was more likely was that the man was trying to spare him a great deal of embarrassment, which he appreciated, despite his resolve to unearth DOTE's nefarious activities. He continued, "We could use more people like you in our group."

Jake's smile was sheepish. "Because I start fights with random strangers in bars?"

"Forget about that, would you? You show me a man who claims to have never made a fool of himself, and I'll show you a man who's either a liar or has been living the life of a saint." He placed an arm on Jake's shoulder. "You're only human, my friend."

He's good, Jake thought. So good that he might start to buy into his self-serving doctrine, if he wasn't careful. Handsome, charismatic, and willing to pick a struggling man up when he was down. Was he simply a good person or too good to be true? "Okay, so is it because of my band?"

Rodent let out the sort of soft laugh that made it difficult to imagine him ever losing his temper. "Fame never hurts, of course. Americans, well, you know what they're like." *They're,* like he wasn't one of them.

"Once you become a star in the US of A, if even a minor one, people trust anything you tell them. The blind faith is astounding. Fame, it's like a religion, and celebrities are the gods."

"It really is," Jake agreed. "Like a religion."

"And everyone wants to be one, a god." Rodent shook his head. "But it's not your fame either. Though you have fire in your belly and clearly never back down from a fight, and though you have the background with your band, what I like about you, Jake, is your *passion*. Most people don't have passion for much of anything these days. Nothing important, anyway."

Rodent was off again, before Jake had a chance to comment.

"Nobody goes out of their way to enrich or challenge themselves anymore, to learn a new skill or repair themselves in an area where they might be lacking. No, they're perfectly okay staying unexceptional. They fret over the number of followers they have on social media, how many likes they get for a 'spontaneous' photo that took them fifteen tries to perfect, the ten-word statement they spent half the morning and all their brainpower honing. They can't eat a meal or work out or take a shit or kiss their dogs and kids and lovers without first getting photographic evidence of it. They take away the specialness—the *intimacy*—of every facet of life in their quest to get it all down on film because, if they don't, it's like it never happened. They do stupid, pointless challenges that compromise their morals, their safety, their *basic common sense* simply because the internet tells them to. They waste hours of their day online arguing with strangers on the other side of the globe over complete bullshit while ignoring the people sitting right next to them. They compare their own lives with the phony ones others have created to make them feel less worthy, and then they go out and buy up every frivolous object that crosses their path—because you've gotta spend that money like a good little consumer, don't you?—in a vain attempt to play catch-up, though the reality is that they never will. They exist in a state of half awareness. We've become a society in which mediocrity and narcissism are the new norm. Nobody cares about anything *real* anymore."

"You're absolutely right," Jake said, stunned to realize that he'd been nodding along, like he'd been hypnotized. Maybe he had.

"If we keep going the way we are, I can't imagine what the world will look like in fifty, a hundred years. We're living in some seriously dark times, man." Rodent's eyes traveled over the youthful party attendees. "I mean, have a look at these younger generations. They're so . . ."

"Inauthentic? Attention hungry? Desperate?" Jake finished for him. They watched a girl snapping a selfie by a carved marble bust of a long-dead general, her fingers making bunny ears at the back of his head. She checked the photo on her phone and then began frantically tapping away, undoubtedly uploading the image to the same social media Rodent had just ridiculed.

With a nod, Rodent placed a hand on his shoulder. Normally, this would've irked Jake, since little people tended to be handled like children by those who were uncomfortable around them—a pat on the head, words spoken in a singsong voice: *you're sooooo cute!*—but he didn't mind now. Being touched by Rodent felt both unsettling and righteous, he realized with some dismay, as if he'd been granted approval he hadn't even known he'd been seeking. It was not difficult to imagine how he could hold sway over dozens of sheltered twentysomethings.

"It's refreshing to come across someone real, like yourself, Jake. You think you embarrassed yourself the other night?" Rodent made a sputtering sound and tilted his head toward a group of boys shotgunning beers. "No, it's *these* fools who are the embarrassment. At least you behave as if you are *alive* and have some real thoughts and emotions rattling around in your head. You have *soul.*"

Once again, Jake found himself nodding. He shook his head, as if to dislodge Rodent's seductive words from his brain. *If you only knew why I was here,* he thought in response to the praise. "Does this mean I've passed your test, then—are you asking me to join DOTE?" Strange as it was, Jake found that he was seeking approval from the man. But not just seeking it, *craving* it, and not only because of his clandestine investigation.

"One thing at a time," Rodent said easily. "I would like you to go on a little errand with us. Consider it more of an invitation than a test."

The message was clear: test or no test, he would need to prove himself, if he wanted to join them. It was exactly what Jake had been striving for, yet he was uneasy. "An errand—where?"

Rodent shook his head. "Where we're going, that's a surprise, my friend! But it'll be great. I'll let you know when the time is right."

Jake held out his hand for Rodent to shake. "Count me in," he said, feeling as if he'd just made a deal with the devil.

CHAPTER 19

At the FBI office, Susan asked Johnathan if she could pick his brain about DOTE for a few minutes. She wanted to know why the group would be interested in a dam, since she'd found evidence of their presence at one inside the birdhouse. "As an environmental group, I mean," she said. "CliffsNotes version," she added, knowing that he'd talk her ear off, given half a chance.

"That's a fairly easy one," Johnathan said. His academic background was in environmental science, and he was often asked to consult with other agents on such issues. Susan suspected that he would have probably been given the case she was working on currently, had it initially been more apparent that Chung's murder might be connected to DOTE or the dam itself. "Dams are notoriously terrible for the environment."

Susan shook her head. "I don't really know much about dams, but I was under the impression that they provide green energy. So wouldn't that make them a good thing?"

"Yes and no. Dams do provide renewable energy, but at a great cost to the natural environment. Essentially, it's only humans who benefit from them—although sometimes humans are also hurt by them, too, because of pollution and home displacement." Johnathan ticked the list off on his fingers as he spoke. "But, as far as the environment, dams can cause flooding, damage wetlands and oceans, increase sea levels, destroy entire ecosystems, displace and destroy wildlife, impede fish migration . . . I could go on. Nasty stuff. Have you heard of the Condit Hydroelectric Project?"

"No."

"Basically, the Glines Canyon Dam was built in Washington State around, oh, 1920 or '30. The dam completely destroyed the wildlife system in the area, and did some awful things to the fish population too—pretty much eradicated salmon, as well as other species. So, a few years ago, it was decided that it would be far more expensive to update the dam than to keep in line with new environmental protection acts. So, they demolished it."

"The whole dam?"

"That's right. I mean, they didn't just go there one day and blow the whole thing up—that would be disastrous. It was carefully planned demolitions. Anyway, now that the dam is gone, the wildlife is flourishing again. There are all kinds of shellfish—clams and crabs, etcetera—and the birds and salmon are back. It's easy to see how bad the dam was for the area now that it's gone."

Susan thanked Johnathan for the information and went back to her desk. She checked the time and saw that she was running late for her appointment at Zelman Industries to have a chat with Marcus Zelman about his hiring of Chung Nguygen. It had taken a bit of finagling with Zelman's admin assistant—and ultimately a veiled threat that had come in the form of Susan reminding the woman that she was speaking with an FBI agent—before an appointment was granted with His Majesty. She could already predict how cooperative Zelman was going to be and anticipated him having his lawyer present. Guys like him always did.

Though she did have to go through a fair amount of rigamarole with yet another assistant once she arrived at Zelman Industries, which occupied a sprawling campus with clusters of smaller buildings spread throughout, Zelman surprised her by attending their meeting sans lawyer. His face was unlined with just enough shine to suggest he'd had cosmetic work of some type performed recently, but underneath the artificialness of his appearance, he was a handsome fiftysomething. His eyes were blue and sparkly, his hair sandy with a dash of gray, and his tanned skin hinted at weekends spent on a yacht.

He sat behind a large floating-top executive desk that looked like teak and as if it weighed five hundred pounds. Once she settled down across from him into a hard leather chair that dug into her back uncomfortably, he offered her a beverage. He made it a point to tell her that it would be no trouble at all for him—as if that was her chief concern, saving *him* trouble—since he'd have "one of his girls" fetch it. Because, of course, the big boss wouldn't dare degrade himself with such a menial task.

She declined. "I don't plan on taking up too much of your time, Mr. Zelman. I'd just like to ask you a few questions about Chung Nguygen."

Sometimes, a seemingly innocent person who was not even a blip on Susan's radar would make the smallest gesture that spurred acute suspicion, and this was one of those times. Had Zelman simply nodded, she would have probably asked him a few questions and then gone on her way. But he didn't do that, which was a big mistake on his part.

He leaned forward, squinted. "Who? I'm sorry, that name doesn't ring a bell."

Bullshit, she thought. And, just like that, he was on her radar. "You sure, because you only hired him a short time ago."

"You sure I can't get you a drink?" he asked. Stalling.

"I'm fine. So?"

His frown was so contrived it was theatrical, a stage actor projecting his emotions for those way back in the cheap seats. "Hmm . . . you know what, hold on a sec." He raised a finger and made a show of calling his admin assistant. "Hi, Joy, do I know a—what was the name again?" he asked Susan. She told him, and he repeated the name back into the phone. "Right, okay, thanks," he said and then hung up.

"Well?" she asked, trying to conceal that she was losing her patience. He hadn't lawyered up thus far, and she wanted to keep it that way.

"I hired Mr. Nguygen to conduct an environmental survey of Cambridge Downs. It's a low-income community that my firm had a hand in developing."

"Is that what you do here, property development?"

"Mainly. And some other things."

It was strange that he did not elaborate. Usually men like Zelman could not help themselves from tooting their own horns. Perhaps he did not feel as if she were one he needed to impress. "Where is this development, Cambridge Downs?"

Zelman shifted in his seat. "It sits just below Gruben Dam."

Susan kept her expression neutral. "And what was the environmental survey for?"

"Why do you ask?"

"It's just a question," she said mildly.

He provided her a put-out sigh. "If memory serves me correctly, I hired Mr. Nguygen to test the soil for toxins, since it sits below the dam. I don't know if you are aware, but dams have an astoundingly negative environmental impact."

"I'm aware," she said. "Do you frequently have lapses of memory?"

A flicker of anger touched his face, but he got himself under control. "I'm not following."

"You said if memory served. We're talking about not even a month ago."

He gave her a greasy smile. "Unfortunately, I don't have the type of job where I can remember the name of every contractor I hire. There's just too many people I work with, and I'm very busy."

Congratulations, she wanted to say. "So, why were you concerned about the toxic soil levels in Cambridge Downs? I can assume you have no interest in acquiring a home in the neighborhood?"

He gave her a patient look. "As I mentioned, it was one of our developments, so I like to check in."

"Do you make it a habit to check in on other projects you've developed?"

He ignored the question. "What do you want from me? I've been blessed with the good fortune of wealth. I like to help underprivileged souls by ensuring their neighborhoods are safe from pollution. I had the survey done as an act of community service." He swept his hands out across his desk. "It's the least I can do."

Underprivileged souls? What a sanctimonious ass, she thought. She believed he was about as charitable as she could throw him. No way was this guy doing anything for the underprivileged out of the kindness of his heart without there being some payoff for him. Tax write-off, perhaps?

"Were you aware that Chung Nguygen was murdered while on shift at the dam?"

"Why would I be aware of such a thing? I hired Mr. Nguygen to conduct the survey. He did his job, gave me the information I needed, and I paid him for his time. That was the end of it. I never saw him again."

"Aren't you curious what happened to Nguygen?"

He shrugged. "Why should I be? I didn't know the guy. He only worked for me once."

A real humanitarian, all right.

"And, what did the survey reveal?" she asked.

He shook his head. "It revealed nothing. The soil is fine."

"That part you remember."

"Well, I'd remember it if there were toxins on the land, so it must have been okay."

"Fair enough," she said. She was getting the sense that he was getting riled. Good. Angry people were more likely to slip up. "Could I see a copy of that report?"

159

"I'm afraid that's confidential."

She leaned forward and smiled easily. "I'm with the FBI. We keep things pretty confidential."

He sighed. "I'll have to see what I can do. It might take some time to locate the report. And, of course, I'll need to okay everything through my attorney."

"Of course." Susan had no doubt that Zelman had no intention of ever sending her a thing. He was hiding something, but what? Could it be that the report had not come back as clean as he was claiming?

He stood. "If you'll excuse me, I have work that I need to get back to. I'm—"

"Yes, you're very busy. I understand," she said. "Just one more question."

He glanced at his watch. He seemed nervous, as if he couldn't wait for her to leave. "If it's quick."

"You ever get any threats from environmentalist groups?"

"No, never." He answered just a little too quickly. He hadn't even taken the time to consider the question, which was odd.

"You familiar with a group called Defenders of the Earth? DOTE for short?"

"Never heard of them," he said, but his eyes told a different story.

Susan made a move to leave and then paused. Along the wall near the door was a series of photographs that celebrated Zelman's grandness in one fashion or another: standing front and center at a skyrise, cutting a yellow ribbon with ludicrously large scissors that could have doubled as hedge trimmers; shaking hands with some middle-aged blueblood who was undoubtedly a politician; giving a toast at some corporate shindig.

It was the photo on the bottom right that got Susan's attention.

"Who is this that you're with in the picture?" she asked, though she already knew.

He hesitated. Why he would over an image he had hanging for everyone to see was odd. She suspected that she'd rattled him, so now he was keeping all his information close to the vest. Or was there some other reason he'd be reluctant to tell her, something shiftier?

Finally, he said, "That's Lucy and Don Neville." He squinted at the photo, as if seeing it for the first time. "I believe we were at a dinner benefit for a cystic fibrosis foundation; fifteen hundred dollars a plate. Or maybe it was prostate cancer. I go to so many of these things I can hardly keep them all straight." He gave her a look as if to say, *You know how it is.*

Unfortunately, she didn't. High-dollar dinners were far beyond her pay grade. "Do you know the Nevilles?"

Zelman frowned. "Why do you ask?"

Susan tapped the frame. "Because you're sitting by them."

"Oh, right," he said. "Our relationship is mainly professional. We've worked together indirectly on a few developments. And, of course, there's the charity functions we mutually attend."

"You must have heard about their daughter?" Susan asked, watching his face carefully.

His expression gave away nothing. "Yes, I heard. Very sad," he said, not sounding sad at all.

CHAPTER 20

Eric was in no mood for a visitor, though this was something he could hardly say to the young woman who appeared suddenly in his office doorway. He shook his head to gather himself, having been deep in a daydream prior to the interruption, though what he'd been dreaming about he couldn't say. Whatever it had been, it had left him feeling cold and shivery, as if he'd just come into a warm house after being outside in the snow for countless hours.

The girl entered his office without so much as a hello and then continued to linger mutely. He slowly stood and edged around his desk, moving a chair toward her in an invitation for her to sit. He stifled a yawn, wishing very much that he could curl up with a warm blanket and hibernate through the next few seasons.

"Brrr, it's cold in here, isn't it?" he said to the girl offhandedly, though she gave him no reply and only continued to stare back blankly at him. Must not be one for small talk. Shivering, he returned to behind his desk, pulling on the blazer he'd had draped over the back of his chair.

The girl, he saw, still had not sat down. He realized now that she had no backpack or purse, and she was dressed far too lightly for the chilly weather in an airy sundress that looked a little grimy. Frankly, she could use a shower too. She wore only one sandal, which was caked in mud that had dried in between her toes; there were brown streaks on her ankles, too, where mud had splattered up on her skin.

Was she a homeless person, maybe, who'd wandered onto campus? How peculiar it was, then, that it was he who she'd encountered first, in his office, located in the Social Sciences building, which was out of the way from the campus quad, in the most inconvenient of areas, at the end of a long, twisty hallway.

The hairs on the back of his neck prickled to life. He closed the blazer over his chest, the room and his body and his bones cold-cold-cold. "What can I do for you?" he asked, or maybe he only thought it, since she said not a word in reply.

In a gesture that felt like floating, he crossed the room and went to her. His hand seemed as if it was moving through water as he raised it and then let it sink to her shoulder. She turned to face him, and when she opened her mouth to speak, water, not words, came flooding out. He was scarcely aware of the strangled moan that escaped him when pebbles and twigs and small pieces of trash came out in the rush, hitting his shoes and carpet with soft plinking sounds, as if it was raining inside his office. He looked into her eyes, finding nothing, no sign of life, only a black abyss that was as vacant as the expression on her face. His mouth worked, shifting the bones in his jaw, yet he was unable to ask if she was okay. He already knew she wasn't.

All he could do was wait for her to tell him why she was there.

And so he waited, waited, falling deeper into the blackness in her eyes, so cold and so bottomless that if he tumbled into them he would sink forever until the flesh on his body rotted away and all that remained were his old bones, so white and out of place in the soft, muddy graveyard that stank of stagnant water and motor oil and dead insects and oh how he wished he could dive into those eyes—he'd swim down, down until his lungs—

"Professor Evans, are you okay?" a young voice asked. "I was just on my way to see you . . ."

But Eric did not answer—could not answer. He wiped away the warm hand that had rested on his arm. A few doors down from his office now—how had he gotten there?—he could not stop. He continued trailing her down the hall, this girl nobody but him could see.

He followed her outside the building, across campus, and outside the confines of Lamount University. He heard the incensed honking and detected the cars zooming past as he walked along the shoulder of the highway. Going where, he had no clue; he only knew that he needed to walk.

Branches scraped his cheeks as he moved through a wooded area, the violent cacophony of rushing water nearby violating his ears like a scream. No, he realized, it was *he* who was screaming, inside his head. He wanted, so desperately, to break free of the trance that had taken over his mind, to run away from the water as far as his legs would take him.

Still, he followed the girl.

Mud squished around his shoes as he walked down an embankment toward the river's edge. It was only at the shoreline that she stopped for the first time since their journey began to ensure that he was still behind her. She raised her hand, providing him a beckoning wave, and then she entered the water.

He waved back.

And then he followed.

His jaw fell slack and all the air whooshed out of his lungs in a single breath when the river crept into his shoes like icy fingers. The water continued to envelop him, frozen needles moving up his ankles, his calves, his thighs, his groin. His panicked heart thudded against his chest, until it, too, was swathed in water.

Please, I can't swim! he thought frantically, though deep in his consciousness he knew this wasn't true. He could, in fact, swim very well. Better than most people he knew.

Eric was up to his neck when he heard the two men shouting from the shoreline. He registered their voices, desperate and pleading, on some primal level. Yet, the black tide that had swept over his mind washed them away, eroding their words with each new wave that clobbered him until the only word he could understand—the only word that seemed to matter—was *follow*.

So he followed the girl, followed her down until he became one with the river, the water filling his mouth, his ears, his nostrils, shrouding the crown of his head. He allowed his eyes to slide closed, and then he sank into the darkness, where he knew she was waiting for him below.

And he would have kept sinking, had it not been for the muscular arms that curled over his shoulders and ripped him back into the daylight and, more importantly, back into himself. He was aware, instantaneously, that he was somehow drowning, despite sitting peacefully behind his desk only moments ago.

"You're all right, buddy. Come with me. That's good—swim," one of the men coaxed, yet Eric suddenly found that he was going nowhere.

The two hands that tugged on his ankles held him in place. He endeavored to kick them away, but their grip was unyielding as the girl's face emerged from the darkness below. She grinned up at him hideously, decaying right before his eyes, and he understood with sharp, frightening clarity that she intended to pull him down to the bottom of the river.

Panic caused him to thrash his legs involuntarily, and for a moment, he was loose.

She seized him once more and yanked hard, pulling him free of the men's helping hands. He swallowed a gulp of bitter water as he descended down into the darkness, and through the terror he could hear her pleading as clear as if she were speaking directly into his ear above water. *Please! I'll give you everything I have—I'll burn my notes and destroy my computer. I've already deleted the photos. I promise, I won't say a word. Please, you don't have to do this. Just let me go and I'll leave town. Please don't hurt me! I can't swim! I can't swim!*

Suddenly, he was weightless, his head bobbing above the surface and his aching lungs filling mercifully with air. The man gripped his biceps, hauling him to the shore before he had an opportunity to break free again. There, he vomited until he thought his stomach might come out with the bile and then flopped down on his side in the mud, panting.

"Christ, guy, if you're trying to kill yourself, there are easier ways," a gasping voice said from above.

"Kill myself? No . . . I . . ." Eric trailed off with a frown, gazing dumbly at the river before him. "Where am I?"

"You mean you don't know?" This voice sounded decades younger than the previous.

Eric glanced up at the two men, likely a father and his teenage son, who he now saw were dressed like fishermen in brown, rubbery waders. They wore near-matching flannel shirts and baseball hats with lures stuck to the bills. Their poles had been cast away hastily nearby, one sticking up from the muddy shoreline, halfway in the water and halfway out, like a fractured bone. They were gaping down at him as if he were a frightening alien form.

He shook his head. "No idea."

"We saw you come walking up to the shore, and we thought it was weird you'd pick this place to take a midday stroll. The only reason people really come down here is to fish," the older man said.

Eric opened his mouth to ask if they'd seen the girl he'd been following but then quickly snapped it closed. Of course they hadn't. Not unless they, too, had the uncanny talent of communicating with the dead. As far as he knew, there were few others like him in the world.

"We saw you wave, like you were looking at someone. But there was nobody there," the boy said.

"We couldn't believe it when you walked into the water," the man said, shaking his head incredulously to emphasize his statement. "And then you kept going. A few more feet, and the rapids would have swept you away. They're strong out there."

"I don't remember doing any of that," Eric said, though on some level the narrative sounded familiar, like a dream he was struggling to recall moments after waking.

"Were you sleepwalking?" the boy asked.

Eric nodded, deciding it would be easiest to let them think that he had been. He'd grown weary trying to explain the truth to strangers, and he found that it usually did nothing more than scare them anyway. "It happens occasionally. Good thing you two were here to wake me up," he said, genuinely grateful. While he didn't believe the dead would ever try to truly hurt him, he doubted his outcome would have been as successful had he awakened from his trance in the middle of the river with nobody to pull him to shore. He may have very well drowned out of sheer confusion. "How far are we from Lamount University?"

The boy's mouth dropped open. "Is that where you came from?"

"That's about three or four miles from here," the older man said. "Did you walk all that way asleep?"

"I guess so," Eric said lightly, though he could tell that he'd spooked them, despite his nonchalance. Once upon a time he would have lied to himself, too, about what had happened. He would have explained the phenomenon away as a hallucination brought on by too much stress and not enough sleep. Now, however, he was okay admitting to himself that he was scared—not so much for himself, but for the nameless girl who had drowned in the river before him.

CHAPTER 21

Susan received a call from Howell that Dov Amsel's body had been found. "He washed up a little farther downstream from where we found Chung Nguygen."

Normally, such a development would have surprised her, but on this strange case it was par for the course. She asked, "Was his time of death the same as Nguygen's?"

"That's something you'll need to ask the ME. All I know is that he's dead," Howell said in his usual no-nonsense fashion.

"Looks like we've got to change our focus. I'm investigating Marcus Zelman further. There's something about him I don't like; he's hiding something. I don't know what, but he might be tied into this." She shook her head. "Defenders of the Earth might also be involved. This case . . . it's just all over the place."

"Follow your gut. Sometimes, cases are like that. No two are ever alike," Howell said, and then he ended the conversation so that she could get back to work.

Susan wasn't thrilled when the humorless Dr. Mikael Abbonzio picked up at the medical examiner's office. The bright side was that it would save time, since she was already familiar with the case. Still, she wasn't able to provide too much helpful information about Dov Amsel's death.

"His body had gotten caught on some rocks, it appears, or else he likely would have been found at the same time as Nguygen," the ME said.

"Cause of death?"

"It's difficult to determine. His body was pretty beat up from the rocks. I can tell you that it doesn't appear to be a drowning. His lungs indicate otherwise."

Susan asked, "But homicide is still likely?"

The ME paused. "I can't say *likely*, but it is a possibility. There's something else you might want to know."

"About Dov Amsel?"

"About Dov Amsel and Chung Nguygen. You'd asked about the toxicology report last time we spoke, correct?"

"That's right."

"Okay, good. I only wanted to confirm because I deal with so many law enforcement agents," Dr. Abbonzio said, not sounding too thrilled about that fact. "Anyway, Chung Nguygen had heroin in his system."

Susan sat up in her chair. What was the deal with this case? She thought of the call Eric had made to her about Samantha Neville. "Wait a minute. Chung or Dov?"

"Both of them."

Dov, she could believe about the heroin, but Chung, no way. "Are you sure? Is there any possibility that there was a mix-up in the slides?"

"No, I run a very clean lab here," Abbonzio said tartly. "Also, when we find abnormalities such as these, it's protocol to run a second test to confirm."

Quickly, Susan said, "I didn't mean to imply that there had been a mistake made in your department. I guess I just wanted to double-check because it is very, very unlikely that Chung Nguygen was a habitual drug user. Is there any chance that he tested positive for opioids because of some kind of medication he was on?"

Abbonzio sniffed. "I suppose I wasn't as clear as I could have been earlier. I'm accustomed to dealing with other medical professionals who are versed in our terminology."

Susan couldn't tell if she was being insulted or not, so she let the comment slide.

"In the simplest terms," the ME explained, "heroin has a very unique biomarker known as 6-AM. This would not be found if he were merely on prescription medication."

"I understand now. Thank you for clarifying. Do you think it was likely, then, that Dov Amsel was drugged and then hit over the head? Or, maybe already on drugs but assaulted?"

"I can't confirm that for certain. But it's possible he was drugged to make him more compliant. I've seen this sort of thing before. But there's one other thing. I don't usually run tox screens so quickly, but I made an exception in this case because I understand the two deaths are connected."

"Um, thank you," Susan said awkwardly when the ME paused. She seemed to be expecting gratitude of some sort.

"Just don't expect it again in the future," she replied, which might have been her way of saying "You're welcome."

Susan thanked Dr. Abbonzio for her time and hung up. Drumming her fingers on her desk, she thought about the strange connections in the case. Since she was a visual learner, she drew a rough diagram in her notepad. She printed the name of each person who'd come up in her investigation by name and listed the information she knew about them, the hope to find a common link:

—Chung Nguygen: works at Gruben Dam, heroin in system, disappeared with Dov, contracted by Marcus Zelman for single job, murderer unknown.

—Dov Amsel: works at Gruben Dam, heroin in system, lied to obtain job, identical birdhouse at home and work, possible ties to DOTE, possible recreational drug use, oblivious wife, murderer unknown.

—Marcus Zelman: lied about remembering Chung, refused to produce geological report, created housing development below Gruben Dam, claims to have never heard of DOTE, knows the Nevilles.

—Samantha Neville: opioids—possibly heroin?—found in system, member of DOTE, suspected murderer Bryan McDougal but possibly unknown.

—Bryan McDougal: enemy of DOTE, ex to Samantha, possible suicide / murderer unknown.

—Cindy Jenkins: lied to give Dov a job, fired from Gruben Dam, sister-in-law to Dov, rich lover (????), liar.

She let out a long, frustrated sigh and shook her head. What did two college kids, three dam employees, a multimillionaire, and an ecoterror group have in common? How were the murders and heroin linked? What was the deal with the matching birdhouses? What was the common thread she was missing? What was Zelman's link to the Nevilles—was it merely a coincidence?

She decided to start at her most recent developments and work backward. The man at the top of her mind was Marcus Zelman. The conversation she'd had with him had continued to niggle at her mind. She felt in her gut that he was withholding the truth, but about what? He was positively lying about his claim of not remembering hiring Chung Nguygen. But why lie about something like that? She deduced it might have something to do with the survey Chung had conducted for him. And she suspected that he was also lying about never having heard of DOTE—but why conceal such a thing? Had he been threatened by the group because of toxicity levels found at his other projects, or even at Cambridge Downs, which was semiconnected to Gruben Dam through location proximity? Was that the big secret he was hiding? Damn, if she could only get her hands on that report.

Think-think-think.

Her hand shot out, and she snatched up the file on Chung Nguygen as something his wife had said occurred to her. She located the telephone number she needed and quickly punched it in. "Hello, Mrs. Nguygen? This is Special Agent Susan Marlan with the FBI."

"Yes, I remember you."

The line was quiet on Mrs. Nguygen's end, so her husband's relatives had probably gone home. Susan was curious about whether they'd absconded with the heirlooms, but she figured it would be poor taste to ask. She said, "I was wondering, remember when we were discussing antiques, and you said that your husband never got rid of anything? Does that also extend to paperwork?"

"What sort of paperwork? Do you mean his will or—"

"No, nothing like that. I'm interested in the environmental survey he did for Zelman Industries."

"Oh, I know exactly where *that* is. It's sitting right on top of his desk," Mrs. Nguygen said. "I actually came across it earlier this morning when I was looking for some of my husband's life insurance paperwork—I looked right at it."

Gotcha, Zelman, Susan thought. *Let's see you try to lie your way out of whatever it is that I find. And I'm sure it's going to be bad.*

"But I hope you don't expect me to decipher the file for you. I have a hard time understanding what it says—I think anyone would, unless they've got a background in environmental science or geology. There's a bunch of jargon in it about minerals and soil—at least, that's what I think it's about."

Susan kept her voice even, though she was grinning. "That's perfectly okay. I happen to know a geologist. Would it be okay if I came by now to pick up the file?"

As Susan hung up with Mrs. Nguygen, she realized that she was both nervous and happy to call the only geologist she knew. She'd had a great time when they'd met up, and they'd left things on a high note. And, although she sometimes liked to quit while she was ahead, this she found was not one of those occasions. She took a deep breath and brought his number up on her phone.

"Hi, uh, Suze. Hi." Eric sounded distracted, off.

"Are you okay?"

He laughed flatly in her ear. "Guess that depends on what you mean by okay."

"What happened?"

"It's . . . too long and complicated to get into now, but let's just say that I've recently had some unexpected company."

She knew what he was getting at. He'd had one of his visions. "How bad was it this time?"

"Pretty bad."

Eric typically downplayed his visions, so if he sounded that shaken and was admitting that it was bad, it must have been *really* bad. "And you're sure it's not from—"

"No, this isn't a schizophrenic thing. I'm on track with my meds, and I don't feel strange—ill, I mean," he cut in, but not unkindly. "I saw a girl. She found me at the university."

Susan listened as he briefly outlined what had happened, interrupting him only when he got to the part where he'd awakened in the river. "Oh my God, what if those guys hadn't seen you. You could've drowned!"

"But I didn't drown," he said soothingly, though this did nothing to make her feel better. She imagined he was putting on a brave face, since he sounded shaken too. "The strange thing is, I think the girl might be linked to Samantha Neville and DOTE."

Susan sat up straight in her chair. "How so?"

"When Bryan was in my office the other day, he said something about Samantha's flaky roommate abruptly taking off last semester after receiving some artist's grant—Tori Blakenwell was her name. But what if she didn't disappear? What if she was murdered?"

"But wouldn't someone at Lamount take notice of something like that? You said word of Samantha Neville's murder was all over the place there."

"Maybe they didn't know. Maybe they thought Tori dropped out after leaving," Eric said. "I called the Greater Collective, which is the artist's retreat she was supposed to have gone to up near Portland. Guess what? She never showed. They have this program there where they provide free room and board to artists for three months, the idea being that their imaginative minds will be free to create if they're unencumbered by everyday nuisances like paying bills and cooking meals. And this isn't some ragtag retreat; this place is a multimillion-dollar complex set back in the forest. It's gorgeous—*I'd* love to go there. The rooms are like something out of a five-star resort. Not only that; the food they serve is done up by some famous chef."

"I'd love to go there too," Susan commented.

"And that's what is so strange about Tori not showing. Every year, there are only a handful of these grants given out. Artists fight tooth and nail to get a spot, and the application process alone takes about six months. According to the admissions coordinator I spoke to, Tori was over the moon about being accepted. He said she'd called the retreat at least a half dozen times to ensure that her spot was still available, as if she couldn't believe her good fortune. She wanted to go there to pen her first novel."

"So it's *really* odd that she didn't show."

"Right," Eric agreed. "I also checked her social media accounts, which she'd been fairly active on. I also checked her blog, which she'd frequently post writing samples to. On all her accounts, her posts stopped abruptly at the same time."

Susan frowned. "That's suspicious, especially for an aspiring writer." She jotted a quick note to herself on a Post-it to check out Tori's accounts when she had a chance.

"Exactly. And here's where the DOTE part comes in. Bryan said Tori had been writing an article or something about the group that did not paint them in the most flattering light. It sounded like she was doing some kind of exposé, maybe. Also, when I was in the river, she virtually spelled out to me that someone had drowned her over her research. She didn't say DOTE specifically, but who else could it be? Given how dangerous they are, would it be such a stretch to consider that she might have been murdered by one of their members in an effort to shut her up? Maybe she uncovered something they'd rather keep quiet."

"I'd say you sound like a conspiracy theorist nut, had I not experienced similar things happening here at work. Some of the things I've seen around here you couldn't make up," Susan said. "I could run a check on her name and on any bodies pulled from the river around the time she disappeared. Which is strange in itself, because that's where the bodies of the two guys I'm looking into were found. Although, from what I've discovered, the river has seen a few bodies over the years. A lot of homeless have drowned there; sometimes they set up camp down near the water, and then they get too close to the river's edge and fall in. The current then sweeps them away. Anyway, let me see what I can dig up."

"That would be amazing, Suze. Thank you."

"Don't thank me yet," she said. "I was actually calling you to ask a little favor of my own. I'm wondering if you might have a look at something for me? It has to do with geology."

"Of course. Anything for you, Suze."

CHAPTER 22

Eric suggested that he and Susan meet for lunch the following day, since it gave the outing more of a romantic feel. It was an odd thing to do, wooing his ex-girlfriend as if they were partaking in a first date, but he had finally gotten real with himself and admitted that he wanted to win her back. And *soon*—there was no point in denying it anymore. He figured he'd have a better chance of doing that over hearty food than at her impersonal desk at the FBI.

But.

He'd have to play it cool, because maybe she didn't *want* to be romanced. For all he knew, she was seeing someone else, a notion that made him want to vomit. Neither of them had dared broach the topic, though he suspected it was something they both wanted to know about each other.

They met outside Macey's Eats, an outdoor café known for its specialty club sandwiches and gourmet doughnuts. Eric had picked the eatery for its casual yet fun vibe, which he hoped would translate over into their date—not that meeting up to discuss how geology pertained to her current case counted as a date. He felt like he'd been transported back to the first time he'd met up with Susan at his home in Perrick to discuss the Death Farm case. That seemed like a whole lifetime ago, long before they'd been a couple or had even gone out for the first time. Dating déjà vu.

"Good to see you again, Eric," she said and then she made his day by kissing him on the mouth.

That, he had not expected. "Shall we?"

It was overcast but warm, with bits of dull Bay Area sunshine peeking through the clouds every so often, as they took a seat outside underneath a brightly colored umbrella. They ordered food and drinks, holding off on dessert until after they'd eaten—a pesto tuna melt and lemonade for her and a stacked Mediterranean roast beef club and Italian soda for him—and then sat back for a moment of restful silence.

Have you been thinking about me? Are you seeing anyone? he wanted to ask. Instead, he said, "So, you want to show me that file?"

"All business, eh?" she teased lightly, though she seemed disappointed to be getting to it so quickly.

He was kicking himself now. "We could hang out all day if you like," he backpedaled. "I'm done with classes for the day. I was only thinking of your schedule."

She sighed. "No, you're right. We'd better get to it. I've got a ton of work to do." She pulled the file from her bag and handed it to him.

He set the documents aside as they discussed the purpose of their meeting. "So, tell me again what you want me to look for. You think this Zelman guy is hiding something?"

She shrugged, shook her head. "That's the thing; I don't know. What I suspect is that he's trying to cover up pollution that might be present in one of his developments. I don't know particulars about environmental law, but I imagine Zelman would either have to compensate residents in a big, big way, or even relocate them altogether. A whole neighborhood in the Bay Area? That would cost hundreds of millions of dollars. Zelman Industries would go bankrupt."

"Which is why he'd never want this report to see the light of day," Eric said. "But how is that possible? You'd think something like this would become public knowledge. This is like Flint, Michigan, all over again."

"Well, think about it. Zelman hired Chung Nguygen to do this report privately and at his own behest. This wasn't something he was ordered to do by the county or anything to that effect." Susan and Eric sat back and shuffled their napkins aside so their server could set down their drinks. Susan sipped her lemonade. "Mmm, good. Zelman claims he wanted to test the soil for the good of the Cambridge Downs community, but I think it's bullshit."

"Not exactly the do-gooder type?"

Susan shook her head. "Not from what I've seen. Zelman's not doing a thing unless it benefits one person: himself."

Eric said, "So where do the doters fit into all this? You think there's a DOTE connection because of the possible pollution? From the sound of it, they'd be pretty furious about the toxic soil."

"That's what's throwing me off," Susan said with a frown. "The toxins in the soil would be more of a result of Gruben Dam, not Marcus Zelman. He was just the one who put a housing development there. And doters seem more concerned with harm against the environment and critters than humans." She told him about the matching birdhouses she'd found at both the Amsel residence and Gruben Dam, as well as the bags of birdseed. She hadn't mentioned it the other night when they'd had dinner at his place because she hadn't understood the significance. "So it seems DOTE is somehow connected to both Amsel and the dam, but I can't figure out where Nguygen fits in."

"Although, there's a chance that the birdhouse thing could just be a huge coincidence," Eric pointed out. "Maybe the group sells handicrafts for funds. Maybe Amsel liked the birdhouses so much that he bought one for his home and one for work."

"How do you explain the bags of birdseed I found discarded at the dam, then?" Susan asked.

Eric thought a moment. "You said Amsel was a drug addict, right?"

Susan shrugged. "That's unknown. His wife seems to think he'd been clean for some time, as does the sister-in-law in HR. The dam employees, however, have essentially stated that he's a junkie. Then, of course, there's the tox screen that showed that both men tested positive for heroin.

"I'm inclined to believe the employees over Dov's stressed-out pregnant wife and the woman who'd put her livelihood—and her freedom from the sound of it—on the line for the man. Those two would have plenty of reason to lie, as would Dov."

"Okay, then."

"I'm not following," Susan said.

"I'm thinking Dov was probably taking the birdseed out to the edge of the property under the guise of feeding the birds, but what he was really doing was getting high on whatever it was he was taking."

Susan asked, "But why have a matching one at his house?"

Eric shrugged. "Maybe he just likes the way they look."

"I don't know . . . ," Susan said, unconvinced. "Have you talked to Jake?"

Eric shook his head. "Not really. He sent me a text to apologize and let me know he's okay, but he hasn't told me what he's been up to. He's missed a couple of our TA meetings. I'm thinking maybe he's been looking into DOTE, but he's afraid to tell me because the last time we talked, I'd suggested that he stay away from them. He's been avoiding me, but he'll have to face me soon because we've got class coming up."

"Well, I'm glad he's okay, at least. But, if he is looking into DOTE, I hope he's being careful. I'd hate for our Jakey to get hurt. The more I look into the group, the more I start to think that they're really dangerous. I asked Zelman if he'd ever heard of them, and you should have seen his face. He instantly said he didn't, as if he couldn't change the subject fast enough. I suspect that they might be threatening him."

"But, if they were threatening him over the toxic soil, you'd think he'd want to tell the FBI," Eric said.

Susan raised her eyebrows. "Ah, but you're forgetting that doing that would also require him to reveal that there *is* toxic soil, which it seems he's trying to hide."

"Right."

"Oh, I looked into Jane Does found in the river around the time Tori Blakenwell disappeared," Susan said. "There was one, and her physical description matches Tori."

"Is it her, then?" Eric asked, both wanting it to be her and not wanting it to be her at the same time. If she'd been found, her friends and family would get closure, but he would also be saddened to learn that such a bright young soul was dead.

He didn't hold a grudge against Tori about the near-drowning thing. Sometimes, the dead communicated in a bold fashion, perhaps to grab his attention. Ghosts, he'd found, liked to cut to the chase.

Susan shrugged. "I sent the remains to the lab to be compared to Tori's dental records."

"But wouldn't that have been done already?"

Susan shook her head. "Not unless Tori had a record, which she didn't. There isn't some massive database where the dental records of every person in the world are stored. It would help law enforcement out a lot if there were."

"But if Tori was a missing person?" Eric said, frustration in his voice. "Wouldn't her record be on file to aid with the search?"

"That's the thing—she isn't classified as missing."

"How has nobody noticed that she's gone?" Eric asked, incredulous. "Surely *somebody* . . ."

"Both her parents are deceased, and she doesn't have much family beyond that—a couple of distant cousins on the other side of the country I'm guessing she never talks to. I get the feeling that she was a loner," Susan said.

"From the sound of it, Samantha Neville and Tori were on the outs—fighting over her disapproval of DOTE—so she was probably happy to see her leave," Eric said. "And she likely made no attempt to look her up once she'd moved out."

Susan nodded, showing that she was following his logic. "Unfortunately, when it comes to missing persons, a lot of times the squeaky wheels do get the most grease. If family members are constantly hounding authorities for updates and demanding to know what's being done, then naturally the case will get more attention. But, with Tori, there was no sign of foul play, and her body never turned up—at least, as far as police know. And if she was set to leave town anyway, and she had a tendency of taking off on the fly, most everyone she knew probably assumed she left for the retreat. And it sounds like the people running the retreat just assumed she'd changed her mind about coming."

"Still," Eric said, unconvinced. "What about her social media accounts—she completely stopped posting."

"I know you don't use social media, but if you did, would you really take the time to comb through the account of someone you considered an acquaintance at best to see when the last time they posted was? And if you then saw that their posts had abruptly stopped, would you make the leap to assuming that they were a missing person?" Susan asked.

"I guess not," Eric agreed, sullen. "And as far as her not returning to Lamount, they'd just assume she was a dropout."

"I'm going to contact the editor at the paper where she worked, see what I can dig up," Susan said. "Don't worry—I haven't given up on this."

Eric gave her a half smile and squeezed her hand. "Thank you. I appreciate it."

The pair paused while their server brought out their food. Eric's club sandwich was as tall as a water tower, with a long skewer with a decorative paper cow on the tip stuck down the middle of it. He became worried about how sloppy he'd look eating the thing in front of Susan, which was silly. She'd seen him chow down more times than he could count. The sandwich fell apart as soon as he extracted the skewer, and he let out an exasperated breath. "Why do all restaurants insist on doing this kind of thing these days? Whatever happened to just serving food on a plate—why do they have to be all elaborate about it and cram a huge fence post in the middle of it, or serve it in a roller skate or whatever?"

She laughed. "Remember that place we went to, that gourmet ice-cream parlor in Petaluma that put all those plastic dinosaurs on our sundaes, like we were toddlers?"

"Yes! See what I mean? It's ridiculous, but those dinosaurs were too funny." He paused for a minute and then announced, "You know, I miss hanging out with you."

Quietly, she said, "I miss hanging out with you too. I had fun with you the other night."

Eric reached for her hand. "Susan—"

"Can I get you two anything else?" their irritatingly chipper server interrupted. "Need extra aioli for the fries? We've also got a killer spicy tomato sauce—"

"I think we're fine," Eric said, imagining how much he'd like to curl his hands around the little twerp's neck and squeeze until he stopped yapping about condiments. The server must have seen the irritation in his eyes, because he left rather quickly and without another word. Well, there was the moment ruined. He let out a sigh. "I should probably have a look at this report, shouldn't I?"

She sighed, too, sounding disappointed. "I suppose so."

After less than four or five minutes, he stopped reading to ask her a question. "Is this for real? You aren't having a laugh with this?"

Her confused expression told him she wasn't. "I don't know what you mean. I tried reading that thing, but it only looks like gobbledy-gook to me. Why? What are you seeing?"

He ran an index finger along a series of charts and graphs that contained a number of abbreviations. "Do you see this here? Do you know what this signifies?"

She peered at the chart. "No idea. What is that, *serili . . . seilini . . .* I can't say that."

"It's *serilinium.* Oh my God, I just can't believe this." He shook his head. "This is incredible."

"Eric! Fill me in! What are you getting so worked up about? Does this confirm that the soil is contaminated?"

Eric shook his head vigorously. "No, far from it. Do you know what serilinium is used for?"

She gave him a look that said she didn't. "You're the one with a background in geology."

"It's mainly used in the manufacturing of medical equipment and lasers. It's a highly coveted material because, while it has some pliability, it also is tougher than titanium."

"Coveted, as in expensive?" she asked.

"Like you wouldn't believe, and that's mainly because it's one of the rarest minerals ever discovered." He was not aware that he was shaking his head as he gaped down at the report. "If what I'm reading here is correct, the Cambridge Downs development is sitting above what could easily be one of the largest belts of serilinium ever known to exist. Every single one of these low-income homes is sitting on land that is worth an unfathomable amount of money. Billions. Had Zelman not developed and sold the land, he would have stood to be one of the richest men in America, maybe even the world."

CHAPTER 23

Jake was not comfortable giving Rodent his home address, but then he figured he already had it anyway, from the night he'd relayed it to the taxi driver. Even if he hadn't, he probably would have still given it to him.

To deny Rodent would have meant being excluded from whatever esoteric mission DOTE wanted him to embark upon, presumably so that he could prove that he had what it took to join their cause. He'd charmed his way into their circle at the party, so to behave sketchily now would undo all the work he'd put in thus far and rip him from his coveted position inside Rodent's inner circle. And it would be sketchy, wouldn't it, to deny them access to his home?

Jake was self-aware enough to realize how odd it was to be so invested in undercover work he wasn't even being paid for. And, after the party at Kimmy's, he'd lain in bed and questioned his motivations behind his dedication. The truth was that going undercover made him feel the most alive he had in months. It was a sensation on par with being on stage. It gave him a sense of purpose, and it made him want to stay sharp and sober.

Though he appreciated Eric landing him the teacher's assistant gig at the university, he didn't find correcting papers and answering student emails about extended due dates all that fulfilling. Go figure. And being a geology major, busting his butt to pass courses? He really didn't care too much about that anymore either. It wasn't just his depression talking he'd realized once he made himself confront his disenchantment. It was that he'd lost the passion for the subject, which he'd only gotten into because he'd found it to be a fun hobby. But that was the problem with hobbies, wasn't it—they were fun until the moment they became a job.

People fell out of love every day, so was it really so strange that he'd begun to feel lukewarm about rocks? He knew a great deal about geology, and he could ace all his exams in his sleep, sure. But did being good at something mean that he needed to be married to it for the rest of his life?

Weird as it may have been, he was realizing that he had a real passion for undercover work. And he seemed to be good at it. Was it so outrageous that he was *maybe, possibly, perhaps* toying with the idea of quitting school to become a private investigator? He was still young enough that a complete career overhaul was possible—it wasn't like he was nearing retirement age with a sudden proclamation that he wanted to train to be a doctor. So what was holding him back?

He was beginning to understand that part of his reluctance to switch gears was rooted in his having invested so much time and energy in geology. But it wasn't only that. Even though he prided himself on his individualism and his claims of not giving a toss about what people thought of him, he was still deeply concerned about how his parents and Eric would take his sudden turn into the left field of career choices. He felt almost *mortified* by the complete 180, as if the randomness of it made it less respectable.

Like he was a flake.

Of course, he didn't want to get ahead of himself. This was only his first "case." There was still the possibility that the whole thing would blow up in his face. But if he could manage to do some good in the world by seeking justice for Samantha and Bryan—and bring down a group of possible budding terrorists to boot—it might be worth the risk.

He still wasn't sure what to make of DOTE. He found it hard to believe that someone as charming as Rodent could be behind a master plot of terrorism, though he imagined he'd need charisma to get his followers to stay with him until the bitter end.

He'd tried to circumvent them picking him up at home by offering to meet them at the secret location of their "field trip," as Rodent had called it. At least if he knew where they were going beforehand, he could either text Eric the address or leave a note as a precaution in the event he disappeared.

But Rodent had refused. "It would ruin the surprise," he'd said breezily, which had done nothing to ease his concerns. The only other directive Jake had been given was to "bring a backpack," which made him think that they might be hiking into the woods. After the gruesome events that had taken place in Clancy with all the dead bodies unearthed in the forest, he was not looking forward to the trek.

He worried that they might have discovered his true motivations behind befriending them and were really just taking him someplace private to beat him up. Or worse. His trepidation further deepened once he was hunkered down inside their vehicle, a nondescript beige minivan with the back windows tinted so dark that they were almost black. The back seats had also been removed—and he was just small enough that they could do practically anything to him and he would not be seen by passersby, should he try to seek help.

"We going to a soccer game in this mom mobile or what?" Jake joked when they were on their way, though internally he was so terrified he could barely keep his thoughts straight. He commanded himself to calm down—acting shifty was the fastest way to alert the doters that he *was* shifty, at least by their standards.

He also reminded himself that he had yet to uncover any concrete evidence that DOTE were actually committing evil deeds. They could be on their way to pass out flyers for all he knew, though where they'd be distributing them at ten at night was a wonder. No need to get himself worked up over nothing.

Still, he would keep his guard up.

Rodent had not come alone, though he had enough energy for ten people. "It's going to be great, man, great!" he announced out of nowhere, causing Jake to nearly jump out of his skin. Rodent banged his hand on the steering wheel every so often, and then the chant would start all over again, continuing on loop throughout the journey. *It's going to be great, so great, so fucking great!*

He'd been joined by Kimmy and two other senior doters who introduced themselves as Miguel and Marty. Jake recognized them from the fashionable crowd at the party, though tonight they were dressed casually, like college students: baseball hats, worn jeans, sweatshirts. Rodent was wearing a sloppy LU hoodie with frayed sleeves that looked strange and out of character on him, given his polished appearance from the party. He also saw a pile of four backpacks on the floor, which further enhanced their collegiate appearances.

"Hiding in plain sight, man," Marty said in response to Jake's question about their vehicle. "You roll up in a scary-looking kidnapper van, and people take notice. But, you look like a soccer mom taking the kiddies to practice, and nobody blinks."

Jake was surprised when they entered the LU campus and parked. Kimmy placed her parking permit on the dashboard.

"We're here," Rodent said.

"Are we picking someone else up?" he asked, dubious. There wasn't much room left in the van.

"Nope. Grab your backpack."

Jake kept his mouth shut and did what he was told. Given the late hour, the campus was quiet. Still, there were a few students milling about, which wasn't surprising. There was a bar near the quad, as well as a twenty-four-hour gymnasium and several dorms. Rodent and his cronies were onto something with their claims of hiding in plain sight.

With the way they'd dressed, they looked just like LU students, despite being a lot older than the typical attendee. The backpacks completed their look, though Jake was worried about what might be in theirs.

They walked to the STEM side of campus and then headed toward a tall structure that housed all the engineering courses. The building was completely dark and, not surprisingly, the doors were locked. Jake felt relief ease over him.

"Guess that's that," he said, feigning disappointment.

Rodent barked out a laugh. "Man, you're a riot."

Jake laughed, too, as if he'd been joking. "Seriously, though, how are we going to get around the alarms?"

"Already taken care of," Miguel said. "Security cameras too. Everything here's run remotely online. You wouldn't believe how easy it was to crack into their system. Piece of cake. We've got a guy who takes care of this for us."

"Ah, speak of the devil!" Rodent said as a man came sauntering up. Jake was instantly uneasy, though he couldn't put his finger on why. "We all good?"

"All good," the man said, his response sounding garbled. He wiped a smudge of brown away from the corner of his mouth using his sleeve. He was truly a disgusting individual, and Jake was hoping that, whatever they were up to, it wouldn't entail touching this slob.

"Jesus, Wicky, don't you ever stop eating?" Marty sneered.

"Not if I can help it," Wicky said, and then he pulled whatever he'd been chomping on previously out of the waistband of his jeans so that he could resume eating. It was a chocolate bar, Jake saw.

Shaped like a baby.

It's him, Jake thought, *the man Bryan had taken a photo of at Salty's the night Samantha was murdered.* And now here he was, eating her sweets. Unless, that was, he was the charitable type to have his desserts shipped from Africa at twenty bucks a pop.

"That's a trip," Jake said to the man. "Is that chocolate shaped like a baby?"

"Yup. Watch this." Wicky tore off some of the wrapper so that the child's head was exposed. *"Waaaahhhh-waaaahhhh-waahh,"* he wailed, and then he bit the head off with an amused snort. "Quiet, you brat."

"That's hilarious," Jake said easily, using all his energy to hide his repulsion. Bryan had been wrong in his assumption that the man would reek of farts and cigarettes, but he was plenty disgusting nonetheless. "Where'd you get that thing. Is it any good?"

"Naw, man, it tastes like shit. But I'm hungry, so." He shrugged, squinted at the wrapper. "Don't know where it's from—this is written in Chinese or something. I got it off some bitch—"

"You talk too fucking much," Rodent hissed. He handed Wicky a stack of twenties, which Wicky made a show of counting. *"Bye."*

"You don't got to be a dick about it," Wicky grumbled, and then he stomped off.

"Sorry about him," Rodent apologized. "He's a necessary evil, I'm afraid."

"He's a dipshit and a creeper," Kimmy said. "But he can break into any place blindfolded and with one hand tied behind his back."

"Great," Jake said weakly. He was so nervous he felt as if he might pass out. Some private eye he was. He wanted to get on with things. The sooner they completed whatever the hell mission they were on, the sooner he could get out of there.

"You're a teacher's assistant, right? You must've noticed how ridiculous security is here on campus," Rodent said. "I think it's mainly there for show, to give these rich kids a feeling of being safe."

"Oh, I'm only a TA for one class. I don't really know about the security side of things—I mainly correct homework," Jake said dismissively. He was unnerved by Rodent's awareness of what he did on campus for work. The guy wasn't even a student there, but Kimmy was, and he hadn't told her either. He'd told nobody at the party, in fact. He supposed that, given the popularity of Eric's class, it wouldn't be too difficult to learn such information—he had no doubt there were at least a dozen students waiting for him to graduate so they could take his place.

Still, creepy.

The way Rodent had spouted the information so casually had unsettled him. It was almost as if Rodent was providing him a subtle reminder about how much he could find out about his life, should he put his mind to it. A preemptive threat, should Jake ever decide to turn them in.

So, Rodent knew where he lived and what he did for a living. What else might he try to unearth to use against him?

They used their cell phones to light the way toward their destination, which Jake thought was a classroom at the end of the hall. They kept walking past it, however, and then went out the back door and down a path that ended at a warehouse-type structure that was fenced in with the engineering building. Kimmy picked the padlock on the large garage door–style entrance, and Jake cringed as it was noisily rolled up—to him, they were being as loud as a freight train. They rolled it back down again, leaving it open a few feet, so they weren't confining themselves in.

"Relax." Kimmy smiled. "Even if anyone hears us, they're not going to think to come back here."

Inside, it looked as if a gigantic robot had exploded. There were gears, mechanical arms, cogs, tools, and chunks of shiny objects that would have been mistaken for scrap metal had there not been laptops plugged into them. There was also a large excavation machine of some kind at the back of the room broken down into several pieces.

"What are we doing here?" Jake asked.

Kimmy pulled a can of spray paint from her backpack and popped off the red cap. Shaking it, she said, "Do you know where the mechanical engineering department gets a large portion of their funding from?"

She walked to a door and sprayed CORPORATE PIGS! on it, the drips of red giving the words a bloodied appearance. Jake had to bite his tongue to stop himself from screaming—*What the hell do you think you're doing?*

Miguel, extracting large pliers from his bag, said, "It's the same bastards who're responsible for destroying the rainforests in Colombia, Indonesia—"

"Papua New Guinea, Angola, Tanzania . . . ," Marty added, and then he walked to the excavator, tore off an arm, and hurled it at the wall. Jake started as it burst apart into dozens of pieces. "This machine here is a prototype of the ones they're developing for mass annihilation of the rainforests where indigenous populations still call home."

"Fuckers!" Kimmy cheered with a shrill laugh as she helped Miguel tear a laptop away from the chunks of metal.

"Would you like to do the honor, milady?" Miguel asked. He bowed at the waist and handed the laptop over to Kimmy ceremoniously. Kimmy drop-kicked it hard. Its screen shattered as it smashed apart on the concrete a few yards away. The trio of doters burst out in laughter.

"Oops, looks like your grant money has been put to terrible, terrible use," Marty said with a vicious snort. "No excavator for you!" They erupted in laughter once more.

They're like animals, Jake thought. *Crazy, rabid animals.*

Rodent offered Jake a can of spray paint. "It's now or never, friend." When Jake hesitated, he added, "I know it might seem like we're doing a bad thing here *right now,* but you have to think of the bigger picture—the future. Mechanical engineering students are often recruited for mining and drilling jobs before they've even graduated. The corporate vultures come to LU job fairs and target them specifically. By delaying their research now, you're saving future generations of indigenous populations, who are unable to fight against the greedy corporations displacing them. But if you don't have the stomach for this, that's cool. You can walk away now, no hard feelings."

Walking away would also mean giving up on his investigation of the group, and Jake suspected that vandalism was just the tip of the iceberg as far as what DOTE were capable of. And, if he was scared off this easily, what hope did he ever have of becoming a real investigator?

He gave Rodent a wicked grin. "Gimme that," he said, taking the spray paint. He made an incensed sputtering sound. "Walk away? I was only trying to figure out what to write first." He sauntered to a workbench and popped the lid off the can. "I think I'll go with 'no blood for grant money.'"

"Good one. But, before you get to work, come with me," Rodent said, and then he extracted a small glass bottle of clear liquid from his pack. He opened a side door and entered a classroom that was separate but still a part of the warehouse building. He went to the desk at the front of the room and grinned maniacally as he shook the bottle at Jake. "Liquid opium. Students are in for one hell of a lecture tomorrow."

Jake laughed conspiratorially, his alarm bells ringing. Opium, like the opioids that were found in Samantha's system? "What're you doing with that?"

"Got a couple street soldiers on campus who've infiltrated old Professor Pascal's classes. They say he drinks water like it's going out of style during his lectures." Rodent pulled open the top drawer of the desk and extracted several full bottles of water. "Of course, he uses plastic, because why give a shit about the ocean?" he grumbled.

Carefully, Rodent poured out a capful of water from each bottle, and then added the opium. He then resealed them. It was as if they'd never been opened, not that it was likely the professor would take notice of such a thing, anyway, after seeing what they'd done to the machinery.

"Man, I'd love to be around tomorrow when he starts drinking these," Jake said with a snicker. "When's his first class?"

"Eleven," Marty answered. "We've actually got someone in the class who's going to record the event."

"Awesome." Jake, while smirking on the outside, was already trying to think of how he was going to warn Professor Pascal in time. He was going to need Eric's help. Though, he imagined, his friend was not going to be too happy to give it.

CHAPTER 24

Susan sat at home in front of Tori Blakenwell's computer, frowning. For such a so-called flake, she'd sure taken precautions to guard her privacy. Susan was working on yet another password attempt, to no avail. She'd gotten the laptop from Ivor Tuttle, a Lamount grad student and Tori's editor at the school paper, who she was lucky enough to catch just before he'd left for the day.

The conversation she'd had with Eric at lunch had not only made her sad for a girl who apparently nobody cared had vanished but had also piqued her interest. If the body at the morgue did turn out to be Tori's, she'd need to solve who had put her in the river. It may have been premature, but she wanted to get a head start. Based on Eric's vision, she suspected DOTE might have had a hand in her disappearance, since they seemed to be linked to most evil deeds she'd uncovered. Linked, she reminded herself, but with no proof. They were sneaky little bastards—she had to give them that.

While Eric's psychic gift had helped lead her in the right investigative direction on Tori's possible murder, his input would never hold up in court. Despite Eric's notoriety for helping law enforcement, no judge on the planet would convict persons culpable based on a college professor's psychic vision. She needed proof, which might be contained on Tori's computer.

If she could only unlock the damn password.

She could, of course, simply wait until tomorrow and have the FBI's tech team take a look at it. But she knew that she wouldn't sleep a wink, having that puzzle sitting on her kitchen table waiting to be cracked—okay, and she suspected that she *might* still be buzzing from her lovely lunch with Eric. She thought about her conversation with Ivor Tuttle as she went into the kitchen, frustrated, to fix herself another cup of coffee.

According to Eric, Samantha and Tori hadn't gotten along, and she didn't have very many friends. There also didn't seem to be much love lost between Tori and the editor, who'd called her "an insufferable know-it-all" before Susan revealed that she was looking into her disappearance and possible murder.

A few shades paler, Ivor had backpedaled. "I don't mean to give you the wrong impression. I'm not harboring any ill will toward Tori, nor is anyone else here. She just . . ." He let out a long, frustrated sigh, which told Susan everything she'd needed to know. He was fed up, but he was no killer.

He continued, "Tori, she was simply unwilling to collaborate with anyone. She knew best—no, I'm sorry, she knew *everything*. At least in her mind, she did. She would disregard all my edit suggestions, and she'd frequently mock the ideas of others. She's even made a couple reporters cry. She was paranoid and secretive as all get-out; it's like she actually believed that everyone was out to scoop her or plagiarize her work. We're hardly the *Washington Post* here at *Lamount Times*. We do mostly puff pieces about happenings on campus: theater productions, sporting events. That sort of stuff."

So that meant, Susan had realized with disappointment, that Ivor would have had no idea if Tori had been investigating DOTE. He later confirmed as much.

"Tori fancied herself a serious investigative reporter, and more power to her, I guess," he said with a snort. "It was just annoying because I never knew what she was working on until the moment I had her story on my desk. I hate to say it—and I'm sure it's foolish of me to, with her being missing—but when she left, the environment improved around here exponentially. When she didn't come back, we all just assumed that she'd grown tired of trying to boss us around."

Ivor had handed over Tori's laptop like it was a burden he was grateful to unload, explaining that he didn't find it odd that she'd left it. "A lot of rich kids go to Lamount. Judging by the way Tori acts, I'd just assumed she was one of them. I figured a laptop wasn't something she'd have a problem replacing, even an expensive one like this. For all I knew, she had a couple. I was going to keep it for a while longer, and if she didn't come back to claim it, the plan was to use it as a communal computer here at the paper for students who can't afford laptops of their own."

Fresh cup of coffee in hand, Susan sat down behind the laptop, determined to get inside. She'd tried Tori's birth date, astrological sign, student ID, the Lamount mascot—a bald eagle—plus a few other topics she might have an interest in, most centered on journalism. She even tried the old standby, 1-2-3-4. She thought back to her initial conversation with Eric, and how the person running the artist's retreat had mentioned how surprised they were that she didn't show. Susan held her breath as she typed THEGREATERCOLLECTIVE, letting out a quiet cheer when the laptop unlocked.

CHAPTER 25

Back in the van, the doters' energy was subdued. *These maniacs were behaving,* Jake thought, *as if they'd just come in from a warm, relaxing day at the beach.* "That was probably the most excitement I've had in years," he said cheerfully. "Thank you for including me."

"The night isn't over, yet, my friend." Rodent grinned.

Oh no, where might they take me now? Jake wondered. "Oh yah? Where're we going?"

The doters exchanged a look. Laughing in an esoteric fashion that made Jake uneasy, Rodent said, "Let's just call it a necessary evil."

DOTE, Jake thought, *seemed to have a lot of those.*

He was surprised when the necessary evil turned out to be a party in a sleek penthouse in Pacific Heights. Unlike the gathering at Kimmy's, which had been a mix of dopey college kids and spiffed-up senior members of DOTE, *this* gathering was . . . Jake didn't know what to make of it, or how to frame it in his head. *Suspicious* and *skeevy* were the words that rose to the front of his mind.

The party was mainly middle-aged men, most wearing wedding rings. They were plainly rich, paunchy, and some were sweaty, despite the chill in the air. They talked in unnecessarily loud tones, their faces growing increasingly red as the conversations became more boisterous, jaws working in overdrive. But they weren't the ones who were causing him alarm. It was the *other* attendees, who ignored everyone in his group except for Rodent, who they greeted with an aura of awe and possibly . . . fear?

"Silicon Valley bigwigs," Marty explained as he led Jake to the bar area, which was brimming with top-shelf liquor. Next to the drinks were pills of various shapes and sizes, placed in bowls like candy. Marty picked up a crystal decanter of what looked like bourbon and gave it a sniff. "I'm guessing this is Johnnie Walker—these pricks all drink the same stuff. You want?"

Jake shrugged, and Marty poured him a drink, filling their pint glasses nearly to the rim. *A pint of whisky!* he thought. *Drink this fast enough, and I'd be dead before I had a chance to realize how drunk I was.*

Jake thought he'd been doing a good job at hiding his disgust, but then Marty said, "He doesn't *force* them to be here, you know. Rodent."

"Who are they?" Jake asked, looking out at the sea of young girls who were mingling with the old creepers. He placed their average age at about twenty. "Are they, um, working girls?" *They had to be,* he thought given their behavior. When the men spoke, they listened intently, as if they'd never heard anything so fascinating. Their stiff smiles never faltered when the men curled their arms around their waists and pulled them close, whispering lasciviously in their ears. Jake shivered just looking at it.

"Are you asking if they're hookers?" Marty said with a laugh.

"Aren't they?"

"No, not at all. They're doters, like us." Jake frowned, and Marty clarified: "We all have our individual duties. We assess the strong points of each foot soldier and put them to work for the greater good. For some, it's providing manual labor at our headquarters, and for others it's hitting the streets and doing PR. Or it's partaking in missions, like the one you went on tonight. There are many roles for our soldiers to fill."

"And these girls, what is it that they're providing?" Jake asked, doing his best to keep his voice even.

Marty didn't seem to notice his displeasure. Or, if he did, he didn't comment on it. He smirked at Kimmy, who was pouring a drink for a white-haired man who had a nose marred by gin blossoms and his hand on her ass. "Every so often, one of our members will land themselves in legal hot water. It comes with the territory. You can't really make a change without rattling a few cages." He shrugged.

Jake imagined they were doing more than rattling cages. He was sickened by the scene, and he wanted to go home. He glanced at the clock on the wall, horribly aware that time was running out for him to contact Eric and warn him about the opium spiking.

Marty continued, "We need to maintain positive relationships with those who can help us out in a jam." He tilted his head, indicating the men in the crowd. "What you're looking at here are some of the most powerful men in the Bay Area. Since they are indebted to us, they provide us legal and financial help when we need to seek it. And the best part is that it doesn't cost DOTE a thing, because of our member volunteers."

But what was it costing the "member volunteers," who were essentially being pimped out? Jake wondered. "Makes sense," he said as sincerely as possible, and then he forced himself to wait a few minutes before excusing himself.

On the way to the bathroom, he overheard a man close to fifty ask Rodent if he could provide girls who were younger. He fought the urge to scream when Rodent said that he would see what he could do. The two men then shared a few lines of white powder.

Jake was on the phone as soon as the door was behind him. "Eric! Listen to me," he hissed. "I don't have much time to talk."

"Are you at a bar—it's loud. What time is it?" Eric asked, sounding groggy and grumpy.

Eric perked up rather quickly, however, as Jake began to outline the night's events.

CHAPTER 26

"You up for a field trip?" Rodent's voice chirped in his ear.

Jake checked the time on his phone. "What? It's like six a.m."

"Musicians!" Rodent teased, far too chipper for such an early hour. "Come on, man, the early bird catches the worm."

"I don't want any worms. I want to go back to sleep," Jake grumbled, though he was already getting out of bed and pulling on his jeans. He wanted to put up a little fight, be convincing.

"I'll be there in fifteen! Road trip!"

"Uh, how long? I can't be gone all day. I have classwork to take care of," Jake said, trying to get a sense of where they were heading.

"Won't be gone more than a few hours. I'll have you back long before the sun goes down."

"The sun hasn't even come *up*," Jake said sourly, and Rodent barked out a laugh and hung up.

For safety's sake—and because he was still traumatized from the ecotage mission—Jake made a move to shoot a text to Eric, to inform him that he was hitting the road with Rodent and possibly a few other doters. Then, he reconsidered. Eric had seemed really pissed when he'd told him about the vandalism he'd participated in with the group—that, after the drunken voice mail he'd left. But it wasn't just Eric's anger that bothered Jake; it was the *disappointment* he so obviously felt about him. Jake had tried to explain that he'd gone to campus with Rodent and his crew to gain their trust, but at the time Eric had been more concerned with reporting the opium spiking in the classroom.

Jake had quickly explained to Eric what had gone down on campus during the call he'd made from the mansion's bathroom last night. He'd started with the most pressing information, which was that Pascal's water had been drugged. Naturally, Eric was appalled, but he'd told Jake that he would save his scolding for another time so that he could get to campus and remove the tainted water bottles from the classroom—but how he was going to do that was a concern.

The two men had concocted a plan, which involved Eric driving to campus under the guise of retrieving the cell phone he forgot in his desk. While there, he'd place an emergency call to campus security and claim that he had overheard a group of students discussing the vandalism and the drugging, yet—*oh darn it*—they'd run away when Eric had commanded them to stop. The story was hokey and far fetched, but it was the best one they could think of to spare Jake from arrest and certain expulsion from LU.

It wasn't a wonder Eric was not happy with him.

Jake opted not to send Eric a text now. He also decided that he wouldn't discuss DOTE with him again until he had something concrete and useful to report. He needed to prove that he wasn't merely going off on some half-cocked mission before he could get back in Eric's good graces . . . and eventually tell him that he didn't want to be a teacher's assistant or study geology anymore.

But one thing at a time.

This morning, it was only Rodent and Kimmy who came to pick him up. "Here," Kimmy said, handing him a travel mug once he'd settled down into the van.

"Thanks, you're a lifesaver," he said, taking a sip of the coffee. He hoped there wasn't poison in it.

He was feeling paranoid after spoiling DOTE's plans of drugging Professor Pascal, though they probably had yet to get word about it.

"So, where are we going—don't tell me, another secret mission? Not sure my ticker could take one of those so early in the morning," Jake said lightly, though he'd meant what he'd said. He was still feeling ashamed over what he'd done to the engineering building. Whenever he closed his eyes, he saw the laptop shattering on the floor, the mechanical arm bursting into pieces, the red spray paint dripping down the walls. Though he was not patting himself on the back in any sense, he tried to focus on the positive, which was that Professor Pascal probably would have ingested the opium, had he not reported it. It may have been the only silver lining to the senseless destruction.

"Nope! We're taking you to our clubhouse," Kimmy said.

Jake's pulse quickened. "Oh yah? What for?" Where was this place? Not in the city, that was for sure—it was far behind them, and he could see that they were heading into remote territory.

"I was proud of you last night," Rodent said over his shoulder, still keeping his eyes on the road as he drove. "Sometimes, people are all talk, you know? They say they want to make a difference, but when push comes to shove, all they do is run and hide. But you, you got right in there and took charge. I respect that. You have true courage, and that's a beautiful thing."

"Not just anyone gets to come to the clubhouse," Kimmy said.

"That's right. Trust is a shared emotion, and you put your trust in us last night," Rodent said. "I figured it was only fair that we return the favor."

Jake grinned. "Aw, I'm touched." And he was also more than a little terrified. What had he gotten himself into? What was at this clubhouse?

His nervousness deepened as they drove on, drove on . . .

Many people from outside the region assumed that the land surrounding San Francisco was a similarly built-up metropolis. But this wasn't true. One needn't drive outside the city for even an hour to find themselves deep in an area where more wild animals dwelled than people. This was the sort of place they seemed to be heading to now.

Though the winding highway they took was paved, the side roads that occasionally shot off it were not marked clearly and were devoid of any signs that might give Jake an indication of where they were.

"It's pretty out here. What area is this?" Jake ventured.

"We're almost there, friend," Rodent said, evasive as ever. He pulled over onto the side of the road and extracted a long strip of cloth from the glove box. Handing it to Jake, he said, "I'm afraid you're going to need to put this on for the rest of the way."

It was a pillowcase, Jake saw. He glanced at Kimmy and then at Rodent. "Is this really necessary?"

"Don't take any offense," Kimmy said. "I had to wear one, too, when I first started coming here. It's just a precaution."

"Don't you trust me?" Jake asked.

"It's not that we don't trust you. It's that we don't trust *them*," Rodent said, not specifying whom, exactly, he was speaking about. "It's for your own protection. If you're ever taken in for questioning, this way you won't be able to tell them where we're located."

"Good thinking," Jake said and then he pulled the pillowcase hood over his face. Once again he was wondering what he'd gotten himself into.

An indeterminate time later—Jake found it was harder to keep track of time and distance with the disorienting hood over his face, which he supposed was the point—he felt the road change when they turned off the highway and onto a long dirt driveway.

"Okay, you can take the hood off now," Rodent said from the front seat, and Jake wasted no time complying. The hood had been hot and uncomfortable, and his face was damp with sweat.

He bounced to and fro as they navigated potholes and tall weeds that had sprouted up in the road. His heartbeat rushed up to his throat as they approached a wide metal gate, and then two armed guards came up to the van to speak with them, a male and a female. The gun the girl held was nearly larger than her entire frame.

Jesus, they're just kids, he thought, placing their ages at around twenty. It was an echo of the young girls he saw at the party, and he found that he wasn't all too surprised. Young minds were probably easier to exploit and mold into the shape Rodent thought they should be.

Jake also noted that it was the guards who were answering to Rodent and not the other way around. Seemed he was right in the assumption that Rodent was the area's leader—or, at minimum, a high-ranking member. Kimmy handed her cell phone over to one of the guards, and then Rodent turned around in the driver's seat to face him. "They're going to need your phone."

Jake laughed. "You're kidding."

"'Fraid not," Rodent said. "It's the price of entry. Don't worry—you'll get it back on the way out."

At least they're planning on letting me back out, Jake thought. Although he was not happy about handing over his phone, he did it with a forced smile. "Rules are rules," he said.

Once the guards waved them through, they continued down the road a couple minutes longer until they came to a stop on a wide, flat patch of earth. "We're here!" Kimmy said and then hopped out of the van.

"Welcome. Make yourself at home," Rodent told Jake, and then he was whisked away by a few doters who appeared to have urgent business with him.

Kimmy placed a hand on Jake's shoulder. "Come on, I'll show you around."

Jake's jaw dropped as Kimmy led him down a path that opened into a riverfront property that could have doubled for the Garden of Eden. "Beautiful, isn't it?" she said proudly.

"Wow, yes," he answered truthfully, thinking that the land must be worth serious coin. This was no ragtag operation they had set up; it was utterly devoid of the rusted trailers and run-down sheds he'd been expecting after the bumpy journey down the unkempt dirt road that was overtaken by ugly weeds. He wondered where they were getting their funding from. "Don't tell me this belongs to your father too."

If Kimmy thought he was fishing for information, she didn't let on. "No, of course not. One of our wealthier benefactors lets us use the land free of charge."

And why would anyone let you do that? he wanted to ask. Because there was charity, and then there was *charity*, and letting a group of young environmental fanatics squat on the land gratis was pushing the limits of human kindness. "That's so nice."

The space before him was engulfed by trees so tall that the tops were difficult to make out. Near the riverfront, handmade carved wood furniture had been set out for lounging, and a series of pretty birdhouses were attached to thick posts nearby that featured carved animal faces. Off to his far right was a field with the most beautiful flowers he'd ever seen. "Opium poppies," she said, watching him admire them.

Which are used for heroin and opium production, he thought. "Beautiful. What are those?" he asked about a series of roundish structures that had been erected on a leveled patch of land. The frames appeared to be made of wood, with canvas stretched down tightly over the tops. They looked almost like igloos.

"Those are our yurts."

"What's a yurt? They're supercool looking, whatever they are."

"All the higher-level doters have one—it's sort of a reward for long-term service. I'll show you mine later," she said. "They're an ancient form of nomadic housing that dates back about three thousand years."

"Nomadic? Do you guys move around a lot?"

"When we need to," she said.

He wanted to ask more, but Rodent was waving them over to a large square structure that seemed to be the central meeting place. Rodent introduced Jake to some doters, who gave him a quick nod because they were hard at work folding pamphlets. Jake picked one of them up and read it: CALIFORNIA NEEDS ACTION NOW! Beneath the tagline were two side-by-side photos: one was of a dam, and the other was a pile of lifeless, rotten fish covered in flies. "What is this about?" he asked one of the doters.

The girl, who appeared as if she might still be in high school, sneered, "Gruben Dam is a representation of everything that is wrong with consumerism. It's disgusting how people can sit idly by and do nothing as the environment is raped just so that greedy corporations can have the power to run their malls, their hotels, their factories . . . while artificial lakes are created so that rich, greedy pigs have a place to park their decadent yachts. We make these pamphlets so that people are forced to pull their heads out of the sand and face the devastation they're wreaking just so they can watch TV at night."

The girl had really worked herself into a frenzy. Jake wondered if she'd stood in front of the mirror practicing the speech until she'd perfected it just so, because it sounded unnatural and corny as hell. "Right on," he said, though she was no longer looking his way, as her eyes were trained on Rodent with unmasked lust. Perhaps she'd delivered the speech for his benefit, though he seemed to be paying her no attention as he chatted with yet more doters in the doorway, which led off to a separate room. *What must he be,* Jake wondered, *twenty, twenty-five years older than her?* He'd heard that it was lonely at the top, but apparently that didn't apply to budding terrorist leaders. But surely he wasn't sleeping with this girl—this *child.* He noticed Kimmy also observing the girl's behavior with a mixture of worry and disapproval.

Rodent called Jake over so that he could meet more of what he called his "best foot soldiers." Jake was no expert on bomb-making supplies, but that appeared to be what he was seeing scattered on the tables before him: several pressure cookers, brass caps, and various fuses and switches. He also saw other tools of ecotage: hoses with nails in them, metal spikes, and flags with the DOTE emblem painted on them. There was also a copy of what looked like the original seventies version of the *Anarchist's Cookbook*, which he believed included recipes for bomb making, among other things.

"Liberating Earth through annihilation," one of the foot soldiers smirked.

Jake glanced at Kimmy, noticing that she seemed uneasy with the statement, but she said nothing.

"We've got something big planned, Jake, and I think you'd be perfect for the mission," Rodent said. "We're—"

"You've got company," yet another armed guard said as he burst into the room. "It's him."

"Christ," Rodent hissed, and he hurried outside after the guard.

"Come on, Jake, I'll show you my home," Kimmy said, looking relieved to be away from all the weaponry.

"So, what's the deal with Rodent?" Jake asked Kimmy once they were inside her yurt.

"What do you mean?" she asked guardedly.

Jake shrugged. "I don't know. It kind of seemed like you were a little upset in there, with all those weapons laid out."

"No, I wouldn't say I was upset. It's . . . Rodent, he's a genius. A visionary."

"That he is," Jake agreed. He sensed there was a "but" coming from Kimmy.

"Sometimes, though, he can take . . . *ideas* above and beyond what we discussed. I don't know if you've noticed, but Rodent isn't the sort of guy who seeks permission from anyone. He likes to do his own thing."

"You mean he doesn't always have the full approval of the group."

"I don't know. I guess. And God help anyone who dares go against him," she muttered.

"What happens if someone wants to quit DOTE?" he asked casually. He pointed at a large dream catcher hanging above her bed. "That's stunning. Where'd you get it?"

"I made it," she said bashfully.

"No, you didn't—you did? Wow, you're talented." *And hopefully willing to keep talking,* he thought.

After a moment, she said, "Once a person gets to the point where they're invited to our little community, they don't want to leave DOTE."

"So, you're telling me this is the point of no return?" he asked in a joking fashion, wiggling his eyebrows at her.

She didn't seem like she was joking when she said, "Yah, pretty much. I mean, being here, you're committed to the cause."

"Have you ever known anyone to leave DOTE?" he asked, trying to sound as offhand as possible.

"Not alive," she said quietly under her breath—so quietly that it was nearly a whisper.

"What's that?"

"Oh, I was kidding . . ." She trailed off at the sound of raised voices coming from outside.

Jake glanced out the door of Kimmy's yurt indifferently, seeing Rodent arguing with a handsome, middle-aged man in a snazzy business suit. The older man was angrily jabbing his finger at Rodent's chest.

"Speak of the devil," she said, unimpressed by the visitor's appearance. Actually, she seemed almost annoyed by it.

"What do you mean?"

"The wealthy benefactor we were talking about earlier."

"Ah, he owns the land. Well, that explains it; nobody is ever happy to see the landlord," he commented, though it wasn't as if they were paying him any rent. Perhaps that was why he was so pissed off. He couldn't imagine what this man could be possibly getting from their squatting.

"If you're into handmade goods, come have a look at this other stuff I made," she said, indicating a collection of bongo drums and beaded jewelry she had spread out on the table.

"Actually, I'm wondering if I might use your bathroom? That coffee from earlier is kicking in."

"Sure, but I hate to tell you, we don't have indoor plumbing here."

"That's cool; I'll just go off into the trees."

"That's pretty much what we all do. But stay away from the poppies. I don't think anyone would like it if you peed on those."

He laughed. "Gotcha."

Jake exited the yurt and hung a left toward a cluster of trees that was nearer to where the two men were arguing. He instinctively reached toward his back pocket for his phone, frowning as he remembered that they'd taken it at the gate. He would have loved to snap a photo of Business Suit, but it was probably good he didn't chance it. If he were to get caught, he would expect one of the more overzealous foot soldiers to kill him. Maybe even Rodent himself.

In truth, his bladder really was bursting, but that's not why he'd gone outside. As he relieved himself, he tilted his head so he could better listen to the argument the two men were having. However, between the trees shifting and the voices of others, it was difficult to hear and he was only able to catch snatches of conversation.

Business Suit: "... *only* him ... I don't recall asking you to also ... security guard ..."

Rodent: "He had to go ... getting greedy ... I don't apologize ... my actions ..."

Business Suit: "FBI ... suspicion ... any idea what you've done ..."

Jake jerked his head back when Business Suit scowled in his direction. He didn't seem too happy about being overheard.

Jake scowled back at him and said the first thing that came to mind. "What, haven't you seen a little person before? Didn't your mother ever tell you it was rude to stare?"

Rodent smirked when the man muttered a quick apology.

Jake slowly let out his breath. "Didn't mean to interrupt! Was just draining the lizard," he said as obnoxiously as possible, so that Business Suit would dismiss him as just some punk idiot. He zipped his pants up and walked away.

The last thing he heard was Rodent telling the man that he was cool.

CHAPTER 27

Jake sounded manic in Eric's ear when he answered his call. He was still miffed about his participation in the vandalism on campus, so he did not provide his friend the warmest greeting. "I've been wondering where you were. I've been trying to call you. I've got a stack of papers about a mile high for—"

"Eric, listen!" Jake butted in. "You are never going to believe what I've been doing." He sounded out of breath.

"Let me guess, you've gone to the biology lab and broken a few beakers? Or maybe you've gone to the library to burn a few books?" he said dryly.

"I've just come back from the DOTE compound—"

"*What?*" Irritated or not, now Jake had his full attention. "Where is it?"

"I have absolutely no idea. It's far outside the city, off in some wooded area down a dirt road. They had armed guards at the gate. I mean, they were holding automatic rifles like they were staging a revolution or something. And, on the inside? I think they're making a bomb, Eric." Jake took a swig of what he was guessing was booze. He normally would have chided him for his drinking, but he could hardly blame him on this one. Jake sounded wholly freaked; he'd be, too, if what he was saying was accurate. "I tell you, man, it's been a long time since I've been that scared. If they found out why I was there, you probably never would have seen me again. These guys aren't messing around."

"And why *were* you there?" Eric asked. "Jesus, Jake, you're going to get yourself killed."

"Look, I don't want to get into that now. I'm calling because I want to meet up with you and Suze to talk about all this." He paused to take another swig. "While I was there, I overheard them discussing the FBI. I think they've got something big planned."

"Okay, I'll give Susan a call now. But, if I do this, I absolutely do *not* want you going anywhere near these doters again. Do we have a deal?"

"You don't have to worry about that. After what I saw today, I'm so freaked out I feel like moving to another country. These guys are seriously scary, Eric, and as you know, I've seen some pretty bad shit in my day."

◆ ◆ ◆

A couple hours later, Eric, Jake, and Susan were sitting around Susan's tiny kitchen table, sharing a pepperoni pizza. Susan's studio apartment was about the size of a shoebox, which was all the more shocking when she revealed that it cost her three times the rent of her place in Perrick. "But, I'm far happier here," she assured them.

While he was happy that *she* was happy, the declaration hurt Eric. Was she saying that she was also happier without him? They'd shared some good times in Perrick, before they'd both moved to San Francisco, or so he'd thought. Perhaps he was being a trifle sensitive.

Jake's attention, however, was on less romantic things. "I don't understand why you can't bust in on DOTE right now, Suze, based on what I've told you."

Susan finished chewing on a thick hunk of crust. Out of habit (or maybe it was nostalgia), Eric reached over with his napkin to wipe a smear of sauce that was on Susan's face. He snapped his hand back about halfway there, once it dawned on him what he was doing. She gave him a strange look. "Um, you've got some sauce on your chin," he explained.

"Oh, thanks."

As pathetic as it was in his mind, he was relieved to note that there didn't seem to be any signs of a male presence in her apartment—no razor, second toothbrush, or aftershave on the bathroom counter. Not that he'd looked. He still wondered if she'd been with anyone since their breakup, but he forced himself to push that ugly thought right out the back of his mind. If she had, she'd been well within her rights to. It wasn't his place to question her.

Susan said to Jake, "Being in the FBI doesn't give me complete autonomy. I can't just go and raid a private property because someone tells me there's bad stuff happening there. Imagine the sort of lawsuits I'd face if I did something like that."

"So, tell your boss and other agents and get a proper warrant or whatever you need," Jake said with frustration. "I'm telling you, some seriously bad shit is going down there."

"It's not that simple, Jake. Come on, you know that," she said.

"Yah, yah, I know," he said sullenly. "But, for the record, I find it utterly ridiculous. What if they kill a bunch of people while the FBI are messing around with red tape?"

"Unfortunately, that's the way it goes," Susan said. "I need to have some kind of solid proof I can bring to Howell before I can even think about organizing a raid. It would help if you could give me even the location of this compound."

Jake shook his head. "I can't. They made me wear a hood."

Eric said, "Paranoid."

"Tell me about it," Jake agreed. "They also took my cell phone away at the security gate, so I couldn't snap any photos. This ain't their first rodeo. These guys, they're paranoid but they're smart. And organized.

There's a reason they haven't been busted yet. I'm not surprised they keep getting away with whatever illegal things they're doing."

"Tell me about the guy you saw. Mr. Business Suit," Susan said.

"He was your standard old, rich white guy, you know? Cocky posture, expensive clothes. There is one thing. Kimmy—she's one of the higher-ranking doters who I suspect is also in Rodent's harem—said that the guy owned the land the compound is on. She said he's letting them use it for free, though she wouldn't tell me why."

"Could be a tie-in with the opium poppies you saw," Eric said. "Did you see any indication that they were manufacturing heroin?"

Jake shook his head. "No, but I didn't look around that much. I only went into the main building and Kimmy's yurt. But there were a few other buildings and a couple storage-shed-looking things that I didn't go into. I wanted to, but I was afraid of arousing suspicion if I was too nosy."

"What's a yurt?" both Eric and Susan asked and then laughed.

"Yah, I didn't know what the hell it was either. It's an ancient form of housing used by nomads."

"I uncovered some interesting things on Tori's computer," Susan said. "She seemed pretty convinced that they were dealing in illicit drugs. She also mentioned the possibility of an underground prostitution ring."

"She was definitely onto something with the prostitution thing," Jake interjected. "I saw it with my own two eyes at a party DOTE threw. I still get skeeved out when I think about those young girls draping themselves all over those old dudes. Though I can't be positive that they're actually getting paid."

"Either way, it's pretty gross," Eric said.

"I don't know where or how Tori got her information, but she seemed to be on the right track. If that was her who was pulled from the river—which evidence seems to suggest—then she was probably killed simply for being too good of a reporter," Susan said.

"Maybe she snooped through Samantha's things or listened in on her phone conversations," Jake suggested.

"It's very possible. Tell me more about what this guy looked like—Mr. Business Suit," Susan said.

Jake thought for a moment. "He was attractive for an older dude. He had kind of a Robert Redford thing going on—sandy hair, in shape. He was really yelling at Rodent, so he must've done something major to piss him off."

"That sounds like someone I've been investigating for this case I'm working, Marcus Zelman. Did he give you his name?" Susan asked.

Jake shook his head. "If he did, I wouldn't be calling him Mr. Business Suit."

"Right."

"They weren't exactly big on names around there. Rodent called most of his minions *foot soldiers*, like they're staging a coup or something. I'm telling you, this guy Rodent, though you wouldn't believe it just looking at him, he's got a major screw loose. But I think it's a good possibility that it was this Zelman guy, because he said something about the FBI—which could have very well been a reference to you paying him a visit."

"Tell her about the campus ecotage stuff," Eric said.

Jake outlined the destruction they'd done to the engineering lab, and ended with the detail about Rodent drugging Professor Pascal's water with opium.

"And I've got two murder victims sitting on the slab with heroin in their systems," Susan said.

"And don't forget about Samantha Neville," Eric said.

"If the guy I saw *is* Marcus Zelman, the big question is how they're all related," Jake said. "A CEO, ecoterrorists, a young college girl, a bartender, and a security guard and environmental engineer at a dam."

"I've been wondering the same thing," Susan said. "What I can't understand is why a rich guy like Zelman would associate with an unhinged group like DOTE, especially because the group stands against everything Zelman represents. And that conversation you overheard, Jake—you're sure he said something about a security guard?"

"That's what it sounded like to me."

"I'm looking into Zelman further tomorrow," Susan said. "There's something up with the guy."

"And this all seems to connect with the dam," Jake said, getting up to toss his plate into the trash. When Susan glanced away, he gave Eric a pointed smile. "Listen, guys, I hate to pack it in early, but I've got some homework to catch up on. But you two kids should keep bouncing ideas off each other. I'll keep my cell on, so feel free to call me if you think of anything else."

Eric and Susan rolled their eyes at each other as soon as Jake walked out the door.

"Smooth, Jake," Eric laughed.

"Yah, he really needs to work on that delivery. He's about as obvious as a house on fire," Susan agreed.

"He's like a kid trying to get his parents back together after a divorce," Eric said, and Susan cracked up.

She nervously began clearing the trash from their dinner off the table. "He was right, though. It might be a good idea if you stayed here longer, so we could bounce ideas off each other."

"Sure, I could do that."

Casually, she said, "It's getting kind of late, though, so—"

"Oh, do you need me to go?" Eric asked, making a move to get to his feet. The last thing he wanted to do was overstay his welcome.

"No, no," she said quickly. "I was going to say that you could always stay the night, if you get tired."

"Oh." Well, well.

"If you don't mind having to share a bed with me, though," she said. "I don't have a couch, obviously, so the only other option is to sleep in the bathtub."

"That wouldn't work. It's a stand-up shower."

She chuckled. "Oh, right."

"So, really, the only option is to sleep in the bed."

"Well, I'm okay with that if you are."

"Sure, I'm okay with that," he said. Although, when the time came later for them to go to bed, they didn't do much sleeping.

CHAPTER 28

"What time is it?" Eric asked groggily the following morning.

"It's early. Too early," Susan said and then kissed him quickly. "Shhh, go back to sleep. Stay as long as you want. I'm sure you know how to let yourself out."

He sat up on an elbow and watched as she got dressed. "So . . . I guess this means we're back on?"

She let out a long sigh, as if facing a very harsh fact. "Yah, I suppose it does."

"Good." He smiled and lay back down on his pillow. "I love you, you know."

"I know." She finished slipping her shoes on and then crossed the room to give him a kiss goodbye. "I love you too. Now get some sleep."

Excited about the new leads (and, of course, having Eric back in her bed), Susan had hardly slept a wink. The sun was only just starting to come up as she entered the FBI office; on the drive there, she had to repeatedly scold herself for speeding. She was itching to get to work. But first, coffee.

Steaming cup of java in hand, she settled down at her desk. Her first order of business was to look into Zelman's background. Luckily, the IT department was up and running—many of the techs regularly filed into the building so early each day that they made her arrival that morning look slothful—and readily available to fulfill her request.

Within a half hour, a tech named Harry ran up the background report on Zelman that she'd ordered. "That was fast."

"It wasn't really any trouble at all, since you only wanted financials," he said modestly.

"Good work, Harry," she said anyway, which clearly pleased the agent.

Susan cracked into the report. Zelman, she wasn't surprised to see, was an extremely wealthy man. "Must be nice," she muttered dryly as she took in the long series of numbers that made up his numerous cash accounts. He had enough money at his disposal that on any given day he could go to the neighborhood she was raised in and buy up a whole block of houses, if he'd fancied.

Which, she saw, was actually the sort of thing he'd been doing.

During the last couple of days, he'd made payments to several individuals, each in the ballpark of $400,000. After a quick call down to Harry for their addresses, she learned that they all lived in the Cambridge Downs development. She had a pretty fair idea what those payments were for.

She was surprised to recognize two names to whom additional payments had been made. Cindy Jenkins had recently been paid $4,000. In fact, as Susan searched further through the accounts, she saw that Cindy had received *several* payments from Zelman, which ranged from a grand all the way up to $8,000. Dov's widow, Anne, had also recently received a single payment for $9,999. *Clever,* Susan thought. By keeping the number just under $10,000, he'd avoided prompting any red flags.

Still, wily as he'd thought he'd been, he couldn't hide what he'd done from the FBI.

Susan gulped the rest of her coffee and grabbed her jacket. First, she'd take a trip to Cambridge Downs, and then she was going to question Anne Amsel and Cindy Jenkins about their financial gifts from Zelman.

As she discovered, many of the residents at Cambridge Downs were elderly. Which was good, since older generations tended to get up at the crack of dawn—at least, that's what she'd always heard. Why this was the case, she didn't know, but it seemed to be true now. Trudy Thompson, Ellen Marr, and Bradley Medina, the residents she first spoke to, appeared to have been awake for hours. Though all three residents were extremely cooperative, Trudy Thompson was the chattiest of them all.

"I just couldn't believe my luck," she told Susan. "A representative of Zelman Industries just showed up at my door one day and offered me three hundred and fifty thousand dollars for my home. It was like winning the lottery."

She probably wouldn't be saying that if she knew about the rare mineral her land was sitting on, Susan thought. Then, a number or two would have been added to that check. "Tell me what happened."

"Well, there wasn't much to it. The man offered me the check, and I laughed and asked him what type of maniac would pay that kind of money for a trailer—you know that's what this entire development is, don't you? They're called 'modulars' or 'manufactured' homes, but at the end of the day, Cambridge Downs is essentially a trailer park."

"So then what did he say? And did he tell you why he wanted your home so badly?"

"He told me that the reason behind the purchase had no bearing on the transaction between us," Trudy said with a shake of her head. "He was actually kind of a rude little twerp—you can always tell when a youngster is uncomfortable around us old folks. He told me he'd add another fifty thousand to the check if I'd change my mind. I told him if he made it seventy-five, he'd have a deal. I was joking, of course, but then he wrote out a check for four hundred twenty-five thousand dollars and handed it to me."

"Then what?"

"Well, first, I had to pick up my jaw off the floor. Then, he said I had thirty days to vacate my home. And that once the check cleared on my end, I was to send him all the appropriate paperwork. He also advised me not to share with other residents what I'd been paid." She smiled. "I was convinced that the whole thing was a joke or maybe a scam until the check cleared, but even after that I had my son use the Google on his computer to look up this Zelman. He's a legitimate businessman, all right."

"Then what?"

Trudy shrugged. "I got to packing. My son lives over in Florida, so I'm buying myself a little one-bedroom condo on the coast right in their neighborhood. Once I die, he can have it. The rest of the money is going to pay for my granddaughter's college education. I can already taste the oranges," she said with a cute little giggle.

Susan smiled warmly. "Good for you." She didn't have the heart to tell the old woman that she'd been duped. She seemed happy enough with her decision, so she just let it be. Ellen Marr and Bradley Medina had told similar stories, but it was Trudy who'd squeezed Zelman's man for the most. Poor Mr. Medina got only $320,000 for a home that was identical to Trudy's. So, in a way, she'd made out the best.

Susan asked, "Do you know of anyone in the neighborhood who doesn't want to sell?"

"Oh, there's a couple people." She flapped a hand. "Crazy old fools, too set in their ways to make a change. You know what these trailers are to them? Coffins."

"Can you think of anyone who's been particularly vocal about not wanting to move?"

"Oh yes, Davis Pelt. He's been going around putting letters in everyone's mailboxes. He's steaming mad about all this."

"Why?"

"Oh, I don't know. I haven't bothered to read any of his letters—been too busy packing. But I heard he's been saying some pretty unkind things about those of us who've sold." She cupped her hand and loudly whispered, "*He's kind of a pill.* His wife, Dana, God rest her soul, was much nicer. She was the only reason half of us tolerated him. He's positively unbearable now that she's gone."

"Which house is his?" she asked. She thanked Trudy for her time and wished her luck in Florida.

"And you, good luck with old grumpy pants," she said with a wink, and she gently closed her door.

"Mr. Pelt?" Susan asked when a tall man with a shock of snow-white hair pulled open the door to a squat green "modular."

He took one look at her and began shutting the door. "I'm too old to change religions, and I've already got plenty of steak knives," he snarled.

She quickly produced her badge and held it up for him to see. "Mr. Pelt. I'm with the FBI."

This got him to open the door fast. "So Johnny Law has finally started to take me seriously, have they?"

"Who?"

"Are you not listening? The police!" he yelled loud enough to scare some birds out of a nearby tree. "You must be deaf or something."

I might be after all your yelling, Susan thought. "*I'm* with the FBI."

"Eh, same thing."

No, it really wasn't, but she was not going to debate the differences with the cantankerous old prune. Trudy wasn't kidding. What she found most astounding was that he'd actually gotten this lovely Dana woman to marry him—any woman, for that matter.

"May I come in?"

"Let me see that badge again."

She held it up for him to scrutinize like he was appraising a priceless oil painting. Others had done it to her before, and each time she'd wondered what made them think they were qualified to spot a fake. He must have been satisfied with what he saw, because he finally let her in. He didn't offer her a beverage or a seat, which was perfectly fine, since she was intending to spend as little time with the man as humanly possible.

As soon as she brought up Zelman's name, Davis erupted in a series of curses.

Susan patiently waited for him to finish. She'd dealt with worse than him, but not much. "Care to share with me why you're so angry?"

"I thought you already knew! I told the police—"

"I'm FBI."

He waved a hand at her, grunted. "That creep's been hounding me nonstop to sell my home. He's offered me close to a million dollars to leave, but I don't want to. It's harassment, is what it is! He's been doing it to other folks in the neighborhood who're on the same page as me."

"Why don't you want to sell, if you don't mind my asking?"

"My wife passed away in this house, and I plan on doing the same thing. Look at me! I'm an old man—I can barely make it to the bathroom on time most days. You think I'd be able to move homes in my condition? And even if I could, where am I supposed to go? Do you know how much houses are in this area? Sure, I could *try* to buy one with all the money Zelman's man wants to give me, but then how am I supposed to pay property taxes on it? I don't have any family anywhere else, and all my friends are here."

You actually have friends? Susan nearly blurted. "What is the split of people who want to stay in the area versus those who want to leave, do you think?"

"Oh, I'd say it's fifty-fifty. We're afraid it might escalate to violence. Zelman's men have been talking about 'being forced to take alternative measures,' if we don't comply, whatever the hell that means. Wouldn't take much to put me in the grave."

CHAPTER 29

Ever since he could remember, Jake had been a light sleeper. As a boy, his young, overactive imagination had translated the creaks and groans of his parents' old Georgian mansion to the clomping footsteps of a hockey-masked serial killer coming to murder him. The wind became the battle cries of banshees declaring war upon him; the branches of trees scratching against the side of the house, witches clawing their way in to steal his eyeballs.

And now, as he heard the whispers inside his small studio, he was imagining that very bad individuals who intended to do him grave harm were coming to get him. Problem was, this time he was right. He didn't dare open his eyes, for fear they were watching him for signs that he was stirring. He hadn't heard them come in; either he'd been sleeping deeply or they'd slipped in through the bathroom window. His hand was closing in on the baseball bat he kept next to his air mattress; and, had he reached it, the morning might have turned out very differently for him.

But they got to him first.

Suddenly, Jake was feeling himself being yanked to his feet. Dirty fingers wiggled in through his lips, prying open his mouth. He gagged as a splash of liquid was poured down his throat. He managed to spit a little of it out, but most of it had gone down.

And then he was falling, falling down deep into a pit of nothingness.

CHAPTER 30

Outside his home, Eric had just exited his vehicle when a minivan screeched up next to him. The window rolled down, and then a young twentyish girl he thought he recognized from campus asked if he knew where the nearest gas station was.

As it so happened, he did.

He stepped closer to the vehicle, and the van's side door slid open. It was then that three things occurred to him simultaneously. The first was that there was a group of masked individuals jumping out from the van, one of them holding the same pillowcase he'd seen in his vision of Bryan being thrown off the roof. The second was that Jake was lying hog-tied on the floor of the van, which had no back seat. The third, and most important, thing was that he should scream for help.

But by then it was too late.

CHAPTER 31

After Susan escaped Davis Pelt's angry clutches—she thought she'd never get the man to stop raving—she hit up the Amsel residence next.

She was met with great hostility from Dov's wife, Anne, who wasted no time telling her, "You've got a lot of nerve showing up at my house to interrogate me while I'm mourning my husband's death!"

"Anne—"

"I told you he was no killer, didn't I?" the widow shrieked, shaking a fist in her face. She burst into wild sobs. "I told you so!"

Susan had had about enough of people screaming at her. She was stunned when a dainty arm sporting a David Yurman watch on its wrist curled around Anne's shoulder, and then Cindy Jenkins came into view. "Geez, lady, why don't you just leave her alone? Harassing a pregnant woman! What's wrong with you?"

Susan allowed the spectacle to continue for precisely thirty seconds longer before she decided she'd had enough. Davis Pelt had prickled her nerves, making her surly, and she used the aggressive mood to her advantage. She became further incensed when Cindy made a move to slam the door in her face.

"No, I don't *think* so," Susan snarled. "Not unless you two want to spend the night in jail."

"Jail?" Anne shrieked. "We didn't do anything wrong!"

"I know about the payoffs, you two," Susan said, and both women's faces went white. "So, unless you want me to take you away in handcuffs, you'd better let me in and start talking. *Now.*"

Both women sat down on the couch, holding on to one another tightly, as if they were afraid they might float away. They stared at Susan expectantly, as if they were under the impression that this was to be an interrogation-type situation. Susan only glared down at them silently.

It was Anne who broke first. "Look, I know it was wrong to take the money. But I'm pregnant, and my husband is dead. I'm broke. What do you expect me to do?"

"No, you first," Susan said to Cindy. "What's the deal with you and Zelman?"

She shrugged. "What. He's my boyfriend."

"He's married."

"So? Married men can have girlfriends, you know," she said unpleasantly.

"Not ones that they're paying on a regular basis," Susan said. "That is what you call a *prostitute*, not a girlfriend. Is that what you are, Cindy, a prostitute?"

"How dare you! I'm most certainly not—"

"Then you better start talking, or else I'll take you in right now and charge you with prostitution. How'd you like to have that on your record?" Susan had no intention whatsoever of doing that, but her threat put enough of a scare into Cindy that she began babbling.

"All right, I'm not his girlfriend! Marcus pays me every so often to do little chores for him."

"What kind of chores?"

Cindy sighed. "Weird stuff. Not anything that would hurt anyone, I swear!"

"I'm waiting," Susan said. "I'm going to need specifics. *Weird stuff* doesn't cut it."

"Well, like one time, he wanted me to go into the control room at the dam and take a bunch of photos on a disposable camera he gave me. He never said why, but a couple weeks later he then wanted blueprints of the building. So, I borrowed the ones from the business office, made photocopies after everyone had gone home, and then put everything back. Nobody was ever the wiser. No harm, no foul, I figured."

"And how were you transporting everything to Zelman?" Susan asked.

Cindy's eyes guiltily moved to Anne.

"What are you looking at me for? I wasn't involved in any of this!" Anne said.

"But Dov was, wasn't he?" Susan deduced.

"What? Cindy!" Anne shrieked, wriggling out of her stepsister's arms. "You can't be serious!"

Cindy sighed. "I'd do the requested tasks and then give everything to Dov to put in these birdhouses Zelman set up for him at different locations. Then he'd have somebody else pick them up. He—Zelman—was paranoid about being seen with anyone he was paying."

"Just when I think that things can't possibly get any worse!" Anne cried furiously. "We've got one of those birdhouses *in our front yard*! Why would Dov do something like that?"

Susan answered for her. "Because your sister furnished him with a security gig he never would have gotten had she not covered for him."

"Is that why you gave Dov a job, so you could blackmail him into doing your bidding?" Anne demanded.

"Look, it wasn't like that. He offered, because he knew I'd put my ass on the line for him." Cindy made a move to put a comforting hand on Anne's shoulder.

"Don't you touch me!" Anne shrieked. "How could you do this to us, you rotten little bitch? This is *so* like you. You can never do anything for anyone else without expecting a favor in return!"

Susan was watching the exchange the way she would a tennis match, her head moving back and forth. *This is great,* she thought. *I don't even need to speak. They'll just incriminate themselves, arguing the way only two sisters can.*

Now Cindy was angry. "I'll have you know that your sweet little hubby wasn't as innocent as you thought! You know what he did? After a few drop-offs, he decided that he wanted to get in on the action. He felt that he should also be getting paid, since he was the one risking his butt."

"And rightfully so!" Anne shouted.

"He also started stealing from their supply—a lot of drugs. It's probably what got him killed, so . . ."

Anne gasped as if she'd been slapped. Cindy folded her arms across her chest and glared back at her.

"Hold on a sec," Susan said. "What are you talking about, Dov getting himself killed?"

"I never once asked Marcus what any of the things I was giving him were for, because I didn't want to know," Cindy said proudly, as if this somehow absolved her of all responsibility. "But Dov, he was a snoop. All he was supposed to do was take everything I gave him and put it in the birdhouses. Simple directions, right? But he starts peeking. And I guess he saw some things he thought he could make some money on—I don't know if he was blackmailing them or running errands for them or what. But I think he got greedy, kept asking for more money. My guess is that they got tired of it."

Anne stared out the window expressionlessly. She blinked once and murmured, "I didn't even know the man I was married to."

"Who are *they,* Cindy?" Susan asked.

"Some environmental group Marcus was in bed with."

"DOTE? Defenders of the Earth?"

"That's the one," Cindy said.

"Anne, I need to ask you a quick question," Susan said. She snapped her fingers in front of the woman's face; it was like she'd gone catatonic. "Anne?"

Anne blinked, her head bobbling loosely on her neck. "Yes?"

"I need to know why Marcus Zelman paid you ten thousand dollars."

"Oh. It was for a set of keys."

"Keys? To what?" Though Susan could already guess.

"He wanted Dov's key ring from work. The one for the dam."

Which would give him complete access to the dam and everything inside it. "When did you give Zelman the keys?"

"I didn't . . . it wasn't Zelman."

"Who was it, then? Anne! Listen to me: Who took the keys from you?"

"Some guy came here this morning and picked them up. He had a funny name, like rat or something."

"Rodent?"

"Yah, that was it," Anne said, and then she turned her expressionless face back to the window.

CHAPTER 32

Eric's skull felt as if it had been caved in. His vision was blurred, watery.

No, he began to understand—he was truly *surrounded* by water.

Where am I? What happened? He could remember a group of masked individuals.

His head began to clear, though it was still muddy. He could see now that he was on the walkway at the top of a dam. Jake was sprawled on the ground next to him, no longer tied up but clearly drugged.

Had he also been drugged?

No, he didn't think so. But he'd definitely been hit over the head. Even blinking hurt.

"Jake," he whispered. "Jake?"

Jake pried his eyes open, groaned. They immediately dropped closed again.

"Jake! Jake?"

There were two other men on the walkway, he saw. One was middle aged and dressed in a business suit; the other was younger, handsome but crazy eyed. Marcus Zelman and Rodent, he assumed.

He could feel a weight pressing on his chest, but something told him he dare not touch it. He sat up, blinked to clear his vision, which remained slow and confused. Still, when he looked down at his chest, he had no doubt that he was wearing a bomb.

CHAPTER 33

On the way to the dam, Susan placed a call to Howell. She quickly explained her suspicions, and her boss then immediately began to organize a backup team to meet her there. By the time she pulled up at Gruben, Howell, Johnathan, and several other members of the FBI were waiting.

And it was a good thing, since Susan's hunch had been right. Off in the distance, she could see movement on the platform of the dam. A few snipers had begun to set up rifles, and Susan asked them for an update. "Looks like we've got two perps and two hostages."

Susan borrowed a pair of binoculars and let out a cry over what she saw: Rodent angrily pulling Eric to his feet by the vest he was wearing.

Which was attached to a bomb.

"Hold your fire!" she screamed. "They've got one of the hostages strapped to explosives!" Knowing that they didn't have the time to wait for a hostage negotiator, she sprinted for the platform, ignoring the shouts of the other FBI agents. "Stand down! Stand down!" they chanted.

She would face a serious reprimand for this, if she managed to make it out of the situation alive, but she didn't care. Not when the only man she'd ever truly loved was in real danger of being blown up.

When she reached the platform, Rodent, brandishing a trigger switch, began shouting. "If you come any closer, I'll blow us all to smithereens! I'm willing to die for my cause—are you, Special Agent Marlan?"

Susan was stunned that he knew her name, but then she remembered Zelman, who was standing off to the side of the platform, staring out at the water. He didn't appear to be a hostage, but he wasn't exactly coming off as a willing participant either.

She raised her hands. "It's okay, Rodent. I've only come here to talk. No need to escalate things."

"Take out your gun," he commanded. "Slowly. You do anything stupid and—"

"I know, you'll blow us all up. Just take it easy, take it easy." She really didn't have a plan, which he probably knew. She wondered what was happening with the SWAT team, if they saw that he was holding a detonator. If Rodent were to be shot, every one of them—and that included Gruben Dam employees and all the residents of Cambridge Downs—would be goners.

"Throw your gun into the water," Rodent instructed her.

Susan did what she was told. It was a horrible feeling, giving up her gun, but she couldn't see any other choice. She cast a quick glance at Jake and Eric. Jake seemed so out of his mind that he probably wouldn't remember the incident—if they didn't die there today, that was. Her boyfriend, though, looked beyond terrified. "How you doing, Eric?"

"I've got a bomb strapped to my chest," he said, in case she hadn't noticed.

"I can see that. Just hang in there, okay?" She was moving closer to him and Jake as she spoke. "Don't make any sudden movements, all right? Rodent and I are going to have a little chat—"

"You come any closer, bitch, and I'll detonate. I swear to God!"

"Okay, okay." Susan stopped in her tracks. "I learned some interesting things in the last couple days, Rodent. Would you like to hear?" She continued on as if he'd answered, keeping her hands in the air. "You and your foot soldiers are being used as pawns by Marcus Zelman. He may have been telling you otherwise, but he doesn't care about the environment."

Rodent's eyes flickered between her and Zelman. "What is she going on about?"

Zelman turned to face them fully, and for the first time since arriving on the platform, Susan could see that he had a gun. "I have no idea, though I might shoot her just to shut her up."

Susan's pulse thudded in her ears. "Oh, I don't think you want to shoot a federal agent, Mr. Zelman. Do you see all those snipers down there on the ground? You take a single shot, and I guarantee they're going to open fire. One of their bullets might hit Rodent, and you don't want that to happen, do you?"

Zelman hesitated, his bravado deflating before her eyes. She understood then that he'd probably thought that he and Rodent would blow the dam quietly. That they'd toss Jake into the water, tie Eric to the platform, and then leave before anyone was the wiser. It was only once they were at a safe distance that they'd detonate the bomb.

But then the FBI had to show up and ruin their plans.

It was only Rodent who was relishing the attention.

"You don't want to die, do you, Mr. Zelman?" she asked. "You're only in it for the money."

"What's she talking about?" Rodent snapped.

"I have no idea," he said, turning his gun on Susan.

Behind her, a voice from a bullhorn rang out. "Drop the weapon, Mr. Zelman!"

"See, they know who you are," she said. "You'll only make things worse if you shoot anyone. And we don't want that bomb going off, do we?"

Zelman hesitated. "What do you want me to do? I don't want them to shoot me!" He was sweating bullets.

"Drop the weapon! Now!" The bullhorn again, and it was spooking Zelman. He was beginning to shake.

Susan made a slow gesture with her hand to silence the snipers. They were going to get everyone killed if they didn't zip it. "Look at me, Mr. Zelman. That's good. I want you to slowly lower your weapon, turn around, *slowly*, and toss your gun into the water. Slowly. That's good, great."

Her relief at seeing Zelman relinquish his weapon was short lived. She still had Rodent and his bomb to contend with. "Now, Rodent, I want you to listen to me. You do not want to blow this dam, because you're going to flood Cambridge Downs and kill all those people, and that's exactly what Zelman wants you to do."

"The lives of a few are but a small sacrifice for the greater good," he chanted like a credo.

"But it's not for the greater good, Rodent. It's for the good of Zelman's pocketbook. Listen to me. The land underneath Cambridge Downs contains a rare mineral that's worth a lot of money—billions of dollars. The only reason Zelman has convinced you to blow this dam is so that you flood the neighborhood. He's been purchasing properties in Cambridge Downs, but some people don't want to leave. If you kill everyone there, he'll be able to buy up the victims' land and then begin excavating it once the water is cleared. If you do this, you'll actually be hurting the environment far worse than the dam ever would, because Zelman plans to mine it."

"Th-that's ridiculous," Zelman sputtered, but his expression was pure guilt.

"Think about it, Rodent. He had your people kill an environmental engineer, didn't he? Doing his dirty work is one of the reasons why you're able to live on his land for free."

Rodent didn't answer, but his expression confirmed she was right.

"Zelman probably spouted some bullshit, too, about sparing the world from evil engineers, right? But the *real* reason he wanted Nguygen dead was because he'd hired him to do a survey of Cambridge Downs, and it was then that Nguygen discovered the mineral. Zelman couldn't risk the secret getting out, so he had your group kill him. I'm sorry, Rodent, but you've been played."

"She's lying!" Zelman shouted, cowering away from Rodent, who looked like he was considering ending his life.

"Ask yourself, Rodent, why he'd be buying up properties in Cambridge Downs if he knew you were going to flood it. There's no other reason that makes sense than the one I'm telling you, and you know it. So, by saving the dam now, you'll be turning your vengeance on Zelman, who used your group for his own agenda. He's the bad guy here, Rodent, not a bunch of poor elderly people in Cambridge Downs who are struggling to get by."

Susan didn't know if Rodent was even listening anymore. He was huffing and puffing like a big bad wolf, and his narrowed gaze was trained on Zelman. Suddenly, he was rushing him. "I'll kill you for this!" he shrieked, animallike, his eyes devoid of humanity. Spittle sprayed from his mouth. "You deceitful bastard! I'll kill you!"

Zelman let out a frightened, pathetic squeal, tripping over his own feet as he scrambled backward. He groaned as he landed hard on his butt; Susan's own tailbone ached in sympathy. "Stay away from me! Help!" he commanded to no one in particular.

Rodent waved the detonator in his hand as he and Zelman tumbled about. Susan could see that it was only a matter of time before the bomb would be set off. She quickly ran to Eric and unstrapped the vest from his chest. She rushed to the ledge of the dam and threw it into the water, half expecting it to detonate upon impact.

She and Eric watched the vest float away in stunned silence.

Seconds later, the bomb went off. Though the water around the vest swelled up into a minimushroom cloud, the dam remained intact. Moments later, FBI agents were swarming the platform, but Susan and Eric were oblivious, having collapsed in each other's arms.

EPILOGUE

With the sun shining so brightly, Susan, Eric, and Jake decided to meet at Fisherman's Wharf for steaming clam chowder in bread bowls, a celebrated if not gimmicky specialty in San Francisco that they all equally enjoyed. The area was a bit of a nightmare to navigate—traffic, expensive parking rates, mobs of tourists—thus, they saved Thurston's Seafood for special occasions. While taking down a terrorist cell certainly counted as one, Eric and Susan had another reason to celebrate.

The trio sat in contented silence as they dunked crusty sourdough chunks in chowder and watched people from all over the world snapping photos and milling about. For the first time in a very long time, they were content and looking forward to catching up on each other's lives. They all agreed: it was nice to finally be able to relax.

Eric shooed away a seagull that was lurking at an empty table nearby and then spooned up a mouthful of steaming bliss. He let out a soft moan. "God, this is good—I don't particularly love clams or potatoes, but together they're—"

"Heavenly," Susan finished for him, before letting out a contented moan of her own.

Eric said, "I'm wishing now that I'd ordered two of these."

"Me too," Jake said, and then Eric asked him when the big day was.

Jake tapped the diamond solitaire sparkling prettily on the ring finger of Susan's left hand. "Me? I think I should be asking you guys that question."

Susan flapped a hand nonchalantly, but she was feeling pure bliss. "We're in no hurry. We only just got engaged."

Eric seconded the statement and brought them back on topic. "So, when do you start?"

Jake beamed at the couple as he mopped up some chowder with a hunk of sourdough ripped from a bread bowl that was bigger than the plate it sat on. "Got my first class Monday." He popped the morsel into his mouth, and once he swallowed his bite he told Eric, "I'm not sure if I ever mentioned this, but I really appreciate your blessing on this. You have no idea how long it took me to muster the courage to drop the bombshell about me leaving university."

And when he had, his friend had seemed surprisingly unperturbed. It was the push Jake had needed to sign up for the program to become a private investigator. (His parents, while initially far less understanding, ultimately had given Jake their blessing as well.)

Eric shrugged, shot Susan a wink. "You only get one life, so you've got to do what makes you happy."

"What do you think the lesson will be about?" Susan asked.

"I don't know, but I hope there's a section on how to properly hide out in the bushes," Jake joked and wiggled his eyebrows. "While a trick of the trade, I feel that could also be a great general life skill."

Susan rolled her eyes and laughed. "I'd keep that one to myself, if I were you."

"Well, you'd better not screw up, because I've already hired another teacher's assistant," Eric said.

"Please don't say you replaced me with Nate Boyle. He's such a little brownnoser," Jake said with a groan.

"'Fraid so. He's a brownnoser, but a smart one. I'd fire him in an instant, though, if you ever wanted to come back."

Jake shook his head. "Nah, I think I've found my calling. And how about you, Suze? You still in hot water at the FBI?"

Susan shrugged. "Guess it depends on who you ask. While their official stance is that I acted recklessly and put the lives of civilians and my fellow agents in danger, Howell personally commended me for my bravery. So, I guess the takeaway is that I've been warned not to do anything like that again."

"Let's hope you won't need to. But I'm glad you did," Eric said.

"Me too," Jake agreed. "Or else you'd be sitting at our funerals now."

"And the funerals of other people," Susan reminded them.

The full extent of Rodent's insanity had become apparent during the FBI's raid of the DOTE compound. The intended explosion at Gruben Dam was only the beginning, and shocking evidence of further premeditated destruction was uncovered; many of the FBI agents on-site said it was the worst they'd ever seen. Ammonium nitrate, acetone, gasoline, gunpowder, and large quantities of pool sanitizer were among some of the large-scale bomb-making supplies discovered. Scrap metal, broken glass, and nails—materials intended to make explosions all the more lethal—were also found. Additionally, there were supplies for pipe bombs, Molotov cocktails, and homemade hand grenades: enough pipes, batteries, fuses, bottles, and timers to fill a medium-size storage container. DOTE had also amassed a sizeable cache of AK-47s and tear gas canisters. An informant who'd traded secrets for immunity later revealed that DOTE had been providing opium to a militia with ties to white supremacy. In exchange, the group members, many with dishonorable discharges from the military, furnished DOTE with weapons they'd procured in the Middle East.

The informant also revealed Rodent and his Bay Area unit's grandiose plans for expansion. While there were branches of the organization across the United States, Rodent, unhappy with the passivity of other chapters, had been planning a statewide takeover, though his *ultimate* goal was to absorb the clubs across fifty states and become the president of DOTE America. A lofty ambition, but his followers wholeheartedly believed it was one he was on his way to achieving.

"How's all that business with the doters coming along?" Jake asked Susan and then under his breath added, "Bunch of freakin' lunatics."

"You know that saying about ignorance being bliss?" Susan said. "I'm starting to think there might be some truth to that, after some of the things I've learned about DOTE."

During the compound raid, the FBI had uncovered plans for a mass drugging that was to take place in Sacramento the following month. Throughout the course of a single day, a group of doters was planning to visit fifteen different cafés that serviced workers at the state capital building and spike communal creamers with liquid opium. A few of the doters who'd cracked under interrogation revealed that there had been additional talk of swapping the opium for arsenic. It sickened Susan whenever she thought of how many unsuspecting individuals might have lost their lives while simply going about their normal routines. It was knowledge of evil deeds such as these that she kept to herself, and not only because her job required her to. She didn't want to disillusion anyone she loved with the truth of how the world really operated. Though, she knew, Eric and Jake were already plenty aware.

Jake put up his hands. "Don't tell me anything that'll keep me up at night! I've got enough to worry about with my classes coming."

"Tell him about Zelman," Eric suggested.

Susan dabbed at the corner of her mouth with a napkin. "I can honestly say, Jake, that few instances on the job have given me more pleasure than informing Marcus Zelman that he'd be facing federal charges for acts of terrorism. Whenever I'm feeling down, I like to imagine him getting by a single day in prison without having 'one of his girls' do everything for him. Well, that, and the way he sobbed like a toddler when we took him into custody."

Jake laughed. "What was the deal with him and the Nevilles? Didn't you say you thought something was hinky there?"

"*Hinky,*" Eric said with a snort. "More like *hanky*, as in hanky-panky."

Susan nodded. "He and Lucy Neville—Samantha's mother—were having an affair. I found that little tidbit out from Samantha's father, Don. Funny thing was that he didn't seem too bothered about it, probably because he's having affairs of his own. *That* I found out from Lucy. Seems he and a few of the female residents at the mobile home parks the Nevilles own have been getting friendly."

"The felons?" Jake asked, incredulous.

"Guess he likes bad girls," Susan said with a chuckle.

Jake laughed too. "I guess so. And what about our bad boy Rodent?"

Susan puffed her cheeks and then blew the air out. "Where do I even begin? If convicted of even a quarter of the charges brought against him, Rodent—a.k.a. Edward Terrance Mowse—will be spending the next three hundred years locked up."

"What's he being charged with?" Eric asked.

"Tax evasion, terrorism, kidnapping, sex with a minor, conspiracy to murder, drug trafficking . . . you name it. I'm guessing he'll try to plead not guilty by reason of insanity. He might end up at Broanville State Hospital for the Criminally Insane instead of Millstone Penitentiary, where I'm sure he'll try to garner new disciples."

Eric said, "Honestly, I don't care where he's locked away, as long as he is."

"Oh, and you were right about Brett Warwick, Jake," Susan said.

Jake frowned. "Who?"

"Oh, right—I guess you know him only as Wicky."

"The chocolate-baby eater," Jake said. "That guy was such a prize."

Susan said, "We found his fingerprints all over Samantha Neville's fridge—and on the food packages inside. Guess he'd gotten hungry after he killed her. The forensics team hadn't bothered to check for prints inside the refrigerator."

"So, he did it, then? He killed her?" Jake asked.

Susan nodded. "He confessed everything because he just felt *so guilty*."

"Really?" Eric asked.

"No, not really," Susan said with a wry smile. "He traded information for a plea deal, of course. He claims that Rodent solicited him to execute a hit on Samantha after he suspected her plans of leaving the group. She'd been a regular presence at the compound and had assisted with the harvesting of poppies and the sorting of weapons and supplies. She'd also served as a notetaker at their meetings—Rodent's plan was to compile the notes into a single crazy manifesto that he intended to self-publish, if you can believe it."

"Oh, I can believe it," Jake commented.

"Basically, Samantha knew too much and had to be 'put down,' as Warwick said it," Susan added. "Rodent had specified that the murder should not in any way be connected to the group—that it should look like an entirely unrelated crime gone wrong. Hence the staged attempted sexual assault. He also copped to killing Tori, though he claims he didn't act alone on that one."

"I'm glad she'll be finally put to rest," Eric said.

"How did Bryan fit into all this, then?" Jake asked.

"He didn't," Susan said. "He was nothing more than a convenient fall guy. We got a young doter willing to offer testimony about the murder on the parking garage roof. Seems she'd been duped into participating in the attack by other doters who'd told her that they were only playing a prank on the bartender. It wasn't until Marty Dennis gave the order to throw Bryan over the ledge that she understood that they planned on killing him."

"Why didn't she come forward sooner?" Eric asked.

"She said she feared for her own life. I have to believe her on that one, given the lengths they've gone to, to keep their secrets from getting out."

"Well, if anything, at least all this will give you something to put in your book," Jake told Eric.

"Nah, I think I'm going to put the book writing on hold for now. I guess I've lost steam on the whole thing. Turns out I'm pretty terrible at typing." Eric laughed softly. "Besides, I'd rather focus my energy on happier things."

"And there's a lot to be happy about," Susan commented.

"Like this clam chowder," Eric said.

Susan gave her fiancé an easy smile. "Sure, but the number one thing is that we're all still alive."

"Okay, let's think about being here in this moment, then. Enjoying this beautiful clam chowder on this beautiful day with beautiful friends," Jake said, the trio clinking their spoons together in celebration.

ABOUT THE AUTHOR

Vivian Barz grew up in a small town with a population of less than three thousand, and with plenty of fresh air and space to let her imagination run wild, she began penning mysteries at a young age. She kept writing, later studying English and film at UC Irvine. She resides in California, where she's always working on her next screenplay and novel.